THE
CIPHER

Also by Stephen Cole

Featuring Jonah Wish
Thieves Like Us
The Aztec Code

The Wereling trilogy
Wounded
Prey
Resurrection

THE BLOODLINE CIPHER

STEPHEN COLE

BLOOMSBURY

First published in Great Britain in 2008 by Bloomsbury Publishing Plc
36 Soho Square, London, W1D 3QY

A CIP catalogue record of this book is available from the British Library

ISBN 978 0 7475 9396 6

All papers used by Bloomsbury Publishing are natural, recyclable products made
from wood grown in well-managed forests. The manufacturing processes
conform to the environmental regulations of the country of origin.

Typeset by Dorchester Typesetting Group Ltd
Printed in Great Britain by Clays Ltd, St Ives Plc

1 3 5 7 9 10 8 6 4 2

www.bloomsbury.com/thieves

For Ele

'The longer we dwell on our misfortunes,
the greater is their power to harm us.'

— Voltaire

CHAPTER ONE

Feels like the end of the world's coming, thought Jonah Wish.

He hurried sweatily along the West Hollywood sidewalk, eyeing a sky both black and brilliant. Massive banks of charcoal cloud loomed over the low-rise tenements, backlit by the early-evening sun. The air felt charged, as if this whole beat-up neighbourhood was waiting for something to happen. As if a storm was itching to break.

It was all screaming *Bad Omen* at Jonah.

Once upon a time thoughts like that wouldn't have bothered him. He had grown up a computer freak, a hacker-turned-cracker who didn't believe in much unless it was made up of ones and zeros. But this past year, Jonah had seen enough to make him believe in all kinds of dark stuff. 'Weird and creepy?' he murmured. 'File it under "Life".'

'Say what?' The surly American voice came from Motti striding alongside, a goateed vision in crumpled black.

'I . . .' Jonah swallowed. 'I was just thinking it looked like rain.'

'Man, I sure lucked out when I got given you as

back-up on this mission,' said Motti, glowering through his round-rimmed spectacles. 'I mean, your sparkling conversation, that big fun vibe you give out . . . who could want more?'

Jonah smiled wryly, letting the sarcasm wash over him. Motti's default setting seemed to be 'bad mood', and insults were just his way of interacting with the world.

'No, please, I'm the lucky one to get you – a long-haired block of grumpiness who thinks it's still cool to be a Goth. And who has egg roll in his goatee.'

Motti scrubbed his fingers over his beard. 'Go to hell, geek.'

'Halfway there already, aren't we?' said Jonah, taking in that unnerving sky and the careworn faces of the people bustling past. He paused and unfolded a map from the back pocket of his jeans. 'I'll just check how long till we need to hang a left.'

'Would you put that thing away?' Motti growled quietly, looking around for trouble. 'Tourists are an easy mark round here. We're standing out like a nudist at a funeral.'

Jonah quickly checked the route and set off again. The whiff of dustbins and salt beef caught in his nostrils, turning his stomach. He wished he was safely back in Geneva in the minimal white coolness of his room, or in the hangout with the rest of the gang; Patch pouring the beers, Con swaying to the sound system, Tye smiling into his eyes and the good times rolling. *But you've got to earn your keep*, he reminded himself. *Not that a lot of people round here would agree.*

Jonah had imagined Hollywood to be all glitz and glamour. But this stretch of crumbling brickwork and chainlink fencing was a long way from the boutiques and boulevards of stardom. Here was a place where hunters and the hunted mixed openly, weighing risk against need and acting accordingly. Jonah could see it in the way the young mothers and aging couples kept their heads down as they walked, striving to ignore the loitering gangs on the street corners. A pair of drunks slouched past Jonah with exaggerated care, as if wary of slipping through cracks in the pavement. Hooded eyes stared out at him accusingly through stained cafeteria windows.

All this is waiting for you, they seemed to be saying, *if you try and walk out on Coldhardt. He feeds you, clothes you, he's made you rich . . .*

You just have to live long enough to enjoy it.

Jonah kept a Ferrari F430 back at Coldhardt's Geneva base – not a bad set of wheels for an eighteen-year-old learner driver – and it was parked right beside Motti's BMW M6 convertible. But big wheels stood out, not least in a district where most parked cars sat jacked up on bricks. So Motti and Jonah had taken a cab from Van Nuys airport and now trudged along on foot, picking an inconspicuous path towards Santa Monica Boulevard.

Jonah watched a half-hour crawl across his wrist-watch, counted it out in shaky breaths, footfalls and quickening heartbeats.

At least the rain's holding off, he reflected, as the ashen sky went on darkening.

The evening was soon lurid with neon. Glowing

shop hoardings lined each street, pushing everything from tattoos and tarot readings to help with income tax. The crowds grew thicker and noisier. Booming beats spilled out from dark doorways. Flashing signs screamed the names of cinemas and steakhouses, girlie shows and petrol stations.

'Happening neighbourhood,' Motti observed.

'Coldhardt said this creep Budd was the biggest and greediest fence on the West Coast,' Jonah recalled. 'He must be loaded. So why arrange for a meet in a dump like this?'

'Maybe he's being watched.' Motti glanced over his shoulder automatically. 'Maybe he thinks someone would spot him in his usual haunts.'

'Could be.' Jonah nodded towards the pink neon sign flickering above a nearby club. 'Or maybe Budd just gets off on clocking "Live Girls Dancing".'

'Beats watching dead ones on a piece of elastic, I guess.' Motti gestured across the street. 'Anyways. We want the ground floor apartment opposite that clip joint.'

'We're early,' Jonah realised. 'The meet's in twenty minutes.'

'Wait here and I'll check the place out, make sure we ain't walking into a trap.'

Jonah nodded. 'Try not to get caught. I'm the code boy, not the cavalry.'

'Don't I know it.' Motti slouched off towards the apartment, his dark ponytail brushing between his shoulder blades.

Jonah leaned against the wall, trying to act casual as Motti disappeared up a side alley. *It's OK*, he told himself. *Let the man do his thing.* As the security expert of their little gang, Motti specialised in getting them in and out of wherever was necessary. He was a pro. In their different fields, all Coldhardt's talent were. Tye the human lie detector, Patch the youngest locksmith in town, Con the mesmerising linguist who had ways of changing the most stubborn minds . . . Each of them an asset to the team.

Why else would the old man keep us around, Jonah reflected moodily. *Because he cares?*

The tense minutes edged by. Then Jonah breathed a big sigh of relief as Motti sauntered back across the boulevard. 'OK, geek,' he said, clapping a hand on Jonah's back and ushering him away. 'The place checks out and no sign of spooks. We're on.'

They were halfway across the street when the first heavy drops of rain started to fall. Soon it was a downpour, like the skies were sweating out their frustrations. Jonah quickened his step beside Motti as they entered the grimy, litter-strewn front garden of Budd's hideaway.

Motti hammered on the door, knocking off great flakes of paint. 'C'mon, we're getting soaked out here!'

The door was opened almost at once, and a big black man practically hauled them out of the downpour and into the dim hallway. His expensive-smelling aftershave was just a little too subtle for his sweat. Jonah held very still as the big man expertly frisked him then moved on to Motti.

'They're clean,' the big man called back through the open doorway behind him.

'Or at least we were till you wiped your clammy hands all over us,' Motti complained.

'Bring them through,' came a rough, Northern accent. Jonah was surprised to feel a pang of homesickness among his general nerves and nausea. He hadn't been back to the UK for a whole year – not since Coldhardt had sprung him from a Young Offenders' Institution to recruit him to the ranks.

Jonah was bundled after Motti into a near-empty living room. Stubby candles littered the threadbare carpet, sputtering in the draught of their arrival, filling the air with cloying scent. The curtains were closed, shutting out the street life outside, and ornately patterned velvet throws had been pinned up on the walls. Jonah and Motti were directed to stand with their backs to the window, facing a high-backed leather armchair in the middle of the room. There, sat rigidly like a mannequin, was a short, stocky man with slicked-down blond hair. His eyes were wide and blue and crafty – real psycho eyes – and his thin lips hovered somewhere between smile and grimace.

The man watched them intently. 'Well, well,' he said more softly. 'Seems Coldhardt is recruiting younger and younger.'

Jonah shrugged, licking his dry lips. 'You're Budd, right?'

'Nice place you got here,' drawled Motti.

'I'll never see it again after tonight. I rent a different place for every drop. No tracing me that way.' Budd gestured to the black guy, who came and stood just behind him. 'This is Clyde. My protection. Just in case you were thinking of trying anything.'

'We're here to trade, not to take you on,' said Motti. 'So let's do it.'

Budd nodded. 'You've brought payment?'

Motti slowly raised his hand and gave Budd the finger. Jonah felt a stab of alarm – until he realised this was Motti's way of showing off the gleaming band he sported there.

'As specified, one enamelled gold ring. Thirteenth century BC.' Motti twisted it up and over his knuckle and tossed it in his palm as if weighing it. 'Taken from a Mycenaean tomb in Cyprus.'

'Adequate payment.' Budd took a deep breath and stood up, practically quivering in anticipation. 'Give it to me. I want to see it.'

'Nuh-uh.' Motti slipped the ring in his pocket. 'First, you give us the merchandise as arranged – this Morell guy's laptop. Right now.'

'You talk awfully hard for a bloke with a ponytail.' Budd smiled and turned to Jonah. 'Clyde here could kill the two of you in a second with his bare hands.'

Jonah took Motti's lead and tried to act the big shot. 'I'd wear some rubber gloves if I were you, Clyde. You don't know where we've been.'

'But I'll tell you where you're going if you mess with us, Budd,' said Motti coolly. 'All the way down. Coldhardt was set to steal that laptop before Morell got murdered and his LA pad burned down. He ain't happy about having to pay for the thing now.'

'Then he should've tracked it down ahead of me, shouldn't he?' Budd's smile grew wider.

'How'd you find it?' Jonah demanded.

'Cops reckoned it was kids who did over Morell's

place. A mansion crammed with priceless relics, and before they torched it they stole his flatscreen, his stereo, his computers, credit cards . . .' Budd shook his head, amused. 'I know the kind of guys who fence stuff like that. And I know the likes of Coldhardt cough up a fortune for the kind of deep, dark secrets Morell liked keeping . . .' He snorted. 'Surprised he can't afford better than a couple of low-rent kids to do his dirty work for him.'

'You're right about one thing,' said Motti. 'Coldhardt wants the info encrypted on that laptop's hard drive. He wants it real bad.' Motti tapped the ring in his pocket. 'So either we can deal and you earn yourself a piece of history, or else you and Clyde can try to dick us "low-rent kids" around and *become* history. Your choice.'

Budd didn't answer. Clyde stared at them impassively.

The rain rattled at the windows, loud as machine-gun fire in Jonah's ears. 'Well?' he said, fighting to keep his voice steady.

'Well . . .' Budd fixed Jonah and Motti in turn with those unnerving pale blue eyes. 'You've shown some balls as well as the proper payment. Suppose I can show you the laptop.' He turned back to his chair and pulled out a slim, titanium laptop from beneath it. 'You want to watch it, boys,' he said more casually. 'If you get mixed up in black magic like Morell, bad stuff happens.'

'Thanks for the tip, but we don't spend too much time hanging in graveyards sacrificing chickens.' Motti nodded at Jonah. 'For a start, he's a veggie.'

Jonah nodded. 'We're just out to find –'

'Save it,' Budd snapped. 'All I care about is my fee. If Coldhardt's prepared to pay for some devil-worshipping weirdo's stolen goods, that's his business.'

Devil-worshipping weirdo? 'Antiquarian book dealer with a passion for the arcane' had been Coldhardt's description of Morell, but Jonah reckoned he knew which description probably nailed it. 'You're certain it's the right laptop?'

'What, you think I'm an amateur or something?' Budd glared at him. 'I had the prints on the casing matched.' He was drumming his fingers absently as if echoing the rain on the glass behind the heavy velvet curtains. 'Now, I don't know what Coldhardt hopes to find on this thing – and I don't want to know.'

'We'll keep it a secret so you sleep good at nights.' Motti nodded to Jonah. 'Go ahead, geek. Check out the files.'

Budd placed the laptop on the floor amongst the candles and started it up. He looked balefully at Jonah. 'On your knees, then, boy.'

Jonah hunkered down – with no other furniture there wasn't much else he could do. The computer prompted for a password. Despite the tension in the air, Jonah found himself loosening up as his fingers jabbed at the keyboard, hacking into the operating system. Minutes cracked away like dismantled code, meaningless, as he scanned the contents of the hard drive, looking for files created on the dates Coldhardt had specified. Once he'd located a handful of encrypted email attachments, he pulled a smart card from his back pocket and loaded it up.

'What're you trying to do?' Budd demanded.

Jonah didn't look up. 'Checking the digital signature on these encryptions. We want to be sure the files were created by Morell.'

'So do it, already,' snapped Motti.

'Just did.' Jonah gave a low whistle of relief. 'The timestamps and signature tally.'

'Could Buddy boy here have tampered with this shit?'

'Nope.' Jonah closed the laptop and got back up. 'Any changes to the file or attempts to copy it would invalidate the signature. We're good.'

'I don't cheat my clients.' Budd nodded to Clyde, who had produced some glasses and a bottle of Scotch from somewhere. The big man started pouring. 'So. Seal the deal with a drink, shall we? Little tradition of mine. Then we can all clear out of this crap-hole – once you've handed over my ring, that is.' Budd stabbed his hand out impatiently as Motti reached in his pocket and pulled out the ring. 'Come on, let me have it!'

As if timed deliberately, a metal arrow shot through the window and thudded into Budd's chest. By the time Jonah's ears had processed the sound of breaking glass, there was blood soaking Budd's shirt, pumping out in a flood.

'Oh God,' Budd gasped hoarsely, eyes screwed up tight. 'What hit me? Clyde, what hit me, what is it? Is it bad?' But even as the big man started stumbling over to see, Budd pitched forward on to his face.

Jonah stared, transfixed with horror. But Motti was already running for the door. 'C'mon, geek,' he yelled. 'Outta here!'

Before Jonah could follow, a masked female figure in a black fitted combat suit climbed lithely into the room through the broken window, wielding a sighted crossbow. With a bellow of anger, Clyde ran to tackle the intruder before she could reload. But the mystery woman yanked down one of the velvet curtains and flung it over him, then kicked him in the stomach. Clyde fell back on to a collection of candles – then screamed and thrashed about as the heavy fabric burst into flame.

On instinct, Jonah snatched a throw down from the wall, thinking he could smother the fire. But the woman acted first, firing another bolt into Clyde's body, silencing him as the flames took stronger hold.

Then the woman turned to Jonah, raising the crossbow once again.

Sickened, terrified, Jonah turned and ran, clutching the laptop to his chest. Motti was waiting for him at the front door, white-faced. 'Move it!'

But as they pounded out on to the wet pavement, a further bolt shot past them and shattered the window of a parked car beside them; a deafening alarm blared into the night. Startled pedestrians close by shrieked and stumbled out into the road – into the path of a bus, which slammed on its brakes. Jonah heard the chaos and confusion but was already careening along the street hot on Motti's heels, weaving between pedestrians, puddles and streetlamps, the thought of a steel spike thudding into his back pumping his heart faster, pushing him on. The rain stung his skin, the thud and blare of bars and strip joints became the soundtrack of his flight. He and Motti ran and ran and didn't stop running, not till they'd covered the best part of a mile.

Checking over his shoulder that there was no sign of their pursuers, Jonah staggered against a shop front, his legs cramping and his stomach going into spasm as he relived Budd and Clyde's death throes. He doubled up and retched – then jumped as he felt a hand land on his back.

'Hey.' It was only Motti. 'You OK?'

Jonah wiped rain from his eyes and thick saliva from his mouth. 'That woman killed Budd and Clyde in cold blood.'

Motti frowned, panting for breath. 'Woman?'

'Well, if it was a bloke he had serious man-boob issues.'

'Whoever she was, where the hell did she spring from?' Motti spat in the gutter. 'She must have had Budd under obs. Wanted to get that laptop as bad as Coldhardt.'

'Probably working for someone like him,' said Jonah darkly. 'Someone untouchable.'

'Wicked world, ain't it?' Motti took the computer from Jonah. 'Well, now that we've got the damn thing, let's get out of here and back to Coldhardt right now.'

Jonah nodded, searching the rain-swept street for a yellow cab. But he couldn't push from his mind the image of the bolt protruding from Budd's chest, the blood, the flames, Clyde's screaming. He breathed shallowly, willed himself not to be sick. Motti came and stood beside him.

'Was Budd right about Morell and the devil-worship bit?' Jonah asked softly. 'Is this book Coldhardt's after some kind of black magic bible?'

'Who cares what it is?' Motti smoothed wet hair away from his eyes. 'All we gotta do is go wherever the hell these files tell us to go, steal the thing and hand it over. End of story. Right?'

Jonah stayed silent, shivering as he looked up into the gusting, rain-soaked blackness of the sky. Something told him this particular story was a long way from being over.

CHAPTER TWO

Tye circled her opponent warily, bracing herself for the strike that could come at any moment. Years of smuggling around the Caribbean, fighting her way out of a hundred scrapes, had left her an expert in combat at just seventeen – but she knew she couldn't afford to drop her guard for a moment.

Not with Con.

Arms up in front of her shoulders, fists in front of her chin, Tye kept up her defensive position. This might only be a workout – a friendly tussle in the gym on Coldhardt's enormous Geneva estate – but whatever the location, whatever the odds, Con didn't like to lose.

As if on cue, Con burst into sudden movement, stepping forward and lashing out her right hand. The tips of her fingers and backs of her first knuckles grazed against Tye's eyes. *Eye slap. Nice.* But even as she processed the pain, Tye tucked in her chin, aligned the first two knuckles of her right hand with Con's ribs, aimed *through* her target, not at the surface – and jabbed out, extending shoulder and hips into the punch for power. Con gasped with the impact and staggered back.

'Bitch!' Con's green eyes flashed dangerously. Then

she laughed suddenly, displaying teeth as white and perfect as her skin. 'I really must stop going so easy on you, yes?'

Tye gritted her teeth. 'Yes, maybe you should.' Con's cultured, slightly Slavic accent sounded cool and chic, but at times it grated like hell. She ran at Con, elbow raised parallel to the floor, and struck her in the chest. Con took the impact but stood her ground, retaliating with a left jab swiftly followed by a double hand punch to Tye's cheek. Tye bit back her cry of pain and backed quickly away, arms up once again in defensive posture.

'I'm surprised you did not see that coming, sweets.' Con wiped stray strands of white-blonde hair away from her eyes and winked. 'You are the expert at reading body language, no?'

Tye forced a smile, keeping it light. 'Well, you can *speak* fifteen different languages – p'raps your body's picked up a few too, just to throw me.'

'I will very happily throw you,' said Con, advancing again. 'Over which shoulder would you prefer?'

Tye circled round once more. Somehow, when she fought with Con it was never just about keeping in shape. Con, with her European education, her poise and intelligence, represented the privileged life Tye had spent her whole lonely childhood longing for, trapped in the dismal slums of Haiti. While Tye had clawed a life for herself out of her limited options, Con had been handed everything on a plate – except the attention she so desperately craved.

Tye was about to aim a roundhouse kick at her opponent's slender waist when Con jerked out of her fighting stance, held up a warning hand and rounded on the pile of crash mats beside her. 'What the –?'

She lunged forward and hauled out from hiding a familiar, scrawny figure dressed in scruffy jeans and a grey hoodie. His freckled face was dominated not only by his black velvet eye patch but by a cheeky smirk. 'All right, ladies?'

'Patch!' Tye glared at him. 'What have we said about you spying on us?'

'It's not my fault!' Patch protested. 'I just happened to notice you had locked the gym door – you know I can't resist a locked door. I'm a professional, aren't I? When I see a locked door, I gotta open it.' He grinned. 'And when I see two fit babes in Lycra working out, I gotta stick around.'

'I'll stick a fist in your face if you try it again,' Con warned him.

'Look, I'm fifteen! It's hormones, OK?' Patch was speaking to Con's chest. 'Hey, I saw Tye whack you in the boobs. Maybe I could rub them better?'

'Rub *this* better,' she said, and kneed him lightly in the groin. Patch groaned and sank to the floor. Con turned to Tye and held out her hand to shake. 'End of workout?'

'End of workout,' Tye agreed. But as she took Con's hand, Con gripped hold of her wrist, pulled Tye off-balance and kicked her legs out from under her. Tye swore in Haitian as she wound up on the floor beside Patch.

'Oops.' Con looked down at her, eyes sparkling. 'I lied.'

Tye leapt up angrily, ready to fight Con to a standstill if she had to – when the shrill trill of a phone cut through the air.

The sound of fun-time ending.

Tye swallowed back her anger and helped Patch up, while Con ran to answer the wall-mounted phone by the doors. 'Yes, Coldhardt?'

Tye and Patch swapped uneasy looks. There were no meetings with the boss scheduled until first thing tomorrow, when Jonah and Motti were due back with the dead guy's laptop.

'Something's gone boobies-up,' said Patch.

Tye scowled. 'Could you keep breasts out of the conversation for, like, five minutes?'

Con hung up, her lips pursed. 'Coldhardt wants us in the hub in fifteen minutes. Council of war.'

'Is it . . . ?' Tye bit her tongue, tried again. 'The boys . . . I mean, are they –?'

'Don't worry, Jonah is fine,' said Con, her eyes glittering more coolly now. 'And so is Motti. They got back an hour ago.'

'Good,' said Tye, trying to ignore the prickle of heat in her cheeks.

'Now,' Con reached up with her arms above her head, 'we must stretch and shower before this meeting starts, yes?'

'See you there,' said Patch, heading meekly for the exit.

Con stopped mid-stretch and blinked in astonishment. 'He didn't make any cracks about soaping my back.'

Tye headed for the changing rooms, shaking her head. 'Guess things *must* be serious.'

* * *

A few minutes later, Tye was done with the shower. Wiping water from her eyes she stepped out – straight into a warm, soft towel as big as a sail being held out to her. Gasping, eyes snapping open, she clutched the towel against her naked body – and saw Jonah right in front of her. He looked dog-tired, but he was smiling appreciatively.

'What the hell do you think you're doing?' she hissed at him, acting angrier than she really was. 'If Con sees you in here –'

'She's already taken off, slowcoach. Raced off to her master's side.' He raised his eyebrows. 'Like I've raced to my mistress.'

'Oh, so I'm your mistress, now?' Tye teased, securing the towel under her arms. 'What happened, you and Motti get married out in California?'

'Well, you know how it is – we took in Vegas, saw this Elvis impersonator passing . . .'

Tye couldn't help it. A grin caught at the corners of her mouth. With his ragged blond hair, neat, straight features and nervous eyes, Jonah had used to put her in mind of a choirboy with dirty secrets he couldn't wait to share. But these days he worked out regularly, his body had grown toned and muscular, and he carried himself more confidently. He was changing from angelic back-row chorister to indie-band front man. But right now, she realised, his rigid stance was at odds with his relaxed tone. She studied him for a second. He was trying to act like stuff was OK when it clearly wasn't. His eyes were glassy, like he hadn't slept, and his shoulders looked tense.

'What is it, Jonah?' She put her palm to his chest. 'How come you're back early?'

'Don't say you're disappointed?'

'Duh.' She leaned in and kissed him, wet and warm, on the lips. He responded a bit too eagerly, trying to slip his hand inside her towel.

'Hey,' she whispered, pushing him back gently. 'I'm glad you're back safe, but no one's meant to know we're more than friends, remember? Anyone could walk in.'

'They're already in the hub. Me and Motti had to report straight to him, I've been let out to grab some air.'

'But instead you're grabbing me.'

'Tye . . . ?' Jonah held out his arms. 'Just . . . just hold me a few seconds longer, will you?'

She frowned. 'Jonah, what happened out there?'

'The men we went to meet . . .' He looked down at his shoes, his voice as blank as his eyes. 'They were both murdered. Shot point blank with crossbow bolts, and set fire to, right there in front of me. And I was almost next.'

'Shit,' Tye muttered, putting her arms back around him and pulling him close.

She'd been nine the first time she saw someone get killed, and had seen so much blood spilled since then that violence rarely shocked her. It was easy to forget Jonah's life had been so different. His teenage years were spent in foster homes around Britain, hiding out in darkened bedrooms making sense of codes and encryptions on borrowed computers, growing his talent. Sure, he'd gone to prison, but his crime had been a one-off. He'd diverted funds into his foster mum's bank account, trying to help her start a new life – little realising that in doing so he'd actually started a new life for himself, outside the law: a life working for Coldhardt.

Since then, the blood had flowed a lot more freely. She went on holding him tightly.

'I'm never gonna be cut out for this life.' Jonah rubbed his face against her neck. 'Am I?'

She sighed. 'It gets easier.'

'But do I want it to?' Jonah's grip slackened and he pulled back.

'Sometimes it doesn't matter whether we want things to happen or not,' she told him quietly, her eyes searching his. 'You know that.'

Jonah didn't say anything.

She pulled him close again. 'It'll be OK.' The words sounded empty to her, but he seemed comforted. For a long moment they hugged and then she felt him start to relax and his hand reached inside her towel again.

'Hey!' She pulled back. 'Stop that! We've got to go.'

'You sure?' Jonah watched longingly as she started to dress.

'Sure I'm sure.' She pulled on her blue top, pale against her dark skin. 'We're late enough already.' But while she sounded firm, inside she was smiling. Despite everything she'd seen in her life, everything she knew about life, Jonah did sometimes make her feel like things *could* actually be OK. Maybe that was the reason why sometimes when she looked at him she felt . . .

No. Tye hastily stopped her thoughts there. Life

was way too complicated as it was. She pulled her braids out of the back of her top and kissed him feather-light on the lips.

'Come on,' she said, turning and heading for the exit. 'Friendly workmates time again. Try to act normal.'

Jonah sighed as he set off after her. 'Just tell me where to start.'

Everything seemed just a little too calm and tranquil as Jonah followed Tye through the quiet pathways of Coldhardt's rambling estate. The evening sunlight gleamed off sash windows and ornamental pools. The fresh green stripes of lawn looked as though Premiership groundsmen were flown in each day to tend them.

Coldhardt moved routinely between bases as and when his business dictated. Over the last twelve months Jonah had found himself living in a castle in Siena, a ranch in New Mexico, a plantation in Jamaica, a converted hotel in Bulgaria . . . But his adventures had begun here in Geneva after Motti, Tye and the others sprang him from the Young Offenders' Institution. Maybe that was why he had come to think of this place as his only real home.

The estate overlooked cornfields and hillside vineyards and, in the distance, postcard views of Alpine France. It was littered with old outbuildings; they seemed quaint and ramshackle on the outside, but most concealed flash facilities within. The state-of-the-art fitness centre was just a short walk from a giant indoor pool, an amusement arcade and games room, the underground garage – and of course, the cavernous hangout where the Talent could chill or party all night long if they felt like it before staggering upstairs to crash in their luxurious personal suites . . .

No, working for Coldhardt wasn't all bad, Jonah reflected. And after the start he'd had in life, he hoped he would never take such luxury for granted.

Of course, there was nothing like knowing you might die at any moment on some dangerous, spooky mission to make you appreciate what you had.

Or *who* you had. Jonah's eyes lingered on Tye walking up the path to the chateau ahead of him, on the way her braided hair bobbed against the smooth dark skin at the nape of her neck. 'Hey,' he called, 'can you give me another driving lesson after this debrief?'

'You need to rest,' she said lightly, pushing some ivy away from beside the front door to reveal a high-tech keypad. 'Wouldn't want you to crash.'

He lowered his voice. 'Not even round your place?'

She tapped out the entry code. 'Down, boy.'

Certainly brought me to heel, Jonah noted, as they entered the spacious marble hallway. He and Tye had acknowledged an attraction between them some months back, but she wanted to take things slowly, keep it secret. Jonah knew Coldhardt wouldn't approve of two of his operatives sharing a romance. Results depended on the Talent working as a team, each member having equal priority, judgements unclouded by messy emotions.

But secrets were hard to keep round here, particularly from Coldhardt, who had practically invented the word. As they walked through the cloisters with their vaulted archways and stained-glass windows, he went through the tips Tye had given him on how to act and disguise his body language, so he wasn't so easy to read. But though he knew caution was sensible it was also driving him crazy. And last night had hammered home that life was all too short.

Here he was, about to relive those events in detail once again, for Coldhardt and the gang.

Tye opened the double doors at the end of the cloister and they stood together as a section of the stone floor lurched beneath them, descending to the secret underground world below.

Coldhardt's hub was a spacious chamber, part boardroom, part workplace, part spooky sci-fi bunker. A huge oval table dominated the space. A regimented row of black filing cabinets stood against one wall, enduring the blank glare of twelve plasma screens mounted opposite.

Motti, Con and Patch were already seated around the table in brushed-steel chairs. 'Jonah!' Patch called, cheery as ever. 'You made it!'

Jonah shrugged. 'Just about.' Tye sat between Motti and Patch, smiling at them both, leaving Jonah to sit beside Con. 'You picked a good job to miss,' he said.

'And I usually miss so little,' she agreed, looking at him with those unsettling green eyes of hers. It was like she was trying to see through you and read what you were thinking. Trouble was, since Con was a self-proclaimed expert in neural-linguistic programming and mesmerism – or *hypnotism* to anyone else – she could catch you off-guard and do exactly that. Jonah had heard people spill their deepest secrets to her under the 'fluence as casually as they would order a drink.

'Pass us a coffee, Mot?' Jonah stretched.

Motti grunted at Patch, who filled a white porcelain cup with the dregs of the coffee jug. Tye slid it across to him.

'Jeez.' Jonah looked at the dark oily liquid. 'Concentrated caffeine. Should stop me sleeping on the job.'

'None of us will be falling asleep on this particular job, Jonah.' The voice was rich, seasoned with age and with a slight Irish gravel to it.

Coldhardt's voice.

CHAPTER THREE

The boss man riveted Jonah's attention as always. Coldhardt had entered from his private office at the far end of the hub, a tall, gaunt figure crowned with a regal mane of white hair. Despite being well into his sixties he moved with the casual confidence of someone a good deal younger. But his pale blue eyes told a different story – that of a man haunted by the memory of something so bad he couldn't forget it for a second. And as he settled himself at the head of the table, his dark velvet jacket and crisp white shirt couldn't disguise how painfully thin he was. He had aged visibly this last year.

Jonah, like the others, waited for him to speak.

'My apologies for convening this meeting a little earlier than intended,' Coldhardt began. 'The problems Jonah and Motti encountered on what should have been a routine pick-up require our immediate attention.' He looked between them both. 'Tell us what happened. Every detail.'

Between them, Motti and Jonah outlined their experiences, from arriving coolly in Van Nuys yesterday morning to their midnight race to LAX and mercifully uneventful flight home.

'Sounds like Budd should've got a better Buddy-guard,' joked Patch nervously.

'Coulda used some protection ourselves.' Motti wasn't smiling. 'Hey, geek, maybe we shoulda asked that bitch with the bow if she had any friends.'

'I'm glad she was alone,' said Jonah, turning to Coldhardt. 'So was Budd right? Is this book you're after an occult text?'

'It's a *grimoire*,' said Coldhardt. 'An ancient book of supposedly magical beliefs and practices. The Guan Yin manuscript, to give it its full title.'

'Guan Yin?' Patch frowned. 'Sounds like it came out of a Chinese takeaway.'

'She is the Chinese goddess of mercy,' Coldhardt explained patiently, 'although her origins are in Buddhist mythology. The grimoire depicts her image on its title page.' He paused. 'Believed to have been compiled in the fourteenth century, written in an unknown language, the Guan Yin manuscript is said to contain a most precious secret. Something that wise men from Europe to the Orient coveted fiercely. They called it the Bloodline Cipher.'

'A fourteenth-century code?' Jonah straightened a little in his seat. 'Things were just starting to hot up at that time, cipher-wise. The first cryptology manuals were published in 1379, mainly substitution alphabets –'

Motti yawned loudly. 'Medieval cryptology manuals. Right. Remind me to get them out the library.'

'Bloodline Cipher?' Con looked puzzled. 'What does that even mean – some sort of scrambled family tree?'

'Maybe it was written by a Buddhist, tracing all his different reincarnations,' said Motti flippantly. 'You know, he starts as a bug, becomes a fish, then a cat, then a guy . . .'

'Sounds like a real blockbuster,' said Tye, pulling a face.

'Whatever the contents, bad luck allegedly dogged the Guan Yin manuscript's owners over the centuries.' Coldhardt's tone warned them the time for joking was past. 'The book was believed lost for good after a Turkish museum displaying it caught fire in 1867. It is my hope we will know more about its contents after you have stolen it.'

'It is worth a very good deal, yes?' asked Con, all but licking her lips.

'A colossal amount. To me, its worth could be incalculable.'

Jonah shuddered. 'The woman who killed Budd and Clyde – or whoever sent her – must know its value too.'

'There must be lots of secrets on Morell's laptop, surely?' Tye wondered. 'We don't know she was after the same info about how to find this grimoire thing.'

'Except that Morell practically advertised the information's existence,' said Coldhardt drily. 'He was a learned man but also naive. It seems he stumbled upon the location of this grimoire, and wanted to acquire it for his own collection. It wasn't for sale – apparently it had been acquired in secret, illegally – so he needed someone to steal it for him. Morell contacted several people – myself included, naturally – to get quotes for the job. I gave him a most reasonable estimate.'

Con smiled. 'Because if he accepted and told you where the grimoire was, you could steal it yourself, yes?'

Coldhardt returned the smile without warmth. 'My dear Con, how well you know me.'

'I still don't get why anyone should twig he had the info on his laptop,' Patch complained.

'From the moment he contacted me, I arranged for him to be watched – and it seems others had him under observation too.' Coldhardt steepled his fingers. 'Morell was concerned about sending such compromising emails from his home address for fear they could be traced – either by the police or by . . . other authorities.' Again, that wintry smile. 'He double-encrypted the messages, drove to a hotel with Wi-Fi access and sent them from the car park so they couldn't be traced back to him.'

Jonah tutted. 'Piggybacking on someone else's wireless connection without consent?'

'Gee, that's, like, breaking the law,' Motti deadpanned, and Patch sniggered.

Tye turned to Coldhardt. 'So was Morell going to give us the job of stealing this grim-thing or not?'

'No.' Coldhardt's eyes narrowed. 'He intended to take his custom to one of my competitors – Karl Saitou, a competent if unimaginative criminal.'

'How d'you know what Morell *intended* to do?' Tye pressed him.

'Because Coldhardt got hold of the keys to decrypt the guy's mail,' Jonah explained. 'That's how come I knew the encrypted files were really from Morell and not tampered with.'

'And those I have read so far make for very interesting reading,' said Coldhardt. 'In any case, before he could give the go-ahead to Saitou and arrange payment, Morell died. His body was too badly charred by the fire that consumed his house to be sure of exactly what killed him.' Abruptly he slammed his gnarled old fist down on the table, making them all jump. 'Such a waste.'

Jonah cleared his throat. 'I suppose you must have known him a long time.'

The old man gave him a withering look. 'I was referring to his collection.'

Figures, thought Jonah, looking down at his cold coffee. 'So Saitou won't steal the grimoire 'cause there's no cash coming.'

'Bit of a coincidence that Morell was killed and his house ripped off by kids who happened to torch the place, isn't it?' Tye looked around at the others. 'I mean, nothing suspicious there.'

'He was into black magic and stuff . . .' Patch had lowered his voice. 'And that creepy manuscript was meant to have burned. Maybe it cursed him.'

'And maybe your real name is Ass,' Motti suggested.

'It must be kids,' said Con uneasily. 'That's why they left all the really valuable things in his house and took the electrical stuff they could sell on quickly, yes?'

'Some youths have been arrested and charged,' Coldhardt agreed. 'But one of them claims they were coerced into committing the crime.'

'They would, wouldn't they?' said Patch. 'Everyone falls back on that old sob story when they get in bother.'

'Well, in any case,' said Jonah, 'I checked all Morell's secure files on the flight back, and none of them had been opened or tampered with since composition or sending. So it couldn't have been one of your competitors who robbed his place, could it?'

Coldhardt waved his hand impatiently. 'Such speculation is ultimately pointless – we have the laptop, and as Jonah has pointed out its information has not been accessed by anyone before us.' He glanced at Motti. 'We should be thankful to Mr Budd. Perhaps I didn't part with my Mycenaean ring in vain.'

'Sorry 'bout that.' Motti took a stab at looking contrite. 'But with Lady Crossbow on the warpath, smoke and fire and stuff all around . . .'

'The house burned to the ground,' Coldhardt went on thoughtfully. 'As yet the ring has not been recovered.'

'Probably pocketed by someone at the site,' said Con.

But Coldhardt had already moved on, reaching for his multi-remote. The plasma screens flicked on to reveal the output from Coldhardt's computer – one of Morell's files, now decrypted.

'This reveals the precise location of the Guan Yin manuscript,' Coldhardt announced. 'You expressed an interest in viewing Jonah's medieval cryptology books at the library, Motti? Well, the library you'll be visiting will most likely stock the originals. It belongs to one Professor Dominic Blackland in San Antonio, Texas.'

'Ride 'em cowboy,' said Motti wryly.

'Now, agreed, Morell's files have remained intact,'

Coldhardt went on. 'But the fact remains he could well have passed the information to others verbally. I can't afford delay. I want a workable plan delivered by this evening, and the Guan Yin manuscript stolen tomorrow tonight.'

Tye must have decided it was 'state the obvious' time: 'That doesn't give us long to work things out,' she began falteringly, 'I mean –'

'I do not *have* long,' Coldhardt said flatly. Jonah wondered what he meant by that, but it was anyone's guess. 'And remember, all of you – that manuscript is of paramount importance to me. Take no chances with its welfare. I must have it intact – damaged it is of no use to me . . .'

Jonah swapped the briefest of looks with the others, then dutifully studied the screens as they were. But his mind was crowding with images of fire – consuming Clyde's body, engulfing Morell's house, spreading through the silent rooms of some old and musty museum. A book of dark magic, followed by bad luck and flames?

Coincidence, he told himself, swallowing hard. *Too corny to be true.*

'We're coming to get you, grimoire,' he heard Patch mutter gloomily. 'Is that your owner's bad luck . . . or ours?'

Twenty minutes later, Jonah led the way out of the hub, blinking in the sunshine, heading for the hangout. He felt completely washed out, and the strong coffee had left his head buzzing like a dud transformer.

'Tomorrow we could all die,' Con announced. 'Let's have a picnic.'

'Let's have sex!' Patch suggested.

'Before or after we eat the picnic, stud?' Tye teased him.

'The one-eyed monster and his one-eyed monster.' Motti held his stomach. 'Suddenly I lost my appetite.'

'I wish I lost my virginity,' said Patch wistfully.

Jonah smiled. 'Shouldn't you wait till you hit puberty?'

'What would you know, geek,' Motti shot back. 'You're *still* waiting!'

'Ha!' Patch raised his knuckles and Motti knocked his own against them. 'What would I do if I didn't have you to make my wisecracks for me? You are officially not allowed to get cursed by this book and die.'

Motti's mood turned on a sixpence. 'Just quit with the curse stuff, mutant, OK?' he snarled, walking ahead. 'I hate that hokey crap.'

'Thus endeth the banter,' said Jonah, shooting a look at Motti as he passed. 'But I suppose if I'd lost an incredibly precious ancient ring I'd be in a bad mood too.'

Motti wouldn't be drawn beyond a grunt and a glare. But just as they both reached the door to the hangout, Con slipped ahead of them and blocked their way.

'I mean it,' she said again. 'About the picnic. Let's all cut out for a few hours.'

Tye frowned. 'Did you miss the bit where Coldhardt told us to work out how we break into a fort by tonight?'

'No wonder poor old Morell had to cast about for cheap quotes for this job.' Jonah sighed. 'I mean . . . what the hell is this guy doing with his own fortress? Why can't he own a bungalow?'

'Everything's bigger and better in Texas,' said Motti moodily.

Patch looked up at Tye. 'How long is the flight going to be?'

'Too long,' she answered. 'Maybe a bit of fresh air today wouldn't be so bad.'

'Good.' Con smiled, looking pleased to have got her own way as ever. 'We could go to le Salève.'

'And have a go on the cable car! Sweet.' Patch nodded. 'Tell you what, I'll make us all some of my trademark super-stuffed sandwiches!'

Motti grunted. 'I just lost my appetite again.'

Two hours later, Tye sat in the back of her silver BMW Hydrogen 7 with Patch and Motti. Jonah was up front with Con – he'd got his wish for a drive in the country, but she guessed it was a little less cosy than the one he'd had in mind. Con refused point blank ever to travel in the back seat – it gave her panic attacks so severe she flipped out; her parents had died in a car crash when she was a little girl, and she'd been trapped in the car with their corpses for hours before she could be cut free. Maybe it wasn't so weird that Con had grown up determined to keep the world at a distance, Tye decided, or that her closest relationship was with her Swiss bank account.

Tye winced as an unexpected gear change sent the car lurching forward.

'Jeez, Jonah,' Motti complained, 'could you pick a gear and stay there? A ninth grader on his first jump gives a better ride than you.'

'Well, you'd know,' Jonah retorted over the frustrated roar of the engine.

'This is the last time I lend you my car,' Tye promised. 'I know you've got to practise, but . . .'

'At least you get a break this way, Tye, no?' Con pointed out. 'You're always having to drive us.'

'And please, God, you always will,' Motti muttered.

Tye smiled and rolled her eyes. 'Just 'cause I'm the only one responsible enough to buy a saloon while the rest of you get sports cars.'

'Got my image to think about, haven't I?' said Patch, thumbs hammering at his gloss silver Nintendo DS Lite. 'God, I feel sick. I think I'm gonna be.'

'Big surprise,' said Jonah, hitting the rear electric windows to give him air.

'Throw up in here and you die,' Tye warned him.

'On the other hand,' said Motti, 'throw up in your sandwiches and no one will know the difference.'

'Scenic stop ahead,' Con announced, indicating a layby where travellers could pull in and admire the view. Even before Jonah brought the car to a halt, Patch threw open the door and chucked his breakfast after it. Noisily.

'Uh-huh.' Motti smirked as he helped Tye out of the car. 'He's got his image to think about.'

They set off up the hillside with a coolbox packed with booze, a rucksack jammed fuller than a restaurant's fridge, and a couple of briefcases filled with the notes, maps and papers that would help them plan the heist. None of them spoke as they meandered along in the sunshine, enjoying the summer sunshine and the breeze. Tye looked at a map of Texas, figuring out their route, the transport and clearances they'd need – transporting them there and back in one piece. She looked wistfully over at Lake Geneva far below, a vast pool of blue hemmed in by trees and buildings like sentries guarding its depths in their hundreds.

'Here's as good as anywhere,' Con decided, sitting down on a small plateau halfway up a hillside.

Patch dropped his rucksack and set about removing the food. 'As her ladyship commands.' Con grabbed a chicken leg and bit into it hungrily.

'Route-wise,' said Tye, 'to keep a low profile I think I'll fly us into the tiny airport at San Angelo and take a hire car down to San Antonio. Should take us three, maybe four hours on the interstate.'

'Or twelve if Jonah's driving,' Motti put in.

'Ha, ha,' said Jonah. 'And what do we find when we get there? What's the dirt on Blackland?'

'Coldhardt gave me his file.' Motti cracked open a beer. 'Blackland's from a rich family, Texan to the T-bone. Had his own fort built from scratch in honour of his ancestors who fought in the Texas War of Independence.'

'Sweet,' said Patch, hefting a huge, clumsily cut sandwich with chutney oozing out of it. 'So Blackland don't need to work, he just sits on his bum reading weird old books all day, is that it?'

Motti shook his head. 'Daddy was big in the oil biz, but Blackland prefers digging other shit out the ground.'

Con hazarded a translation. 'An archaeologist?'

'All nice and respectable on the surface. But Coldhardt reckons he's more of a tomb raider on the sly. Not declaring all his finds and smuggling them off to his stronghold.'

'Just how fortressy is Blackland's place?' Tye asked, hunkering down. 'I mean, it's not like we're going to be storming the Alamo, right?'

Motti pulled a face. 'Can't promise you Mexican bandits, but we'll have a small security force in the grounds to take care of.'

Jonah nodded. 'I hacked into Blackland's bank account, found the firm supplying his security and checked out what he's bought from them. Afraid the rest of that fort's defences are a little more high-tech than men with old rifles wearing racoons on their head.'

Motti took a big swig from his beer bottle. 'Don't diss my heritage, geek.'

'So what shouldn't we know about this place?' asked Patch.

'I'll come to that,' said Motti. 'But once we're past security, biggest problem we might run into is that every book in Blackland's library has been fitted with long-range active RFID tags, our target included.'

Tye frowned. '*What* tags?'

'Radio Frequency Identification,' Jonah clarified, as Motti passed him a picture of the house. 'Kind of like barcodes with go-faster stripes. Inductively powered chips that transmit all kinds of information using radio waves.'

'Including their location?' Con wondered.

'Yep.' Jonah lowered the picture. 'And it looks like Blackland's got high-gain antennae to keep tabs.'

'So even if we can make it away with the manuscript,' said Patch, spitting sandwich everywhere as he spoke, 'its little tag's gonna be shouting for help.'

Motti nodded. 'And an aerial like that could track it a hell of a way.'

'Can't we take it out?' asked Tye. 'I mean, if it's a tag –'

Jonah shook his head. 'They can be as small as half a millimetre and thin as a piece of paper. A tag'll take time to find – time we may not have. But maybe if we make a conductive foil box to damp the tag's signal . . .'

The five of them planned and ate and drank all afternoon, discussing the problems they would face, throwing thoughts and doubts and suggestions at each other. And as the plans began to crystallise, Tye felt a twisted surge of pride. *All our lives we struggled to be something, to be taken seriously. And look at us now. We can do this.* And since Blackland had most likely got hold of this manuscript illegally, it seemed only fair that he should lose it in the same way . . .

While Patch helped Motti type up their proposals to show Coldhardt, she and Jonah busied themselves packing up the remains of their feast and Con went off to bin the empties. Then a thought hit Tye with a prick of sudden coldness: *It won't always be like this.* She'd had so little stability in her life, and yet this last year, since Jonah was recruited . . . Even if he did her head in sometimes, with him around it felt like a proper balance had been reached in the group.

I want to keep hold of today, Tye thought, with the

wide-open blue sky and good tastes on her lips and a safe bed waiting back home when she was ready. Tomorrow they would be rushing headlong into risk and danger. All that certainty would be gone.

Tye looked out again over the city's stone sentries massed amid the trees beside the lake, trying to picture the landscape as once it had been, remembering the wild sweep of the Léogane mountains she had played on as a child before her mum left and her world fell apart. *The only thing that stays the same*, she thought, *is that everything must change*.

She looked at Jonah, away in a world of his own.

Will you?

CHAPTER FOUR

Blackland's fort sat bathed in floodlights beneath the dark Texan skies like a deserted Hollywood set, ringed in by formidable fencing. Jonah watched from the cover of a stand of oak trees in this former ranchland. It was half two in the morning, the constant thrum of the cicadas was wearing on his already frayed nerves, and he wished he was waiting in the getaway car with Tye.

'Another night, another break-in,' he murmured, scanning the straggly bushes before him. Motti had gone ahead first, to scout out the fencepost-mounted CCTV camera and signal when it was looking far enough in the other direction for the others to join him – one at a time, to keep moving foliage to a minimum. Patch had already dashed over; and any time now . . .

At last a hand came up from the twitching foliage, twenty or so metres closer to the fort – and its first line of protection. The fence was ten feet high, marked into sections by concrete posts and crowned with extension arms from which lengths of razor ribbon were tautly strung. Keeping low, Jonah ran quickly and quietly across the scrub to join his friends. They were dressed all in black, as he was.

'Fence looks a bit evil,' Jonah noted, eyeing the vicious-looking razor wire.

Patch nodded miserably. 'I've got a bad feeling about tonight.'

'Our biggest problem's the microphonic coaxial cable running between the fence posts parallel to the ground,' Motti explained. 'The cable converts any movement in the fabric of the fence into electrical noise. The noise is analysed by software that's supposed to know the difference between wind, rain, little birdies and stuff, and an intruder breaking in . . .'

Jonah nodded. 'I'm glad you said "supposed".'

'Thing is, over time, the sensors get jumpy.' Motti turned away, checking the CCTV camera's position again. 'Which means a lot of false alarms for the security team. Which means . . .'

'They make the fence less sensitive so they're not being called out for nothing the whole time,' Patch concluded.

Motti nodded. 'Especially when the fence alone is a good visual deterrent – to anyone who ain't us.' Satisfied with the camera's position, Motti stuck his hand up in the air again. A dark, slim figure clutching a bundle in both hands came scuttling from the treeline towards them. 'Con and a blanket. 'S all we need.'

Patch sighed. 'I could get by without the blanket.'

Con closed the last of the distance and flopped down on the ground beside them. 'Hello, boys.'

'The posts are the weak point, Con.' Motti was wasting no time on pleasantries. 'Provided you don't touch, kick or disturb the wire mesh directly attached to those posts, the alarm shouldn't go off.'

Con looked doubtfully at the bundle she was carrying. 'And the blanket is enough to stop me getting shredded on the barbed wire?'

'It's got a titanium foil lining,' Motti assured her.

'Well, it's actually made from a titanium-aluminum-vanadium alloy,' added Jonah. 'Deals with razor ribbon, muffles the signals from RFID tags . . . A hundred-and-one household uses.'

'Just sling it over the top and flip over,' said Motti. 'You won't feel a thing.' His eyes were back on the slowly rotating camera. 'Now, it's just as we planned. We'll wait till one of the guards passes by – that should leave this section of the perimeter safe from the flatfoots for a bit. Then I'll help each of you over the fence, one at a time.'

'And wait for us as back-up out here till we signal,' Con added.

Patch sighed. 'Why can't I be the one who stays out of trouble?'

''Cause you're our indispensable locksmith who's going to get us inside that fort,' said Jonah. 'And 'cause your glass eyeball is the safest place to carry the plastic explosive that's going to take care of Blackland's high-gain antennae – so no one will hear our stolen manuscript transmitting.'

'See?' said Patch. 'All you've got is good reasons.'

'Let's just get on with it,' said Con quietly. 'As soon as the guard patrol goes by.'

Long minutes dragged by sweatily as they waited.

Motti scowled. 'These clowns are crummier than I thought. It's been thirty minutes and no one's shown.'

'I've got *such* a bad feeling about this,' Patch told them again.

'Let's go over everything one last time,' hissed Jonah, feeling unnerved enough already. 'You can never be too sure.'

'OK. Con's the lightest and the most agile,' said Motti, 'so she'll go in first. Patch, Jonah, if either of you set off the alarm, give the guards the biggest chase you can – buy Con time to get the manuscript. Once you're inside, stick to the shadows and tread careful. There should be dome cameras inside the grounds – faster and more accurate than the CCTV out here, and most likely hooked up to a Video Motion Detection system.'

Jonah nodded. 'Actively analysing any pixel changes in the video pictures the cameras transmit. If they pick up a disturbance big enough to suggest an intruder, the alarms kick off.'

'But we didn't find no records online for Blackland buying infra-reds to help light them,' Motti reminded them. 'He's got this whole ain't-it-pretty-floodlit thing going down, showing off his property, lots of bright light – which means stronger contrast in the shadows. Stick to those and it should be too dark for any pixel changes to matter.'

'We hope,' said Patch.

'Just get in through the first goddamned door or window you come to, OK?' Motti produced a two-way radio handset. 'Jonah, you got the RT. Signal when you've got that manuscript. I'll let off a signal flare through the fence, bring security running this way. You'll hear it go boom – that's your cue to make for the main gates. Tye will smash them open with the pick-up so you can get on board with the goods.'

'And meantime you double back through the woods to the road so we can collect you on our way back to San Angelo,' Jonah concluded.

'Cinch, innit?' said Patch without enthusiasm.

They went on waiting. Another twenty minutes. Jonah saw a light go out at one window, like the fort was giving them a crafty wink. There was still no sign of security in the grounds.

'I don't like this,' said Motti under his breath. 'How long we gotta wait for these a-holes to do their job?'

Con shrugged. 'I say we move now.'

'And what if you're still scrambling over that fence when some old guard turns the corner?'

'I will try to land on him, yes?' She looked at Motti. 'It'll start getting light in less than two hours, then the mission will be compromised. Get me in and I'll scout around, then come back and tell you how things stand.'

'Guess we don't got much choice.' He looked at Con. 'OK, on my signal.'

Con took a deep breath. Jonah held his, as the camera slowly swivelled away from their intended stretch of fence.

Then Motti broke cover – '*Now!*'

He and Con ran to the nearest fencepost. As Con unfolded the blanket, Motti formed a stirrup with his hands. Jonah watched admiringly as she stepped lightly into it, launched herself upwards and placed the blanket over the razor wire to smother its bite.

Then she calmly pulled herself up like a trapeze artist, barely brushing against the chain links, and flipped herself over. She landed sure and safe while Motti sprinted back into the bushes like a man caught short.

As the camera swivelled back to look their way, Jonah ducked out of sight with Patch and Motti. He strained to hear anything from Con over the measured thrum of the cicadas and the pounding of his pulse in his ears.

Finally her voice floated to them through the shadows beyond the fence. 'I think it's clear.'

'Your turn next, geek,' breathed Motti, eyeing the camera. 'Move.'

Jonah felt sick with nerves as he followed Motti to the fence, but it was like jumping out of a plane – there was no going back now. You just had to do all you could to survive the fall.

Motti made a stirrup again, and Jonah hoped that he wouldn't put his foot in anything else. He clutched at the razor wire through the blanket – praying it wouldn't take his fingers off – and with Motti giving him a bunk-up was able to haul himself up and over. His foot caught against the fence post and he braced himself for the sound of alarms – but the impact must have been within tolerance. He scrambled down as lightly as he could, hit the ground the other side a little awkwardly. Wincing, he stared around for any sign of security but caught only a glimpse of Con as she turned and ducked behind a large, decorative bush clipped to resemble a pyramid. He staggered over to join her, to wait there for Patch.

Then he saw what Con was looking at, and had a

shock of realisation at what was propped up against the tight leafy wall of the pyramid: the body of a security guard, arms splayed out, his navy uniform soaked with blood.

Jonah's guts twisted like a wrung cloth. The thick stub of a crossbow bolt was protruding from the man's chest.

'The woman who killed Budd and Clyde,' Jonah blurted, staring wildly all around. 'She's been here. She wants the manuscript.'

'But how?' Con straightened, her catlike eyes almost accusing. 'How did she know it was here? You said the laptop –'

'Morell must have *told* someone – or what about that guy Saitou he was going to employ. Maybe the bow-woman works with him, or she found out somehow, or . . .' Jonah's voice trailed off as he pointed past the glare of a floodlight to where a tree stood in stark silhouette. A dark figure lay at its feet, as if blown from its branches. Jonah stumbled straight through the bright orange spill, no longer mindful of intruder alarms, adrenaline pushing him forward. Security had been torn apart; here was another guard, peaked cap pulled down over his face, lifeless hands locked uselessly around the bolt in his ribs as if he were still trying to pull it out.

Jonah turned away, sickened. 'I think we can guess what's happened to the rest of the patrol.'

'The question is,' said Con slowly, 'has she been and gone – or is she still here somewhere?'

They both jumped as Patch scrambled through the bushes to join them. 'Lovely,' he muttered. 'I'm guessing this pair ain't just sleeping on the job.'

'Unless someone tried to wake them by firing a crossbow at them,' said Jonah darkly, pulling his walkie-talkie from his back pocket. 'Motti, can you hear me?'

'Don't tell me you found it already?' Motti's voice spat from the handset.

'All we've found are two dead guards,' Jonah reported.

'And trouble,' Patch added, grabbing Jonah's arm, pointing behind him.

Jonah saw that a figure had appeared from round a corner of the fort some thirty metres away. Through the fierce floodlit glare it was impossible to make out detail, but he wasted no time shoving Con and Patch behind the tree in case the intruder was armed.

'Motti, we're not the only trespassers here,' Jonah spoke into the radio tersely. 'Looks like the bitch with the crossbow. Get on to Tye – we may need back-up.'

Patch nodded. 'Or a ride out in a hurry.'

'Roger that,' said Motti gravely. 'Watch your asses. Out.'

Jonah peered out from cover to check on the figure – in time to see it vanishing back round the corner.

'Come on, we must follow,' Con snapped, setting off in the same direction.

'Why?' Patch hissed. 'This whole thing's gone belly up, Con. You heard Motti, we should watch your arse. *Our* arse, I mean – or arses . . . Whatever!'

Con kept moving. 'Whoever we saw, they might have the manuscript, or know where it is. If we can find out who they are, there may be a bonus for us, yes? Besides, there's one of them and three of us.'

'Yeah, until they shoot a couple of us dead like the guards,' said Jonah pointedly. Even so, he found himself jogging alongside her, and Patch was following close behind, clutching the foil blanket close as if for comfort.

As they rounded the huge stone corner Jonah glimpsed the figure dart in through a doorway. 'Could be a trap,' he said, pulling on Con's arm, holding her back. 'Ambush. We don't know how many of them are inside.'

'Let's surprise 'em.' Patch carried on running round the outside of the fort walls, and Jonah and Con followed. 'We'll get in through the next door we come to and set our *own* ambush.'

'Could work,' Con admitted.

They soon came to a plain wooden door beside a dark window. 'This is the east wing . . . so if those plans we saw are accurate,' said Con, 'this should be a utility room.'

While Patch rushed to study the lock, Jonah peered in through the glass and clocked a sink, an industrial-size washing machine and a drier just as big. 'Bang on, Con. Patch, how'd you rate the lock?'

'Fifteen pin,' Patch reported, reaching in his pocket for a bunch of keys. 'Five pins on three sides. Good security rating. Unless you get busy with a home-made bump key.'

Jonah kept watch anxiously, praying the Crossbow Girl stayed well away. 'A what key?'

'Bump. It's like a blank key, cut deep, can fit inside a certain type of lock, yeah?' Patch inserted a key as if to demonstrate, then pulled a screwdriver from his other pocket. 'When you hit the key in the lock, only the top pins are bumped up, creating a gap between top and bottom pins. At which point . . .' He twisted the key as he cracked the screwdriver against its base, pulled down on the handle – and the door opened.

'Nice work,' Jonah muttered, as Con nudged Patch aside and stepped in first, heading for the inner door. 'Con, wait, if Crossbow Girl is armed and ready to go –'

She turned back to him impatiently, pulled down the neck of her black top to reveal a phosphor cap pressed to her collarbone – a small glass ampoule that would ignite with a blinding flash under impact. 'They can't hit what they can't see.'

But as she reached for the handle of the door, it swung open towards her – quickly followed by a fist. Con gasped as she was sent sprawling backwards with no time to react. She knocked into Jonah, who fell back against the large porcelain sink, knocking detergent everywhere. *They guessed what we were trying,* he realised, *came to head us off*. Before he could turn, he heard the sickening smack of two more blows finding a mark on Con's body.

'Get off her,' Patch yelled.

Jonah saw the man who'd sneak-attacked Con in silhouette against the bright oblong of open door, lunging forward to grab him. He grabbed a bottle of cleaning fluid, wrenched off the cap and squeezed the contents into the man's face. Jonah caught a snatch of South African accent as the man let stream with some colourful swearing. *Wash your mouth out*, he thought grimly, squirting a blast of bleach down his attacker's throat. The man choked and retched, wiping ferociously at his eyes, and Patch hit him as hard as he could on the jaw. Jonah followed up with a kick to the stomach that sent the man staggering back into the corridor.

Con was on her knees, holding her ribs, and Jonah crouched down beside her. 'You OK?'

Con spat blood on the floor and nodded silently. But behind her, outside in the grounds, Jonah caught a glimpse of movement. A figure in black was running towards the house. A girl, gripping a crossbow.

'Quick!' Jonah grabbed Con by the wrist and hauled her away, Patch narrowly beating them out of the room and into the large, marble-floored hallway. Jonah heaved the heavy door shut behind them, just as a bolt slammed into the wood with a splintering *thunk*. There was a key in the lock and he turned it just in time, as the handle jumped from his grip, worked furiously by whoever was on the other side.

Jonah looked round quickly. They were in a hallway. The fort was as old-fashioned inside as out, only gloomier – it was all antique dressers and grandfather clocks and grey walls displaying old swords and rifles.

Their attacker had already recovered, ignoring the disinfectant dripping from his clothes, looking mad as hell. He was maybe in his late teens, as big as a bull, a tanned, toned powerhouse with blond hair and glaciers for eyes. 'We've been waiting for you to show . . .' His South African accent was curt. 'Coldhardt's little assholes.'

'As far as we know he's only got the one,' Jonah

shot back, tensing for a further fight.

'My name's Sorin.' The guy smiled, red tongue flicking against ice-white teeth. 'And you are Jonah Wish, Patrick Kendall and Constance Beatty.'

Jonah didn't have a smart comeback; like Patch and Con he found himself shifting uneasily at the namecheck. Then the door shuddered under a large blow behind them. Jonah and the others moved away.

'It's all right, Sadie,' he shouted, 'I'm on it.'

Con glared at him. 'Who are you people? Who do you work for?'

Sorin only smiled – as he darted towards them with incredible speed. But Con was just as fast as she snatched the phosphor cap from beneath her top and hurled it down in his path. Jonah flung up his arm as the yellow flare bit away the shadows. Sorin recoiled, shouting in pain and anger – as another huge thump saw the utility room door almost sheared from its hinges.

'Move,' snapped Jonah.

'Wait. That asshole called me Constance.' Con flew forward, into the smoke. Jonah heard the crack of knuckle on bone, ceramics breaking. A few anxious seconds later Con re-emerged, stuffing a Rolex into her pocket. 'One less creep to worry about.'

'Make that one more!' Jonah shouted as the door to the utility room gave way. He grabbed the radio from his pocket. 'Motti, we need back-up. Hostiles in east wing. Get Tye and get here –'

The masked girl with the crossbow, presumbly Sadie, burst out from inside – and then skidded and landed flat on her butt.

'Ha!' Patch waved the blanket like a victory flag as

he chucked an empty bottle of liquid soap at her head. Jonah realised the soap itself had been carefully spilled all over the floor.

But Sadie recovered swiftly, scrambled on to the fallen door where she could keep her footing. She ripped off her mask to wipe her slippery hands – and in a heartbeat Jonah recognised the ring on her finger. *Coldhardt's ring. The one Motti was meant to give Budd,* she *got hold of it.* But as Jonah turned to run it wasn't the glint of gold that shone in his mind, but the image of her: her black, spiky hair, her face porcelain-pale with cheeks as rosy as a doll's, brown eyes caked with kohl, emphasising her murderous glare. He sprinted after Con and Patch, their footfalls together like cold thunder on the marble as they made for the grand staircase across the hallway.

But however fast they ran, he knew Sadie's bolt would be faster.

Jonah threw a desperate backward glance over his shoulder. Sadie was taking aim, her finger curling round the trigger, aiming carefully at –

'Patch!' Jonah bawled.

Trailing the foil blanket behind him like a superhero's cape, Patch had reached the top step. He turned round as the bolt was loosed – and doubled up as it hit him in the stomach.

Patch staggered back, mouthing in silence, then fell and lay still.

CHAPTER FIVE

Parked out on a wooded trail, just out of sight of Blackland's fort, Tye sat in the pick-up, biting her nails. Motti was taking for ever to get here. He'd radioed that he was coming to her rather than waiting at the roadside as planned. Which meant something was wrong. She was tempted to radio him back, but if he was hiding out, lying low, her voice barking out of the handset wouldn't exactly do him many favours. She wished they'd had more time to plan and prepare. She felt a flare of resentment at the thought of Coldhardt sitting pretty in his own fortress while they risked their lives breaking into this one. She should've spoken up, got them more planning time, scouted the location in advance. But Coldhardt had been so adamant they move quickly . . . as if he could sense his enemies closing in.

Just what were Jonah and the others up against in there?

There was a rap at the door of the pick-up. Tye was jolted back to the moment and grabbed the revolver lying in her lap. It wasn't even loaded, but as a deterrent . . .

Motti opened the door, panting for breath.

She scowled and lowered the gun, angry and relieved at once. 'What the hell's happening out there?'

As he opened his mouth to reply, a burst of static belched from his radio together with Jonah's frantic voice. *'Motti, we need back-up . . .'*

'Drive,' Motti snapped, holding the radio to his ear as he scrambled inside.

Tye had already started the engine. 'But if I break through the gates now, security –'

'– is screwed all to hell. Two guards been wasted, at least two. Now *move*!'

Tye put her foot down and fat tyres tore through the turf as the pick-up sped away along the track.

'Gates give on to the west side,' Motti continued. 'If we crash 'em, people gonna know we've arrived – and while they come looking, we sneak out and circle round to the east wing. Plan?'

'Plan,' Tye agreed. The vehicle had been left for them at San Angelo by one of Coldhardt's contacts, customised with special bull bars designed to concentrate and multiply the force of collision. She'd calculated a speed of at least fifty to smash through the iron security gates, but so much depended on where she hit them and from which angle . . . It wasn't an exact science.

She only had one shot at getting it right.

Tye poured on the gas as they thundered along the wooded lane. 'Hang on tight.'

'Duh!' replied Motti as he buckled up and wedged his feet against the dashboard, bracing himself.

The pick-up lurched as they roared and skidded round the corner. The fort came into sight.

And there were the heavy-duty gates – standing wide open.

Tye took in two uniformed bodies, face-up in the gravel with bolts in their bellies. Just beyond them, she saw a huge, white limousine parked on the drive, blocking their way. She stomped on the brakes, spun the wheel, muttered a prayer as she swerved to try and avoid the limo. But the pick-up was like a big red missile and it was going too fast to stop.

There was a kind of sick grace to the collision as they smacked loudly into the back of the car; the limo's boot and bumper crumpled like paper and it leapt into the air like Chitty Chitty Bang Bang's posher cousin.

The impact flung Tye forward in her seat, the safety belt biting into her ribs. Moments later, she had unbuckled and was racing outside. Every bone in her body seemed to rattle as she ran, and there was a prickling thickness throbbing through the back of her neck. *If anyone was inside that limo, they could be dead as those two guards.* The realisation stopped her running. She was suddenly afraid to see.

Motti reached the car first. 'No one,' he reported, glancing back towards the fallen guards. 'And that's all security here terminated.' He shook his head. 'But if this is Lady Bowfinger's getaway vehicle, I think she'll be leaving on foot.'

A woman's scream echoed distantly from inside the fort.

Motti turned at the sound. 'Maybe that's her now.'

'Sounds like someone's terrified,' said Tye.

'Do we care? It wasn't Con,' Motti noted. 'And Patch and Jonah can't reach a note as high as that.'

Tye took a deep breath. 'Well, gates or no gates, we've announced our arrival. Let's get inside and take a look.' She led the way across the drive, kicking up gravel as she ran for the nearest window.

'No!' Jonah felt his world tilt, felt his legs start to shake as he tore up the remaining stairs to where Patch lay unmoving. He reached him just as Con did. 'Is he OK, is he –?'

Patch's eye flickered open and scrunched the blanket he was clutching in front of him around the bolt. 'Good stuff, this titanium foil,' he croaked. 'Don't think she broke the skin.' Jonah tried to help Patch up, but the boy shook his head a fraction. 'Just make out I'm dead and leave her to me.'

Jonah blinked. 'To you?'

Patch winked. 'Eye for an eye.'

'Murdering bitch!' Con shrieked, turning in a fury back to Sadie.

The girl had negotiated the slippery floor and was running towards the stairs, grim-faced. There was no sign of Sorin. Sadie swung up her arm ready to fire at Con, but then had to dodge aside as Jonah chucked a large vase down at her from the top of the stairs.

He grabbed Con's wrist and yanked her away along the landing, panting for breath. The floors and walls were black up here, with strange markings and crude geometric designs scratched into the ceiling, like strange stars overhead. The landing turned at right angles, and once they'd rounded the corner, they stopped running.

'Hope Patch knows what he's doing,' said Jonah.

Con nodded, wiped drying blood from her swollen lip.

Cautiously, Jonah peeped out from around the corner, as Sadie reached the top of the stairs where Patch's body was sprawled. She crouched as if to make sure he was dead – and then Patch lashed out with both legs, catching her in the stomach and propelling her backwards. She gasped, and as Jonah heard her tumble and crash back down the stairs he felt a savage satisfaction. Patch scrambled up and staggered over to join them.

'That was brilliant, Patch,' said Jonah, putting an arm round him. 'You OK?'

'No, it bloody hurts.' Patch pulled up his top to expose a huge, red-purple bruise spreading over his skinny stomach. 'Kiss it better, Con?'

'Shut up, Patch,' she said quietly. 'Jonah, how did these people know we were coming? How do they know us by name?'

'How many rivals must Coldhardt have, how many enemies?' Jonah shook his head helplessly. 'Take out his workforce, you shut down his operations.'

Con swore. 'Now they can get the manuscript and execute us at the same time.'

'I told you I had a bad feeling about tonight,' said Patch miserably.

'Time we split,' said Jonah. 'At least with security dealt with we don't have to wait for Tye to break open the gates.'

'But we can't go back the way we came,' said Patch. As if for emphasis, fresh footfalls started to pound a ragged rhythm on the staircase behind them. 'Sounds like the bitch is back.'

'And where's her mate?' Jonah licked his dry lips. 'We don't know how many of these bastards there are. If any of them reach the west wing staircase ahead of us . . .'

'We'll be cut off!' Con realised.

As one, the three of them sprinted away.

It was maybe fifty metres across the gravel to the nearest lit window in the looming grey stonework. Tye covered the distance in seconds, Motti following close on her heels. White curtains shielded the room from sight.

'Surely someone would have heard the crash and come looking by now?' said Tye breathlessly.

'Unless they're too busy,' Motti suggested, 'taking care of stuff –'

He broke off as suddenly the curtains jumped open and a girl's face slammed up against the window. Motti stepped back in alarm as she beat her palms against the glass, like she was trying to get out. Tye felt her stomach twist. The elfin-looking girl looked maybe eighteen, her eyes as wild as her shoulder-length red hair, terrified. A large brown birthmark stained her chin and neck, but she hadn't been born with the gash on her pale cheek. Someone grabbed a fistful of the girl's hair and yanked on it savagely, tearing her away from the glass.

Then the window was flung open and Tye quickly

flattened herself against the wall as another girl's face appeared, peering out across the driveway. She was older, early twenties perhaps, black with dyed blonde hair, straightened and scraped back off her high forehead.

But Tye didn't get much more of a chance to study the face before Motti punched it. The girl grunted with pain and staggered back out of sight. Tye flashed him a *what was that?* look.

'We don't got our lockpick with us,' Motti hissed to Tye, climbing quickly inside. 'Don't look a gift horse in the mouth –'

'– when you can smack it there instead?' Tye followed him into a simple study, her empty gun at the ready. The black blonde, dressed in a grey pinstripe trouser suit, was getting to her feet, dabbing delicately at her nose, collected and aloof. The redhead, meanwhile, sat curled up and cowering beneath a big wooden desk in the corner – no threat. Tye noticed the black girl had bloodied knuckles and kept the gun trained on her.

'Red there don't look like a pro housebreaker to me,' Motti said, turning to the girl he'd hit. 'And since you were beating up on her, I'm guessing you're a stranger here yourself.'

'If you're guessing, it seems I have you at a disadvantage.' The girl was apparently British and sounded amused. 'You're Anthony Motson . . . and your companion is Tye Chery.'

Tye frowned, sensed Motti stiffen beside her. 'Well, don't that make me nostalgic. Ain't been called Anthony in years.'

'I see the two of you have wrecked our transport,' the girl went on. 'Now we'll have to take yours.'

'Is that so?' Tye kept her face impassive and her grip on the gun tight. 'How'd you know who we are?'

'My name's Bree. Glad you could make it.' Her smile grew wider as she held out a hand to Motti, who ignored it. 'I suppose you're here to help your friends? They could use it. They're in a lot of trouble.'

Motti glowered at her. 'If they're in trouble, Breezy, *you're* in trouble. Now what say we go find them all together?'

'Don't trust her,' the redhead told them, in an accent difficult to place. But wherever she was from, she was speaking aloud Tye's own thoughts: this Bree girl seemed too relaxed, too confident by half. 'She's a psycho,' the girl went on. 'She and her friends tore this place apart, they've got Mr Blackland –'

'Ignore Maya here,' Brie interrupted smoothly. 'She's a student librarian, and really not very helpful.'

Maya flinched. 'I'm only here for the summer,' she whispered.

'I'd say your employment's terminated.' Bree turned back to Tye and Motti. 'We've acquired the Guan Yin manuscript. The Bloodline Cipher is ours. And pretty soon we'll have all your friends, too. In pieces.'

'Then the cavalry's arrived just in time,' snarled Motti. 'You're gonna take us to them right now.'

Suddenly Tye noticed Bree's eyes flick twice between them and the inner door. *That's why she's so confident.* 'Mot, she's been stalling for time.' Tye took a warning step nearer the girl, both hands on the gun. 'Someone's coming –'

The handle of the door jerked suddenly, and the heavy wood swung open to reveal a man standing in the doorway, paunchy and grey. Motti was already running to intercept. He punched the old man in the stomach and chopped him on the back of the neck as he crumpled to the carpet.

'No!' Maya shouted as she saw him fall. 'Mr Blackland!'

The owner? Tye took in the huge bloodstain spreading over the back of the man's pale shirt and swore. *Poor old guy's dead*, she realised with a sick feeling, *a decoy, just propped in the doorway to distract while –*

Motti looked up angrily from the corpse – right into the swing of a baseball bat. He yelled out as the wooden club cracked against the side of his head, shattering his glasses, knocking him to the ground.

'Motti! Tye yelled, swinging the gun round to cover his attacker – but Bree had anticipated the movement and swung her palm down edgeways in a karate chop that almost took Tye's wrist off. The gun slipped from her numbed fingers – but Tye was already turning to kick Bree in the stomach. The blow hit home, and Tye followed through with an uppercut. But her opponent feinted backwards, caught Tye's forearm and bent it back hard. Gasping with pain, Tye was forced to the ground where she got a knee in the face. Tye jack-knifed backwards, hit the floor in a daze beside Motti. He was out cold, a thick crimson dribble running down his temple from the hairline. Tye felt a stab of panic and fought to stay calm. If she could only rest a few moments, get her strength back . . .

Bree had picked up Tye's gun and now surveyed her dispassionately. Abruptly she turned towards the doorway. 'Shall we kill one of them?'

'I don't see why not,' said a new voice – deep and cracked with age, with an accent that spoke of no particular place. Tye hadn't heard anyone else come into the room, but suddenly the hairs on the back of her neck were standing up. 'After all, her friends will soon be captured. And we only need one of them to bring the message back to Coldhardt.'

Then they still haven't got the others. 'What message?' she asked, playing for time; the gun might be useless, but she couldn't run out and leave Motti. 'Who are you?'

'My name is Heidel.'

Tye angled her head back, craned her neck to see who was speaking. She caught a glimpse of a tall man, standing stooped in a black suit. He had a lined, lugubrious face and a mane of silver-grey. A hint of cruelty played about the edges of his lips as he held the bat in two gloved hands.

'What do you say, Ms Chery?' Heidel went on. 'Would you care to sacrifice yourself for your friend, or would you rather he died in your place? He is sleeping rather heavily, he will never know you betrayed him . . .' The old man's tone hardened. 'The way your benefactor Coldhardt betrayed *me*.'

'Benefactor?' *Keep him talking*, Tye thought. 'We're only Coldhardt's employees, we don't mean anything to him beyond –'

'You're his family,' said Heidel angrily. 'That's how it works. The big man gathers his little ones to him.

Insists that they prove their love by risking everything, time after time. Rewards them when they win.' He walked towards her. 'And their luck holds for a time. But then doubt steals in, or the strain gets too great, and . . . in walks death. Or betrayal.' Tye had a clear look at Heidel's eyes now. They were clear blue, no passion there. They looked . . . wrong, somehow – as wrong as a man in a flashy suit wielding a bloody wooden bat. 'So which will it be, Tye Chery – death or betrayal, which would you give a head start?' He smiled coldly. 'Because believe me, each follows the other.'

Then someone cleared his throat. 'Did you get that out of a fortune cookie or something?'

Tye wanted to sob with relief. '*Jonah?*' She propped herself up on her elbows and saw him step through the doorway with Patch.

Then her hopes sank like her heart; standing right behind them were a beach-blond himbo and a pale, dark-eyed girl with jet-black hair.

'Prisoners and escort,' said Bree, and the smile she gave Tye was sickeningly triumphant.

CHAPTER SIX

Jonah tried to take in the scene quickly and coolly – but his mind, like his eyes, couldn't choose where to settle. There was an old man at his feet clearly dead, Motti looking not a lot better on the floor, Tye at the feet of a girl with a gun and some aging mobster type who could have been Coldhardt's brother – oh, and a pixie-like red-haired girl hiding under a desk.

Quite a crowd, Jonah thought. *Here goes nothing.*

'Yep, it's prisoner and escort all right,' he told the black girl with the dyed hair. 'But guess what . . . ?'

'You're *all* our prisoners,' hissed Con behind him, shoving Sadie and Sorin into the study. Sorin had reached the west-side staircase ahead of them and Sadie had cut them off from behind, just as Jonah had feared. But Patch, once again, had managed to turn things round . . .

As Sadie and Sorin stumbled forward, the black girl swung her gun to cover Jonah, and the mobster raised his baseball bat.

'Back off!' Patch shouted.

'Do as he says,' said Sorin, and Sadie nodded – dishevelled and looking mad as all hell. The mobster slowly lowered the gun, but the black girl kept aim.

Tye looked up at her. 'Better give it up, Bree. It's not even loaded.'

'As if,' Bree sneered.

'No loud noises, please.' Jonah glanced at Patch, who was holding his false eye in one hand; now he flipped up his eye patch to reveal the empty socket. 'Patch has got his eye on you. And since you know so much about us, I'm assuming you're aware of how he keeps all kinds of stuff in that insulated glass. Tonight it's stuffed full of plastic explosive – enough, we reckoned, to take out the radio mast that Blackland uses to keep tabs on his books.'

'The arming device is in the pupil,' Con explained, as Patch showed around the fake eyeball like a magician's assistant. 'You press on it once to arm it – then, when you take your finger off, you've got maybe five seconds before it blows.'

'I'd show you,' said Patch, looking pale and sweaty, 'but I've *already* armed it. If I take my finger off the pupil I'll blow up the whole bleedin' lot of us.'

'You're bluffing,' said the old man calmly.

'No, Heidel.' Sorin shook his head. 'We saw him arm the mechanism. Or else we'd have taken them.'

'Kendall wouldn't harm his friends,' Bree stated.

'I don't want to hurt anyone,' said Patch, waggling the eyeball. 'And I get bloody nervous at times like this, so no one make my hands any shakier, yeah?'

'Give me my gun back,' said Tye.

Bree weighed the gun in her hand, then held it out to Tye. But as Tye reached for it she tossed it out of the open window. 'It's useless, remember?' She smirked at Patch. 'Well, Kendall? Going to blow us all sky high for my disobedience?'

Jonah tutted. 'You want to keep your gang under control, Heidel. Any more surprises, we could all wind up dead.'

'Now stand in the far corner, all of you,' Con snapped. 'No tricks.'

Heidel stared at her for a few moments. Then he signalled to his gang and slowly, dutifully, they backed away.

Jonah crossed to Tye and knelt beside her. 'You OK? Is Motti all right?'

Tye shot a poisonous look at Heidel. 'He's breathing.'

'For now,' said Bree casually.

'Unlike that poor old sod on the floor,' said Jonah, straining as Tye helped him half carry, half drag Motti over to where Con and Patch waited. 'Is that Blackland?'

'Yes, it's him.' The red-haired girl under the desk had poked her bruised face out. 'They killed him.'

'And for what, my dear Maya?' Heidel produced a small, brown book from his pocket. 'Ah yes, for this. Blackland's greatest treasure. The Guan Yin manuscript.'

'Give that to us,' Con demanded. 'Throw it on the floor and –'

'Oh, I don't think so.' Heidel smiled faintly. 'That's the problem when one's only weapon is mass destruction – it offers little finesse when negotiating.'

'Oh?'

'You won't detonate that explosive if I don't comply with your demands, Con. In a confined space like this you risk killing yourselves at the same time.' He walked slowly towards them, pausing with his back to the window, holding up the book just as Patch was holding the eyeball. 'Besides, I know just how valuable the Bloodline Cipher is to Coldhardt. I know what depends on it, what's at stake. You *daren't* destroy this manuscript.'

'You're insane,' Maya piped up quietly. 'All of you.'

Jonah remembered Coldhardt's warning back in the hub: *That manuscript is of paramount importance. Take no chances with its welfare . . . damaged it is of no use to me.*

'Coldhardt wouldn't need to know *we* destroyed it,' said Con icily. 'You wouldn't be alive to breathe a word.'

'So you would betray your master, eh, Con? Perhaps there is hope for you.' Heidel glanced at Patch. 'It seems we both hold a trump card. But I shall resolve this standoff now by leaving with my colleagues – and the manuscript.' He looked behind him at his followers. Bree nodded, and sauntered over to the window.

'Wait,' said Con warningly, 'we say what happens here.'

'Oh, let 'em go,' Patch moaned. 'Good riddance!'

'Yes, let them just leave,' said Maya.

'We'll meet again,' said Bree, not bothering to look at them as she swung her legs out of the window. Sorin clambered out after her. Sadie didn't move, staring Jonah out. She smiled, held up the priceless enamelled gold ring on her finger – then pointed an imaginary crossbow at his head and mimed pulling the trigger. The glint in her eyes as she did so sent a chill piercing through him. He looked away, and only then did she follow the others out of the window.

As she left, Con hurled herself at Heidel, grabbing for the manuscript in his hand. The old man blocked her strike with a sweep of his arm, knocking her off-balance. Before Jonah could react, Tye had darted forward to help – but now Heidel had hooked his other arm around Con's neck, crushing his wrist against her windpipe.

'Let her go!' Patch shouted, thrusting the glass eyeball towards him. 'I mean it!'

'You're as impotent as your master, boy,' Heidel snarled, squeezing harder. Con's face turned red, her eyes widened as she struggled for air. 'Give Coldhardt this message,' he hissed. 'Time waits for no men, and I am the proof. The living proof of something he will never own.' He backed away to the window, dragging Con along by her throat, then threw her flat on her face to the floor. She lay retching for breath, and as Jonah and Tye rushed to help her, Heidel scrambled through the window with surprising agility. He looked back, his face impassive. 'I suspect Bree was right; we shall meet again. And when we do, no quarter will be shown.'

'Yeah,' Jonah muttered as Heidel ran into the night. Con's gasps for breath filled his ears. 'You're right about that.'

'Con . . .' Patch stared down at her, his eyes shiny with tears. 'Is she gonna be OK, Tye?'

'Slow down, Con, deep breaths,' Tye urged her. 'Hold your chin up, that'll help keep your airway clear . . .'

Over her straining and spluttering Jonah heard the roar of an engine starting up.

'No!' Patch shouted, running to the window. 'The bastards, they're taking our pick-up!'

'I totalled their limo,' Tye said helplessly.

Jonah looked at her. 'They're going to leave us stranded?'

'They've pissed all over us. Half-killed us. Shafted us.' Suddenly Patch pulled back his arm, making ready to throw the plastic explosive after Heidel. 'Well, bugger 'em – and bugger that stupid bleedin' manuscript!'

'No!' Jonah shouted, staggering up and running for the window. He cannoned into Patch, too late to stop the throw, clocking in horror the eyeball's glistening flight across Blackland's drive. It fell well short of the pick-up, which was already pulling away.

Instead it struck the bonnet of the smashed-in limousine outside.

Jonah yanked Patch away from the window as a massive, scorching explosion of heat punched the window glass into thousands of tiny jagged shards. Each fragment reflected the blast in yellow-red as they rained into the room. Maya shrieked and Tye threw herself protectively over Con. The shadows of the flames danced exultantly over the bare walls of the study.

'You bloody idiot,' Jonah shouted in Patch's face. 'That explosive was our only defence, our one deterrent. Now those psychos can come back and finish us!'

'I'm sorry!' Patch shouted back, trembling.

Maya stepped gingerly over the glass to help Tye move Con over to the door. '*Are* they coming back?' she asked quietly.

'I'll see.' Jonah crossed to the window, a sick feeling building in his belly. The ripped curtains twitched like the night was breathing in on them.

He saw the pick-up unharmed, parked in the gateway to the drive, well away from the blazing wreck of the limo. But Heidel stood watching him from the other side of the flaming wreck, half-obscured by the thick black smoke, his features rippling in the heat haze. Jonah watched, uneasy and transfixed, as the old man produced the Guan Yin manuscript, the book they'd come so far to get from his pocket.

And then threw it into the blaze.

Jonah was too stunned to react. He watched Heidel slowly turn and walk back to the waiting truck. The passenger door was opened and the old man climbed inside. Then the pick-up drove slowly away, no wheelspins or *screw-you* theatrics. Jonah found himself thinking of a hearse leaving a funeral. The flames billowed a brighter orange, flaring up as if feasting on the new morsel thrown to them. When they died back down there was nothing to see beyond save the huddled shadows of the dark landscape and the star-splashed indigo above.

Tye spoke just behind him; he hadn't heard her approach. 'Tell me that wasn't the manuscript he just burnt to ashes.'

The sting of smoke caught Jonah's eyes and he rubbed them. 'It was so dark, I couldn't see clearly. It could have been a trick.'

She looked at him, her dark eyes reflecting the fire. 'Who are you kidding?'

'At least now we know what the Bloodline Cipher is,' said Patch bitterly. 'It's toast.'

A book of dark magic, followed by bad luck and flames. Jonah shivered and looked to where Patch was slumped between Motti and Con, over by the door. Con was breathing more normally now. Maya hovered uncertainly beside the desk in the corner.

'*Are* they coming?' she whispered again.

Jonah shook his head. 'Gone. Like the manuscript.' He slammed his fist against the wall in frustration. 'Except that's gone for ever, and Heidel and his crew will be back, won't they? Back for us.'

'Who are you?' Maya pressed one hand to her bloodied cheek. 'You came for the Guan Yin manuscript too. Why?'

Tye ignored her. 'We'd better get out of here. That explosion will have carried for miles – maybe all the way to the nearest neighbours. They'll be dialling 911.'

Patch sighed. 'D'you think they could spare an ambulance for Mot at the same time?'

'This place'll be full of cops,' said Con hoarsely, tugging the high neckline of her black top away from her throat, turning to Maya. 'What about her?'

Maya took a wary step backwards. 'What about me?'

'She was Blackland's librarian,' Tye explained.

Con's eyes had narrowed. 'She can ID us.'

'God, you're right,' Patch realised. 'That old git used our full names.'

'I won't tell anyone anything,' said Maya quickly,

her grey eyes wide and frightened. 'I don't want to get involved.'

Jonah looked queasily at Blackland's body. 'Bit late for that.'

'I won't talk to the police,' Maya insisted. 'Listen, those people may have taken the manuscript, but there's a copy. It's been scanned, every page. All stored on a DVD upstairs. You can have it, just . . . just don't hurt me.'

The glitter returned to Con's sub-zero eyes as she turned to Tye. 'Is she lying?'

'Seems on the level,' said Tye slowly.

'It's why that bitch Bree was beating me up,' said Maya, her fingers straying to the welt on her high cheekbone again, her lip curling in anger. 'She wanted to know if there were duplicate copies of the manuscript . . .'

Con raised an eyebrow. 'And you didn't tell her?'

'She killed Blackland,' said Maya simply. 'I didn't want to do anything that might help her.' She sighed, looked almost guiltily at Tye. 'I suppose I *would* have told her if you and your friend hadn't stopped her when you did. Thank you for helping me.'

'In return, *you* will help us to help ourselves,' Con informed her.

'Scans of the manuscript,' Jonah muttered. 'Then we're still in the game . . .' He could feel his heart pumping faster as he turned back to Maya. 'So, Blackland kept a digital archive of all his books?'

'Yes, I've been helping him with that project,' she told him, 'not just for cataloguing, but to aid close study and translation. I'm a cryptanalyst.'

Tye looked puzzled. 'You mean you analyse crypts?'

'Duh!' Despite everything, Jonah grinned. 'It means she cracks ciphers.' Tye glared at him, as he turned back to Maya. 'So the entire Guan Yin manuscript is encrypted, not just this Bloodline Cipher thing?'

She nodded. 'Sure. I was thinking some kind of polyalphabetic cipher at first, but frequency analysis shows natural statistical features in accordance with Zipf's law –'

'Oh, sweet Jesus,' Motti drawled. 'Don't say we got another Jonah.'

'Mot!' Patch bounded over to him. 'Thought you was in a coma or something.'

'I wish. It'd hurt a lot less.' As Tye and Patch helped him stand, Motti touched the swollen bruise on his forehead and winced. 'What'd I miss?'

'Just about everything,' Con told him.

'But you've woken up at a good bit.' Jonah grinned at him, then looked back at Maya. 'Has Blackland got transport?'

She nodded quickly. 'A vintage Buick in the garage.'

'And these must be the keys,' Tye announced, crouched beside Blackland's body, her hand inside his jacket pocket.

'Patch, get Tye inside that garage,' said Jonah, nerves sparking in his gut. 'Get the car and park it out front. Con, help Motti outside. If the cops show, get out of here. I'll keep in RT contact and meet up with you later.'

'Who died and made you the boss?' growled Motti.

'You did, nearly,' Jonah retorted.

'I'm the one who *really* almost died!' Patch proudly

lifted his top again to show his spectacular bruised stomach.

Tye grimaced and looked back at Jonah. 'And while we're doing that, you'll be getting this DVD with Maya here?'

'And any other rare stuff you can carry. After this shambles we must curry favour with the boss, yes?' Con glanced at Motti. 'First you lose his ring, then we lose his manuscript –'

'So let's get going.' Jonah took hold of Maya's arm and hurried her from the room. 'Library. Right now . . .'

Tye sat in the driver's seat of the Buick Riviera '65, scanning the shadow-shrunken landscape for hints of electric blue, straining for the first wails of police sirens approaching. She felt sick with tiredness, and her jaw and nose were throbbing. But Motti wasn't complaining about his injuries, so she kept quiet about her own. She checked him in the rear-view, sprawled on the cherry-red leather upholstery beside Patch, one hand in his jeans pocket, resting the good side of his head against the window.

The limo had burnt out quickly, and sat now a charred and twisted wreck. While Con had poked about in the ash for some trace of the manuscript, Tye had filled in Motti on what he'd missed.

'You really think Lady Bowfinger's got Coldhardt's ring I dropped?' he asked.

'She was flaunting it,' Tye told him. 'Rubbing Jonah's face in it.'

Motti groaned softly. 'Damn thing's worth a fortune.'

'What, Jonah's face?' Patch joked. Motti punched him on the arm. 'Ow!'

Con came back to the truck. 'Nothing,' she reported, climbing into the passenger seat, picking bits of black from her long fingernails. 'You know, it seems incredible that Heidel's gang would kill five people and take on another five to get hold of a priceless ancient manuscript – and then just throw it into a fire . . .'

'They did it out of spite,' said Motti. 'You said they knew how badly Coldhardt wanted it.'

Tye nodded. 'It's a big statement of hate.'

'Like killing all us lot would have been,' Patch agreed.

'All except one of us,' Tye reminded him, 'left to bring the message home to Coldhardt.'

'"Time waits for no men, and I am the proof . . . "' Con repeated the words quietly, and Tye saw her try but fail to suppress a shudder. 'The living proof of something Coldhardt will never own. What did he mean?'

'When we pass on the message to Coldhardt, maybe *he'll* know,' said Tye. She checked her watch. 'If Jonah ever gets back, that is.'

'P'raps he stopped to give Maya a quick one in a pile of old books,' Patch theorised. 'All that talking codes got 'em horny.'

'Jonah's not like that.' Con gave Tye a sideways look. 'Is he, Tye?'

Tye shrugged, refusing to rise to the bait.

'I'd do it with her,' Patch went on. 'If you covered up that birthmark she'd be quite fit.'

'As if!' Con retorted.

Patch smirked. 'Jealous?'

'Sore?' She reached back and poked him in the stomach, making him yelp.

'Shut up,' Tye complained. 'I'm trying to listen for sirens. Come *on*, Jonah . . .'

'Here he comes,' said Motti suddenly. 'And hey, look at that. He's bringing his new squeeze with him.'

'Saves me getting out the car,' Con declared. 'I'll mesmerise her into forgetting all about us and send her back inside.'

Tye angled the rear-view. Jonah and Maya were hurrying across the driveway, each carrying a holdall. Jonah opened the boot and they slung the baggage inside. *It doesn't look like just books in there*, thought Tye in surprise.

Jonah opened the rear passenger door. 'You'd better budge up. Maya's coming with us.'

Motti looked at him. 'She's what?'

'She's been working on the Guan Yin manuscript for weeks, made some headway with the translation,' Jonah explained, Maya standing awkwardly behind him. 'Could save us – and Coldhardt – a lot of time when it comes to cracking this Bloodline Cipher thing.'

'So steal her work and we can leave her here,' said Con.

'Why does she *want* to come with us anyway?' said Tye, looking at Maya and frowning. 'Most people wouldn't be tripping over themselves to run away with a bunch of thieves who'd just broken into their house.'

Maya came forward. 'I've realised I don't have

much choice.' The shadows made the dark skin of her birthmark look like a gaping hole in her throat as she leaned in to look at Tye. 'I have no visa. I am here in America illegally, I have . . . trouble back home in Ukraine. I cannot go back there.'

'What trouble?' Patch asked.

Motti snorted. 'We all got our own sob stories to deal with, Cyclops.'

'Sob story is right. She could be a spy,' said Con. 'Left here by Heidel to gain our trust.'

'They beat the crap out of her!' Jonah protested.

'That could have been staged,' Con argued.

Maya looked at her. 'No,' she said simply.

'Yeah, well you would say that, Red.' Motti looked at her doubtfully. 'They heard us crash into the limo, knew we were coming and made you scream to bring us running.'

Jonah was looking at Tye with *please be on my side* eyes. 'I'd know if Maya was lying,' Tye conceded. 'I don't think she is.'

'And we don't have time to wait about here in any case,' said Jonah firmly. 'We're pushing our luck as it is.'

'That's for sure,' said Motti. 'Start 'er up, Tye. We'll get a message through to Coldhardt and he can decide.'

'It's gonna be a squeeze, four of us in the back,' Patch reflected. 'Tell you what, Maya, you can sit next to me.'

Jonah got in first. 'Don't mind Patch,' he told Maya, 'we're getting him neutered.'

'With the world's tiniest nail scissors,' Motti added,

wincing as he budged along to allow Jonah and Maya inside.

'Thank you,' said Maya quietly, shutting the door.

As she started the engine, Tye watched the girl in the rear-view, angling for the tiniest sign of triumph in the girl's sullen face, or eyes, or gestures. But Maya's hunched shoulders suggested anxiety, and the way she was shaking her legs and wetting her lips so frequently were classic signs of stress.

Tye put the car in gear and pulled away from the dark stony stretch of the now-abandoned fort, the car wreck and the corpses; leaving the blackness for where the first stirrings of dawn promised light on the horizon.

CHAPTER SEVEN

Tye had sat through God-knew-how-many debriefs with Coldhardt, but had never known an atmosphere in the hub quite like this one. Motti was quieter than usual, a new pair of glasses perched on his nose and dosed up on special painkillers prescribed by Coldhardt's private doctor. Patch too seemed very restrained; from the way his hand kept touching his stomach, she imagined the pain was reminding him of how close he'd come to dying last night. How close they all had come.

On the long haul back to Geneva, Tye had thought of little else. Even when Jonah took over at the plane controls, the events of their disastrous mission kept looping through her thoughts, staving off sleep.

Jonah and Con weren't here for the debrief either, which was also weird. They were staying with Maya in a safe house in Chamonix across the French border; the girl was being kept well away from the heart of Coldhardt's operation until her story checked out. And as for Coldhardt himself, well . . .

That was really the strangest part of it.

It had fallen to Tye to call him last night from San Angelo – '*you'll be able to read just how bad he's taking it*,' the others had insisted – and so she'd given Coldhardt the bare details of their encounter with Heidel and his party posse; explained Heidel had known the Talent were coming and even known their names . . . And while she hadn't mentioned how his ring had wound up on Sadie's finger – they were still licking their wounds, which tasted bad enough already – she figured he needed to know about the manuscript ending up in the flames.

The weird thing was that he'd taken the news with an air of cold resignation; he was clearly angry, but it was as if he'd somehow expected something like this would happen, and now it had, he had to deal with it.

'*He wanted us to give you a message.*'

'*Did he, now.*'

'*He said, "Time waits for no men, and I am the proof, the living proof of something he will never own."*'

The silence on the line, relieved only by digital noise, had gone on for so long she hadn't dared disturb it. And she knew better than to press him when he changed the subject, his voice dipping into its iciest reaches:

'*Did you manage to salvage anything from the evening's performance?*'

Tye had found herself speaking enthusiastically about Maya and her digital archive, praying that Jonah hadn't been hoodwinked and that Coldhardt still had a shot at getting whatever the hell he wanted out of this grimoire thing.

Now, as she and Patch and Motti worked to pile flesh on the bones of their story, Coldhardt was listening with an air of grave distraction, as if this was merely a ritual to be got through before his real work could begin. Tye sensed there was a hell of a lot going on beneath the old man's façade of attention, and it was a disquieting feeling.

'I'm sorry we loused up,' said Motti. 'Guess we didn't allow for another crew coming on that strong.'

'I didn't give you much time to prepare contingencies,' Coldhardt conceded.

Patch shrugged. 'But how come they knew we'd be breaking in last night?'

'There are two obvious possibilities,' said Coldhardt. 'The first is that they have somehow been listening in on our conversations . . .'

Motti scowled. 'While we were out on that dumb picnic?'

Tye shook her head firmly. 'Me and Con, we checked. No one around.'

'Or else,' Coldhardt went on heavily, 'there is a spy in your ranks. Someone Heidel has recruited and who is passing on all they know.'

Tye felt her veins freezing over. 'That's impossible,' she whispered.

A faint smile warmed Coldhardt's weathered face a fraction. 'I find the spy hypothesis unlikely, but we must all remain vigilant. Every possibility must be accounted for, particularly when we are up against such formidable opponents.'

Tye nodded curtly. 'So who are they?'

'The woman with the crossbow is Sadie Djief, a French girl raised in Chad, and now turned mercenary. She has a reputation for efficiency and sharp-shooting, but she is somewhat unstable.'

'Psycho cow,' said Patch with feeling. 'Still, at least you can't accuse her of talking too much. You know, I never heard her say a word.'

'You wouldn't have. Her tongue was ripped out six years ago by an Indonesian interrogator in East Timor.' Coldhardt spoke so casually he might have been discussing a game of cricket. 'The one called Sorin I've been unable to identify, thus far . . . But the other female is Bree Matthews. She is a formidable planner and analyst, available only to the highest bidder.'

'She's also a grade-A bitch,' muttered Tye. 'But what about this Heidel guy? He said . . . you betrayed him.'

Coldhardt's face might have been carved in granite for all the emotion it showed. 'That's one way of putting it.'

'And he knew about the set-up, the way we're all –' She shrugged. 'Well. Kind of . . .' *Like family,* she wanted to say, but it sounded so lame. And she thought of what else Heidel had said: *They prove their love by risking everything, time after time . . . then in walks death.*

'He must have it in for you, big time,' said Patch, stepping into her silence. 'Who is this bloke?'

'Not someone I expected to hear from again.' The faintest ghost of a smile tugged at the corners of Coldhardt's lips. 'And certainly not someone who would burn a seven-hundred-year-old grimoire lightly.'

Patch shrugged. 'Well, what're you gonna do to sort him out?'

'Oh, I imagine Heidel would just love me to busy myself formulating plans and stratagems against him. I think I shall leave it to him or his associates to make the next move.'

Against us, thought Tye with an uneasy shiver.

'And what about *our* next move?' said Motti. 'What about the e-version of the manuscript that Maya got for us, does it check out?'

'The DVD contains scans of an exotic text transcribed on to vellum, exactly what I would expect the Guan Yin manuscript to look like. But time – and Jonah's talent for decryption – will tell.' He paused. 'Maya has also provided us with a full catalogue of Blackland's RDIF tags and the frequencies upon which they each transmit – so if the grimoire *does* still exist, we may yet track it down.'

'What about the books she brought with her?' Tye asked.

'A good selection.' Coldhardt inclined his head. 'Fabulously rare and extraordinarily valuable. To acquire such a collection of arcane antiquity in one haul . . .'

Motti shrugged. 'Guess we did something right, then, huh?'

'And what about Maya?' asked Tye, still disquieted by the weird atmosphere in the room. 'Is she for real?'

'I've unearthed some information.' Coldhardt pressed a button and a picture of Maya appeared on the screens. Dressed in an unflattering kaftan with big collars, eyes made up like a thick blue snail had crawled over the lids, she looked like something out of the 1960s. 'Maya Marisova hails from a village outside Lviv, in Ukraine. She is nineteen years old. Building on her childhood aptitude for languages, both natural and computational, she spent last year studying history and ancient languages at Moscow State University. This picture was taken from her student files – her academic record is quite outstanding.'

'What about her criminal record?' wondered Motti. 'She said she was in cop-trouble back home, had no visa.'

Coldhardt nodded. 'Earlier this year, one of her tutors disappeared in suspicious circumstances.'

Tye raised her eyebrows. 'How did Professor Blackland get on to her?'

'Perhaps we should let the girl speak for herself.' Coldhardt consulted a fob watch pulled from the pocket of his waistcoat. 'I requested that Con and Jonah conduct a little conversation with the girl that could be shared with us.' He hit another button on his remote and the picture changed to show a blank screen. A few seconds later it flared into life to display an empty leather armchair in a spotlit minimalist room. 'Excellent. The camera's activated. The interview can begin as scheduled.'

Tye and Motti watched as Maya crossed into the picture, her red hair like a torch carried between white wall and wooden floorboards. She was wearing a baggy black cardigan and a short black skirt with stripy tights, a very different look from her student picture. *If you don't want to be found, become a new person*, Tye supposed.

Maya sat in the chair, apparently relaxed, holding a steaming mug of something.

'Hidden camera?' asked Motti.

'Naturally.' Coldhardt turned to Tye. 'Study her closely. I must know if she is telling the truth and is a free agent . . . or if she is working for someone.'

Patch sighed. 'That Heidel bloke?'

Coldhardt didn't answer, staring at the screens as if he could see through them, at something lying in wait.

'If he's one of your competitors, how come you didn't expect to run into him again?' Tye persisted.

'Because I thought I killed him, thirty-two years ago.'

Tye jerked as if her head had slammed the brakes on. 'I'm sorry?'

'I believe you heard.' Coldhardt gave her a casual glance that sent chills through her, bone-deep. 'Please, watch the screens, all of you.'

In a grim silence shared by Patch and Motti, Tye did as she was told.

Jonah sprawled on the sofa beside Con, while Maya sat in a squashy armchair cradling her mug of black tea. She was looking out of the window, a little smile on her elfin face as she took in the *carte postale* view of snowy Alpine crags and huge, conifer-smothered hills, of quiet, spotless streets and hotels with their balconies in bloom, window shutters flung wide.

'Very different from Texas,' she remarked, her English oddly inflected but so much warmer than Con's accent. 'Your Coldhardt must be very rich.'

'And then some,' Jonah agreed. 'But then old man Blackland didn't seem short of a few quid.'

'He wasn't. Much of his income came from the

private sale of artefacts recovered during his archaeological digs . . .'

'That's what Coldhardt said,' Jonah agreed. 'A bit dodgy.'

'I'd do the same,' Con argued. 'Shows initiative . . .'

Jonah looked down at his sweaty hands, felt his stomach gently fizzing. The interrogation had begun.

Coldhardt's camera had been placed behind a two-way mirror, and he pictured Tye and the others scrutinising the pictures and performances back at the hub. He and Con had agreed that they would begin with some quite innocuous questions so that Tye could see how Maya responded when not under stress. Then, when they moved on to more probing questions, any attempts to lie should seem more obvious.

'Did Blackland say where he found the Guan Yin manuscript?' Jonah asked awkwardly. While he appreciated Maya needed vetting before she could be allowed into their circle, this seemed a pretty mean way of going about it. 'I heard the museum in Turkey that was displaying it burnt down.'

'It remained in the country,' said Maya. 'Blackland was out on a dig somewhere near Maçka, I think, a year or so ago, when he stumbled upon a derelict monastery built into the base of a cliff. So beautiful . . .'

'You've been there?'

'I wish.' She looked at him and smiled self-consciously, showing small crooked teeth. 'Anyway, he discovered a concealed vault and inside it were several obscure books, one of which was this grimoire.'

Con nodded. 'And Blackland kept it for himself.'

'Yes.' Maya sipped her tea. 'You know, it is thought

the manuscript was brought back originally from Sudak, in my country. There have been many secret devotional cults dedicated to Guan Yin throughout the ages. It was said she was able to turn hell into paradise, that she reached out to unhappy, ignorant people with a thousand arms.' She paused, and nodded. 'Yes, it seems much powerful magic was practised in her name by these devotional cults. And one such society spawned the Guan Yin manuscript as a reference work for its members.'

'How old is it?' asked Jonah.

'Blackland's friend Morell dated the pages to the fourteenth century, but the knowledge they contain could be much older.' She was warming to her theme. 'Great libraries had been founded in Ukraine as early as the eleventh century. At Saint Sophia Cathedral men transcribed existing titles, swelling the stock of many other libraries in the provinces.'

Con narrowed her eyes. 'So it is possible that more than one copy exists of the original Guan Yin manuscript?'

'Definitely. It's thought that at least three are in existence.'

'And each important member of this devotional cult would have had the key with which the cipher could be decoded,' Jonah concluded.

'You are a bright one, Jonah Wish.' Maya smiled again. 'Any such cult – and the manuscripts themselves – would have been in existence for around a hundred years when the Turks invaded in 1475. Public buildings were ransacked and burned to the ground – it seems most likely the invaders took the grimoires back to their homeland together with countless other treasures.' She shrugged. 'That is what Blackland believed, at any rate.'

'Did you know Morell planned to steal the Guan Yin manuscript from Blackland?' asked Con.

'No,' Maya replied, 'I did not know. Was it Morell who hired you?'

'Morell died before he could hire anyone,' said Con.

'I'm sorry. He seemed a nice man,' Maya reflected. 'But very envious of Blackland's success.'

'How did you find yourself working for Blackland, Maya?' asked Jonah.

'I was studying in Moscow, needed some work for the summer,' Maya explained. 'Blackland and I had certain friends in common there. It was through them he asked me to catalogue his *kunstkammer*.'

Jonah raised his eyebrows. 'Sounds rude.'

Con turned and gave him a look. 'It's a German word, means art chamber.'

'A collection of curiosities and wonder. That's how Blackland spoke of it. He was so enthusiastic . . .' Maya sighed. 'Enthusiastic for me too, I found out. But I did not feel the same.' She shrugged, suddenly quite matter of fact. 'After he realised that, he started to threaten me.' A haunted look crossed her eyes, and her fingers traced absently against the cut on her cheek. 'Threatened me often.'

'Threatened how?' asked Jonah.

'He said he would hurt me, or maybe send me back home.' She sighed, looked down at the floor. 'The police wish to speak to me. A tutor I was close to disappeared, and they learned that he was a member of a secret occult group. A group for whom I had done work sometimes, translating old books on demonology and witchcraft, breaking encrypted spells and blessings . . .'

Con nodded. 'So you're interested in black magic and stuff?'

A gleam stole into Maya's eyes as she smiled. 'I love all the ritual of it. All the rules and the ceremony. The *drama* . . .'

'The danger?' Jonah ventured.

'You believe those lurid tabloid stories, the scary Hollywood films.' Maya looked disappointed. 'The words and the rulings of the occult arts are not dangerous in themselves. As with the rulings of any belief system, it is the men who interpret them who are dangerous.' She leaned forward in the chair. 'Compare the atrocities done in the name of organised religions through the ages with those committed in the name of dark magic. Which cause has inflicted more suffering on a global scale?'

Con got them back on-topic. 'I take it Blackland was a member of this society too?' Maya nodded. 'But surely, if he smuggled you into America, by sending you back he'd be incriminating himself?'

'It would not be the police who would deal with me.' Maya looked away. 'And since I have no living relatives, I have few places I can turn for protection.'

Suppose we can all relate to that, thought Jonah.

'Is my questioning completed?' Maya asked. 'There are many things I would like to ask you . . .'

'Perhaps later,' said Con, rising from the sofa with a

furtive glance to the hidden camera. 'Or perhaps not. We shall see, yes?'

Maya looked at Jonah and smiled again. 'I hope so.'

'Well, Tye?' Coldhardt enquired, as Maya's image flicked off from the several screens.

I don't like the way she looks at Jonah, was Tye's most forthright reaction. When someone was lying and feeling uncomfortable they would often turn their head or body away from their questioner, their hands and arms giving them away with stiff, self-directed gestures. But Maya was mirroring Jonah's own posture – a sign that she was interested in him. *Keep it clinical*, Tye warned herself, trying to quell her unease. *You've got nothing to worry about with Jonah, but if Coldhardt's got doubts about any of us, and I turn in a sloppy job . . .*

'No alarm bells ringing here,' she said, almost reluctantly. 'No real hesitation in Maya's replies, no overly defensive responses, nothing to suggest she's recalling what she's already said ahead of answering, plenty of eye contact . . .' Tye paused. There was a lot more to her human polygraph act than simply reading body language. That stuff she thought of as supporting evidence for her gut instinct; the same instinct that had kept her alive in her smuggling days. But Tye knew Coldhardt preferred opinions to be backed up with facts, so she continued with the surface stuff: 'Maya usually glanced to her left when recalling precise detail. As a right-handed person, she'd be more likely to look to her right if she was making it up.'

Coldhardt nodded brusquely. 'In short, then, you would say the signs add up to someone who is telling the truth?'

'Yes,' said Tye.

'Good,' said Coldhardt. 'That tallies with my own observations. Nothing in Maya's behaviour so far has seemed suspicious. But for the time being she will continue to be looked after in the Chamonix safe house, away from the heart of my organisation. And I will continue my excavations into her past.' He nodded decisively. 'They may throw light on her future.'

'I guess with a man who's been dead thirty years back on the scene,' said Motti, 'it's not a great time to take chances on stray girls.'

'Like each of you in the past, she must prove herself. She and Jonah can work together on translating the Guan Yin manuscript files.'

Nice and cosy. Tye frowned. 'Is the safe house secure enough? I mean, if you're expecting possible trouble –'

'Entrance to the block is secured by fingerprint and retinal scan,' Motti informed her. 'And the windows are made with aluminium oxynitride, capable of keeping out point-fifty calibre armour piercing rounds. Each room is fitted with panic screens – vanadium steel shutters that block the doorway in response to a key phrase –'

'It's secure,' Patch translated.

'At all times there will be back-up for Jonah present in the safe house.' Coldhardt looked at Tye. 'Con can remain there overnight, then the rest of you for twelve-hour shifts. Devise a rota.'

She nodded. *Starting with me*. 'Got it.'

'For now, you may all go and rest.'

They rose to go.

'One last thing. The acquisition of the Guan Yin manuscript marks the starting point of a journey . . . a dangerous journey, no doubt, but one that may prove to be the most important of my life, and of yours.' Coldhardt looked at each of them in turn. 'If Heidel has truly returned . . . if this proof of which he speaks means what I think it does . . .' He trailed off, eyes clouding as he stared into the darkness of the TV screens. 'We must be strong. All of us.'

Tye swapped uneasy glances with Motti and Patch. They lingered for any more pronouncements, but Coldhardt remained silent. The hum of the strip lights, the distant rush of the air-con systems, all the background noise of the hub seemed somehow alien and amplified as they waited.

'Class dismissed,' Motti breathed at last, and led the way over to the lift that would take them to daylight. Tye looked back at Coldhardt, their charismatic leader and mentor. Right now he seemed just another lonely old man, locked into his thoughts, mourning times past.

CHAPTER EIGHT

Jonah shut the blinds on the stunning scenery outside with a nick of nostalgia, smiling as the glow from his monitor lit the room instead of the sun. How many summer days had he spent indoors, engrossed in that digital view while the rest of the world basked in sunshine?

The safe house boasted a desktop PC with multi-core CPU. While Con amused herself with a family-sized bag of crisps and the TV, he'd tweaked the motherboard to run faster and installed a water-cooling kit to stop it overheating as a result of the increased speed. Then, as Coldhardt had requested, he'd hacked into the global network of RFID receivers.

'What's that you're doing?'

Jonah looked up to find Maya had come in, watching the screen with interest.

'A job for Coldhardt.'

'Obviously.'

He kept tapping away at the keyboard. 'This piece of code is designed to worm its way into every airport, library and high-street store that uses the RFID system. The receivers will go on functioning normally, but in addition . . .' He paused. 'In addition they'll be scanning for the transponder-tag inside the Guan Yin manuscript.'

Maya frowned. 'Surely the manuscript was incinerated?'

'It is just possible Heidel switched the manuscript for something else.' He looked at her. 'Suppose there's no chance Heidel didn't know about the tags?'

'No, he was quizzing Blackland about them when –' Maya broke off for a few moments. 'Blackland was using a new, advanced tagging system, you see. Tiny, very powerful chips well ahead of anything on the market, carefully concealed within each book.'

'Well, suppose we might just see what turns up.' Jonah noticed she was holding a DVD in her hand. 'Movie?'

'Guan Yin manuscript.' She loaded up her DVD containing the high-res scans of the ancient vellum pages. In moments, a pin-sharp image of a single page of parchment appeared on the screen. It was covered in small, neat writing in a language Jonah had never seen before. A scratchy drawing of what could have been a tree occupied one corner, with writing bunched up all around it.

Jonah looked more closely. 'Looks like there's a lot of character repetition . . .' He read the file number. 'Hey, this page is from the final quire of the manuscript, isn't it? What about the rest of the book?'

'I always read the end of a book first,' she protested, pixie-eyes dancing. 'Don't you?'

Jonah gave a definite shake of his head. 'I start at the beginning.'

'Well, I'm itching to get to the big finish. Still, if you insist . . .'

Jonah watched as she took the mouse and opened up another file. Her manner seemed far less formal now it was just the two of them, as if she felt able to relax a little. *That's cool*, thought Jonah.

'This is from an early page of manuscript,' she announced. 'Take a close look and tell me what you see . . .'

Jonah pushed his long fringe aside, scanned the text on the screen. 'It's maybe a different language?'

'Right.' She looked impressed. 'There seem to be two distinct languages used in the book – one for most of the manuscript, the other purely for the appendix – the final twenty-five sheets of the manuscript. See, the characters are repeated more frequently, the words themselves – if they are words – seem far longer . . .'

'A verbose cipher, maybe? One which substitutes several ciphertext characters for one plaintext character . . .' Jonah looked between the two pages on the screen with some trepidation. 'I have to say I've never seen an alphabet like either of them before.'

'This manuscript is one of a kind,' Maya agreed. 'Some nineteenth-century scholars thought it might be a hoax – just a jumble of made-up letters. But the script flows very smoothly, as if the author understood what they were writing.'

'And in any case, you said the words and characters are repeated in ways that match the patterns of natural languages.'

'Which would be next to impossible to fake,' Maya agreed.

Jonah paused. 'I'm enjoying this.'

Maya looked puzzled. 'What?'

'You know . . . this.' Jonah felt slightly self-conscious and began to wish he hadn't started the conversation. 'Sparking off someone else's ideas, sharing possible approaches. Face to face, I mean,' he said quickly.

Maya smiled. 'Yes. It is very . . . stimulating.'

Something about the way she said it made him blush. 'Um . . .' He cleared his throat and looked firmly at the screen, trying to get back to business. 'Have those characters been traced over?' he said. 'Looks like two different inks have been used.'

Maya nodded, serious again. 'The main part of the manuscript was written in tempera paint – parts have faded over the years. Certain words and symbols look darker throughout because they've been retouched – probably around the same time the appendix was added. The inks are very similar.'

'Any idea how many years passed between the original and the retouching?'

'Hard to say,' Maya admitted. 'But the later characters are drawn as fluidly as the originals. It could have been the original author, coming back to his work, or at least someone who was familiar with that "alphabet".'

'Let's hope so. 'Cause if he traced any of the symbols wrongly . . .' Jonah enlarged a section where two characters in the middle of a word had been overwritten. The original ink was just barely visible beneath the darker strokes. 'It's going to mess up any text analysis we try.'

'Speaking of text analysis . . . how're you with Chinese languages?'

'Huh?'

Maya leaned forward to enlarge part of a page, affording Jonah a glimpse down her top as she did so. He saw the edge of a tattoo peeping over the top of her black bra and found himself staring. *God, I'm turning into Patch*, he thought, looking quickly at the screen. He forced himself to focus on the weird symbol Maya had highlighted, drawn in muddy red ink.

'These exotic symbols are the only things common to both sections of the manuscript,' she explained, apparently oblivious to any effect she'd had on him. 'They're different to any of the characters in the body of the text, and often written in a different ink.'

'Could be headings, or chapter titles?'

'Or maybe signifying sections of a separate code book that can translate the pages.' She enlarged the symbol still further and looked at him, her grey gaze intent. 'The drawing of Chinese goddess Guan Yin on the title page could be a big clue. Up until the last few hundred years, more than half of the world's literature was written in Chinese characters.'

'Pictograms and ideograms. Symbols representing ideas or things rather than actual words.' Jonah nodded. 'Well, I've broken hieroglyph codes before. They're usually quite logical once you get into the swing of them. What do you think this one means?'

'It looks to me like the character *ròu,* inverted then turned upside down.' Maya drew the pictogram, which to Jonah resembled a box with most of its bottom missing and two up-pointing arrowheads inside it. She looked at him, something unfathomable simmering in her eyes. 'It's supposed to represent a hacked-open carcass. It means *meat* or *flesh*.' She scrolled to the bottom of the page, where a fainter symbol sat close beside a crude drawing of someone screaming. 'And if we invert and rotate this symbol seventy degrees, it starts to look a bit like the pictogram for *ji* – meaning *temple*, or *offer sacrifice to*.'

'So – "*flesh offer sacrifice to temple*". Sounds fun,' Jonah said wryly. 'What was that you were saying about not believing those lurid tabloid takes on black magic?'

'There are many kinds of sacrifice.' Maya paused, and when she spoke again her voice held a more challenging tone. 'Look at the way you and your friends have given yourselves to Coldhardt.'

Jonah frowned. 'You what?'

'Everyone sacrifices their brainpower, their free time, their physical presence to get something back, whether it's an education, a regular pay cheque, power, respect . . .' Maya looked at him. 'What you do is different. You're prepared to sacrifice your *lives* for Coldhardt.'

'What would you know about it?' said Jonah defensively.

'You offer up your flesh and bones in his cause . . .' Maya went on. 'And do you ever stop to think that some day that offering may be collected?'

Jonah shifted uncomfortably. He wasn't used to conversations like this. He resorted to flippancy. 'God, you're a real barrel of laughs, aren't you, Maya? How'd you get so happy?'

'Knowledge makes me happy. Cracking codes. Learning secrets.' In the light of the screen, her freckles looked grey, like dust motes settled on her skin. 'How about you? Does your life make you happy, Jonah?'

The challenge prickled at him. 'I guess. OK, fair enough, I'm not happy with some of the situations I pitch up in,' he admitted. 'But to leave my friends would make me more unhappy. Besides, when I joined up I wasn't exactly turning my back on a brilliant future. I was in a Young Offenders' Institution, a kind of prison – no visitors, no meaning, no hope.'

'So Coldhardt has given you meaning in your life . . .' She grinned unexpectedly. 'As well as cool visitors like me of course.' She paused. 'But what about hope?'

'I hope I'll be around long enough to enjoy what I've got,' he joked. 'Because at the end of the day, I'm bloody lucky.' He gestured to the computer. 'I get to do what I love, what I do best, and I get rewarded for it – tons of cash, a fantastic lifestyle, and friends I can count on for the first time.' He leaned in closer for emphasis. 'Before I met Coldhardt, I was just living. But this last year, I've been really *alive*.'

Maya folded her arms. 'Nothing like risking your life to make you appreciate it all the more, huh?'

'Patch once said we'll live for ever or die trying.' He met her gaze. 'I'm with him on that one. It's the only way to get through the days.'

'Maybe.' Maya's cool grey eyes didn't falter. 'What about Coldhardt, fount of your happiness – will *he* live for ever?'

Jonah half smiled. 'He's working on it.'

There was a pause and then another unexpected grin dimpled Maya's cheeks, easing the tension. 'I'm glad. After all, for ever might *just* be long enough to crack the end of this manuscript . . .'

Jonah shook his head. 'That'll have to wait. Right now, the offering I've got to make to Coldhardt is a decrypted plaintext version of the title page.'

'He asked you just for that?' Maya blinked. 'Why?'

'To show we can do it, I suppose. Or maybe because he prefers to start at the beginning and move on, like me.'

'At his age, I'd have thought he'd be more interested in endings . . .' Maya leaned back in her chair. 'Oh, well. Guess it's your lucky day. We can give him the title page straight away.'

Jonah stared at her. 'What?'

'It was translated way back, by a clerk in the museum that held the manuscript before it was stolen and the whole place burned down. The clerk's notes were folded up and placed within the manuscript. Blackland found them there in the monastery.'

'Why didn't you tell us this sooner?' Jonah demanded.

'It hardly counts as part of the manuscript. It's thought that the cover page is a later addition to the whole, possibly sixteenth century. And it's encoded in a completely different way to the rest of the manuscript, more of a word puzzle. The characters of an invented language had to be transposed into Latin and then only certain letters chosen –'

'OK, OK. So what does it *say*?'

'How does it go, now . . .' Maya cast her eyes

upwards, as if remembering, and Jonah had the feeling she was teasing him. '*The life of a creature is in the blood. Through the mercy and purity of Guan Yin, who gave up her eyes so her father might see, this Bloodline Cipher is disposed to thee. Thy flesh be stitched with threads immortal, they hold fast though the blood sweat fastens.*'

'That's it?'

'That's it.'

'Just a bit cryptic, then.' Jonah frowned. 'Do you have the scan of the title page? I'd like to run my own decryption just to be sure.'

'I did the same,' she said approvingly. 'We can compare all three versions.'

He grinned at her. 'And that way, we needn't tell Coldhardt the work had been done for us already. Nice one!'

He rose to go. Maya caught hold of his hand and looked up at him hopefully. 'So will I get to meet your mysterious Coldhardt? He sounds like he'd fit right in with my crowd back home.'

'He probably would,' Jonah agreed, gently freeing his fingers. He liked Maya but not in that way. 'We'll see what he says. I'll go and call him.'

Crossing the room, Jonah could feel Maya's eyes on his back. And as he closed the door behind him, he hesitated. *You might just fit in with our crowd too*, he thought. *A code-cracker with a passionate, in-depth knowledge of all that creepy stuff Coldhardt's into . . .*

He headed for the phone, a mixed-up feeling inside him. *Maybe I could find myself leaving here sooner than I thought.*

* * *

Tye sat on a brown, cracked leather sofa in the hang-out, brooding on all that had happened.

A guy who's supposed to be dead, clinging to life for thirty years? She chewed her lip. *Suddenly back and stoked for revenge? It's got to be a wind-up.*

What was this guy hoping to achieve?

The sumptuous sofas were arranged around a full-sized snooker table. Drinks and snacks dispensers lined the walls along with arcade video games, pinball tables and fruit machines, hemming in their chill-space with walls of lurid light and colour. There was even a gleaming chrome coffee bar. A room to the left housed a miniature cinema – only eight seats but a full-sized screen; while to the right were two rooms each with an enormous HD TV – one for watching and one for gaming on.

Right now, neither were in use. Patch stood at the coffee bar in a cloud of dusted chocolate, finishing off a cappuccino with hazelnut syrup, while Motti lay sprawled on the sofa beside her with a beer and a comic book. The hangout seemed so big and empty with just the three of them here tonight.

'It was such a weird atmosphere in there today,' said Tye quietly. 'Do you believe this Heidel guy's for real?'

'I didn't see much of the guy, remember?' Motti pointed to the purple swelling like a tattoo on his temple. 'But Coldhardt doesn't normally make mis-takes. If he thought he killed the guy . . .'

'I wish I knew why he seems so rattled by the whole thing.' Tye slumped down a little lower in the sofa.

'How many people do you think he's killed over the years?'

'Maybe he's worried the whole damn lot of them are gonna come back.' Motti rubbed his sore head. 'To haunt him with a baseball bat.'

'This guy obviously knows Coldhardt,' Tye went on, 'and must know all there is to know about us.'

'Gee, d'you think maybe he'll send us cards on our birthdays?'

'He knows about the Bloodline Cipher too . . .'

Motti turned the page of his comic book. 'Whatever the hell that is.'

'We know that the older Coldhardt gets, the harder he chases ways to live longer,' Tye reminded him. 'Elixirs of youth, mad Aztec goddesses . . .'

Motti looked at her. 'What, and now a code in some old book?'

'*I'm the living proof of something Coldhardt will never own* . . .' She shrugged. 'If Heidel's supposed to have died thirty years ago, maybe whatever's in that cipher helped him stay alive?'

'Uh-huh,' said Motti, 'and maybe *Scooby Doo*'s a documentary.'

'I know it sounds far-fetched.' Tye held up her hands. 'But it would make sense of why Heidel threw the manuscript into the flames.'

Motti got her meaning. 'He wanted to make damn sure Coldhardt didn't get the benefit of what's in there?'

An uneasy silence hung in the air between them.

'I hope this Maya bird works out all right,' Patch announced, coming over to join them. 'Then Con and

Jonah can come back and we'll all have a new buddy to get to know.'

Tye half smiled, despite herself. 'You're always first to accept anyone new, aren't you?'

'Safety in numbers! You can never have too many people watching your back.'

'Uh-huh.' Motti took a swig of beer. 'Trouble is, Cyclops, Red can't watch your back while you're staring at her front.'

'Nothing to stare at,' said Patch, forlorn. 'Her shoulder blades are bigger than her baps.'

'Don't be so gross,' Tye complained. She threw a cushion at Patch, spilling hot coffee into his lap. He jumped up, yelling in pain.

'One in a million shot, Tye,' Motti drawled, putting down his beer. 'You actually hit something down there.'

Patch grabbed the beer and poured it over his steaming crotch. Then he sank back in his seat with a relieved sigh.

'OK,' said Motti calmly. 'You got exactly ten seconds to fetch me another beer.'

'Maybe I could wring out my trousers into a glass?'

'And maybe you could wind up with two broken legs.'

Patch hurried away to the fridge. He turned on the sound system while he was there, and strident, doomy guitars thundered out from the speakers scattered about the room. 'That's better!' he yelled. 'Better party while we can. 'Cause when Heidel and Bree said they'd be seeing us again . . .' He itched the skin beneath his eye patch. 'I reckon they meant it.'

Motti nodded. 'This whole thing's got "grudge match" written all over it.'

'So why'd they have to take it out on us?' complained Patch.

'They're against Coldhardt and all he stands for,' Tye reminded them. *The big man gathers his little ones to him*, Heidel had sneered. *Insists that they prove their love by risking everything, time after time.*

'Coldhardt won't take this lying down,' said Patch confidently. 'He'll sort that lot out.'

Motti touched the cold beer bottle to the angry bruise on his head. 'You mean he'll make us do it for him.'

Their luck holds for a time . . . Tye closed her eyes and seemed to see Heidel's, the colour of stagnant water. *But then, in walks death.*

'We must be strong,' quoted Patch, parodying Coldhardt's voice. 'All of us.'

Tye didn't smile, and Motti went back to his comic. They sat with Patch in distracted silence while the music blared on around them.

CHAPTER NINE

Tye woke early. She wondered how Jonah had slept, what his bed was like. How it would feel with him lying beside her. Not just for those snatched, secret hours when the house was quiet, or when the others were too wasted to hear the creak of the floorboards outside her room, but for a whole night, every night. The two of them with nothing to hide.

Nothing to hide? Tye dwelled on the idea with a kind of numb fascination. Reading lies off everyone else her whole life hadn't exactly encouraged honesty in herself. She had feelings buried so deep even she'd forgotten what they were, most of the time.

She stared up at the virgin white of the ceiling. Damn Jonah Wish for not being here right now.

As she turned in bed she caught sight of her smoke-stone lying on the top of her dresser, sparkling in the earliest strands of sunlight through the pale curtains. Weird; she was sure she hadn't left it out in the open. She held it between dirty fingernails; it was beautiful the way a speck of night seemed caught inside it, like a tiny fly in glittering amber. Coldhardt had given one to each of them when they'd joined up; his way of telling them they had proved themselves to him.

The day she'd got hers had been one of the happiest of her life, her entrance into a world she could never have imagined. Now she could hear a lazy little voice whispering in the dawn quiet: *you bought that crap – and he bought you.*

The soft, insistent beep of her pager woke her from her thoughts. Coldhardt was calling another meeting. Surely he couldn't want that Jonah back-up rota off her already . . .?

Or else something happened to Jonah in the night.

Tye rose from her bed, threw on some clothes, half-tamed her hair with a headband and ran from the room.

Fifteen minutes later, back in the stark striplighting of the hub, she was wishing she'd spent a little longer on her appearance. Coldhardt, Patch and Motti were not yet here. Con was back, nursing a coffee. And while Tye sat quiet and dishevelled at the table, Jonah and Maya were chatting bright-eyed and busily like members of some secret code-crackers club.

'My first water coolers were hand-made out of old aquarium pumps and home-made water-blocks,' Jonah was saying. 'Used to piss off my foster families so much . . .'

Maya laughed. 'I can imagine – this weird kid they'd taken in, taking apart their PC and shoving things inside it.'

'Not that weird!' he protested. 'I just couldn't stand the noise of the fans working overtime to vent all that heat . . .' He sighed. 'Now I order purpose-built cooler kits and it's just so easy.'

'Something to be thankful to Coldhardt for,' said Tye, prising herself into the conversation. 'Hello, Maya. We thought you were being kept at the safe house?'

'We had a kind of breakthrough last night,' said Jonah, eyes smiling. 'Told Coldhardt, and got the summons.'

'I had to wear a blindfold!' Maya looked at Jonah with mock reproach. 'You tied it too tight.'

Tye stiffened as the two of them shared a look. What was going on? It was a look that spoke of intimacy. But surely Jonah wouldn't . . . no. Telling herself not to be so dumb, she spoke lightly. 'Don't tell me you broke the cipher already?'

'We've got Coldhardt what he asked us for,' said Jonah; Tye felt he was choosing his words carefully. 'And we were just saying thank God we weren't being driven mad by a mega-noisy cooling fan to offset our overclocking . . .'

Act interested, Tye decided. 'What's that, then?'

'Overclocking?' Jonah looked over as if noticing her properly for the first time. 'It's when you crank up the clock frequencies in your circuits to speed up performance. But all electronic circuits get hot because of the electrons moving through them, right, and the harder you work them . . .'

As Jonah kept on, Tye felt a numbness rising through the base of her skull. She didn't have a clue what he was talking about. And there was Maya, nodding along 'cause she got every word. She looked from one to the other, trying to seem interested and not dismayed.

Tye was glad when Motti walked in and parked himself beside her with a gruff hello, soon followed by Patch, who sat the other side.

But before she could begin a conversation of her own, Coldhardt walked in. Even if the temperature did drop a degree or two, at least Maya and Jonah's baffling chatter stopped. Con stifled her next yawn, acting all ears as the boss sat down to speak. Maya seemed to drink it all in, eyes dark and hawklike, fixed on Coldhardt.

'Jonah,' Coldhardt began without ceremony, 'read out your translation of the title page.'

'Good morning to you, too. This is Maya, by the way.' Jonah smiled at the girl as he pulled out his PDA, as if this were some private joke they shared. 'Couldn't have done this without her.'

Tye felt a stab of jealousy. *Stop it,* she told herself instantly. *He's just been doing his thing. Maya's been helping him.* She fought to keep her face blank. She might be the real expert on body language, but Coldhardt wasn't too bad at it himself, and if he picked up anything . . .

'Get on with it, Jonah,' snapped Coldhardt.

Jonah switched on his Palm's screen. '*The life of a creature is in the blood. Through the mercy and purity of Guan Yin, who gave up her eyes so her father might see, this Bloodline Cipher is disposed to thee. Thy flesh –*'

'*– be stitched with threads immortal . . .*' Coldhardt spoke the words in unison, '*. . . they hold fast though the blood sweat fastens.*'

Jonah looked at Coldhardt as both finished their

recitation, his face clouded with confusion. 'How'd you know?'

Coldhardt smiled. 'You have independently reached the same translation of that opening page as I was given by certain . . . agencies.'

Jonah's face darkened. 'Then you didn't really need us to do this?'

'On the contrary – your translation was vital.' Coldhardt eased back in his chair. 'How else could it be demonstrated that my sources are telling the truth? Now I can contact them and tell them I shall proceed to the next stage.'

'Of what?' Jonah put down his PDA. 'You're making less sense than the translation. Don't you think we have a right to know what's going on?'

'Please, Jonah . . .' Coldhardt's eyes twinkled. 'No showing off in front of our new guest.'

'Now that you know what it says,' said Motti, butting in quickly, 'any pointers on what the hell it actually means?'

'In the old stories, Guan Yin was the pure daughter of an evil ruler,' said Con. 'Her father went blind with plague, and Guan Yin gave him her eyes so he could see. Her sacrifice so moved him that he repented his evil and became good. In turn, his conversion made Guan Yin whole again.' She snorted. 'A ridiculous story!'

Tye looked at her. 'Been swotting up?'

'I had to do something to pass the time while Jonah and Maya were locked away in their private world for half the night.'

The words stuck in Tye's ears like hooks, but she

managed to mask her feelings. 'So whoever wrote this manuscript knew their Chinese myths,' she said coolly. 'What's that stuff about immortal threads?'

'The ancient Greeks believed the course of a human life to be a thread,' Coldhardt remarked, 'spun and measured out by the Fates, and cut at their command.'

'So an immortal thread would be Fate-proof, yes?' said Con brightly. 'Like eternal life!'

'There are lots of possible meanings,' Jonah noted. 'I suppose a bloodline is a kind of thread too – a line of descent from a common ancestor . . .'

'All the way back to Adam and Eve,' joked Patch.

'In the search for serious answers,' Coldhardt interrupted, 'I'm afraid we shall have to leave Jonah and Maya to continue their excellent work on the manuscript. Now that I know the translations tally, I must learn whether the man named Heidel you encountered is truly the man I knew long ago – or else an impostor.'

'Not in any hurry to meet him and his mates again,' said Patch, clutching his stomach.

'Nevertheless, if I am to have the proof I need, you must get close to him, at least.'

'Hmm. An older man surrounded by younger gang members.' Maya, it seemed, had grown a little bolder. '"The big man gathers his little ones to him," that's what Heidel said. The model seems obvious to me, Coldhardt.'

Coldhardt regarded her, a dangerous glint in his eyes. 'Does it, now.'

'Heidel looks to be around your age,' she went on innocently. 'Were you and he as Jonah and Motti are now – selling your skills to a big boss?'

'You could say Heidel and I were together a long time,' he equivocated.

'And now you are the age of your former boss, you're working the same scheme yourself.' Jonah looked at him. 'Is that right?'

Tye held her breath. She didn't even dare look at any of the others. The questions were obvious, begging to be asked; but to do so felt like heresy, somehow.

'An inquiring, analytical mind is a useful tool,' Coldhardt noted, with a smile that seemed genuine. 'Perhaps I shall tell you more – if it transpires that Heidel is truly who he claims to be.'

'That is our incentive to find Heidel?' Con remarked. 'A history lesson?'

'We're thieves, not private detectives,' Patch agreed quietly.

'Each of you shall receive a bonus of three hundred thousand pounds for undertaking this mission,' Coldhardt announced casually.

Tye felt a jump in her chest like her heart just fired a cannon. 'That's more than usual.'

'Danger money?' asked Motti, gruff as ever.

'Sod the danger, gimme the cash!' Patch rubbed his hands gleefully.

Con sat up straight in her chair, her eyes agleam. 'How are we supposed to acquire this proof?'

'Thanks to Maya and Jonah's efforts, I believe I have located Heidel's stolen copy of the Guan Yin manuscript.'

'But it was blitzed in the limo fire,' said Patch. 'Wasn't it?'

Coldhardt leaned back in his chair. 'It seems the transponder tag inside it is still transmitting.'

Tye felt static prickle the hairs on the back of her neck. 'Where is it now?'

'In the early hours of this morning it was detected – thanks to Jonah – by RFID scanners at Heathrow airport.'

'Look, Coldhardt, Tye and I are sure it was the grimoire that Heidel burned.' Jonah looked to Tye for support and she nodded. 'Surely this has to be either a reading error or a trap.'

'My money's on a trap,' Motti agreed. 'I mean, what are the chances of Heidel using regular air travel?'

'Why shouldn't he?' said Coldhardt. 'Not all the players in this business have their own pilot. And besides, there is a credible reason for him being in London. Some rare paintings by an artist he favours are up for auction in central London.'

'Why would he take that manuscript with him on an art-buying trip?' Motti challenged. 'And he's had ages to take out that tag.'

Coldhardt looked at Maya. 'How difficult would its removal be?'

'It was inserted into the wooden spine beneath the vellum, then restored to leave no trace of incision,' she answered. 'But I don't know if Blackland told Heidel the location of the tag before he was killed.'

Now Coldhardt turned to Tye, who nodded. 'She's telling the truth. Heidel bundled in Blackland's body from another room, used it as a decoy.'

'In which case Heidel could have removed the

transponder before he even entered that room,' Jonah pointed out.

Con looked perplexed. 'But if he made such a show of burning the manuscript in front of you, why would he now expect Coldhart to be listening out for the tag?'

'Perhaps because he knows how much this manuscript means to you,' said Maya, regarding Coldhardt. 'He knows you will clutch at any straw.'

A flicker of annoyance crossed his face. 'Heidel is playing a game. And yes, there is a good chance he is baiting a trap.'

'A trap you're gonna send us into,' said Motti quietly. 'He gave you that signal at Heathrow in case the auction thing on its own wasn't enough for you to come running.'

'Perhaps. But this time, you will have the element of surprise.' Coldhardt shifted in his seat. 'Because it's not the manuscript I want, now. It's intelligence on Heidel. Track the tag signal and you track him – or one of his associates, who can *lead* you to him.'

'And then what?' asked Tye.

'I want data – surveillance footage, fingerprints, speech, distinguishing marks . . .'

'Maybe we could ask him to give blood?' Motti suggested.

'One thing,' said Tye. 'What about Jonah?'

Coldhardt gave a regal smile. 'He and Maya will receive payment to the same value should they crack the Bloodline Cipher.'

Jonah and Maya swapped glances, but Tye shook her head. 'That's not what I meant.'

'Yeah,' said Patch, 'you said he needed back-up in the safe house at all times in case . . .' He trailed off, glancing at Maya.

'Given the situation now, Patch, I feel you need the back-up more than Jonah,' said Coldhardt smoothly.

Maya stared. 'You think of me as a threat?'

'I'm not sure quite what to think of you,' Coldhardt replied. 'In any case, Jonah will *have* some back-up, as I will shortly be conducting business of my own at the safe house.'

'Oh?' said Jonah. 'What business is that?'

'When Heidel told you, "Time waits for no men," he was in a playful mood.' There was no trace of amusement or appreciation in Coldhardt's lined, craggy features. 'He didn't mean "no men". He was referring to a particular organisation called *Nomen Oblitum*.'

'That means *Forgotten Name* in Latin, no?' said Con.

Tye suddenly noticed that Maya was looking slightly flustered. 'You've heard of them?' she asked.

'What?' Maya glanced her way. 'Oh, yes . . . Yes, I've heard of them, seen them referred to in old texts. Blackland was especially interested in their history – what scraps there remain of it.' She seemed self-conscious to suddenly be the centre of attention, her fingers straying to her birthmark. 'Nomen Oblitum was the title used by a secret cult of European occultists in the fifteenth century.'

Motti seemed unimpressed. 'They couldn't remember their own name?'

'It is said the cult valued anonymity,' said

Coldhardt, 'both from the forces they claimed to control and the small-minded humans who frowned upon their actions.'

Jonah raised his eyebrows. 'What did they get up to?'

'The members of Nomen Oblitum appointed themselves guardians of forbidden knowledge,' said Maya. 'They located and acquired rare texts, tablets and tapestries, accumulating knowledge on anything from demonology to man's mastery over his body.'

Patch stared. 'What's some dodgy cult from a zillion years back got to do with time waiting for anyone?'

'It seems the order has endured through the centuries,' said Coldhardt quietly. 'Each child carefully nurtured and indoctrinated in the ways of the cult, forever searching for more and more secret works, passing on their knowledge to their own children.'

'Like a bloodline?' Jonah ventured.

His words hung in the air, despite the weight of them.

'I have arranged a meeting with members of this most interesting organisation at the safe house later today,' said Coldhardt coolly. 'I shall use the surveillance devices there to record the meeting for your later viewing, Tye. I want your opinion of what is said.'

Surveillance devices, Tye realised. *No wonder he didn't want me to go into details of how I figured Maya was telling the truth at her interview.* 'That tallies with my own observations,' *he'd said – he must have been watching Maya in private, way before he showed us that arranged interview.*

And now she could see by Maya's hurt look at Jonah that a certain penny had dropped. 'So that's why we had that little "chat" in the living room?'

'All the time you are there you can be spied upon,' Coldhardt informed her bluntly. 'Purely a security measure.'

The girl's eyes flashed. 'And what about our privacy?'

Coldhardt remained unmoved. 'Sadly, Maya, certain things must occasionally be sacrificed in the quest for knowledge. Now, we must discuss in more detail the task ahead. Jonah, would you escort Maya back to your limousine, then return here at once?'

He nodded and rose from his seat. Maya glared at Coldhardt, hardly pacified, and Tye couldn't blame her. It was easy to talk of sacrifices when you weren't making any of them yourself.

This little world of ours is getting darker by the day, she reflected unhappily. *Or maybe I'm just finally starting to see the light.*

'Seems we're always saying goodbye,' said Jonah quietly.

'Goodbyes are crap,' Tye agreed. 'And we've had too many lately.'

It was late morning, and he and Tye had wandered a short distance away from Patch, Con and Motti, at the imposing gates of Coldhardt's estate. The business at the hub was done with, and a black Mercedes limousine was waiting to take Jonah back to the safe house; Maya must have been waiting inside it for most of the morning.

Jonah lowered his voice still further. 'This is like torture. Wish I could just kiss you.'

'Wish by name, wish by . . .' Tye leaned up and pressed her lips against the side of his mouth quickly, her teeth just scraping the skin. It was a friends' kiss – but Patch still whooped and Motti pretended to throw up, while Con carefully examined her fingernails.

Jonah looked over at them. 'Don't worry, I'll be scabbing a goodbye kiss off you lot too.'

'Just don't slip me the tongue again,' joked Patch.

Tye looked over to the Mercedes. 'At least you'll have some company while I'm away. Nice, cosy, geeky nights together in front of the computer . . .'

'You're right,' Jonah agreed. 'I doubt I'll miss you at all.' He pulled a face at her. 'Duh!'

She pushed him in the ribs and they both laughed. Then he shook hands with Motti, gave Con a hug and knocked fists with Patch. 'Just take care of yourselves, OK?'

'Gee, geek, what a great idea!' Motti turned to Con. 'Add that to our list of good plans – "take care of ourselves".'

'You take care too,' said Con. 'Do not sprain a finger typing on that dangerous old keyboard, yes?'

'I'll try.' Jonah felt a double-twinge of guilt; not just from knowing that – money aside – he had a way better deal than they did, but because secretly he felt so relieved not to have to face up to Heidel and his crew. 'Don't you go spending your bonuses all at once.'

'What'll really be a bonus is if I can get that enamalled gold ring off Lady Bowfinger,' said Motti. 'Take back what's ours.'

'Just remember to duck if she takes a swing at you. That thing could take your nose off.' Jonah paused, smiled self-consciously. 'Feels like I'm waving you guys off to war.'

'That's 'cause you are,' said Patch, his chirpy façade slipping just a little.

'Yeah, well . . .' Jonah pulled out his mobile and activated the camera. 'Wave me bye-bye.'

Motti gave him the finger, Patch saluted, Con struck a sassy pose like she'd just stepped off a cat-walk and Tye . . . she just stood there, watching him. The sound of a shutter played. The moment was saved to the phone's memory and to his, and then Jonah backed away reluctantly to the waiting Mercedes. 'I'll see you soon, yeah?'

'You know it,' said Motti, and Tye nodded, watching him go.

Please let it be true, Jonah thought.

CHAPTER TEN

Jonah stared into the retina scanner and waited for the door release to click. Maya seized the door with a scrawny arm and pulled it open, then pushed past him into the air-conditioned lobby. He followed her, leaving the cafés and ski shops of Chamonix outside in the sunshine.

He knew she was still mad about the surveillance stuff. *I didn't know we could be watched the whole time either*, he wanted to tell her, but had decided not to. He'd spent his whole life as the one on the outside coming new to groups, trying to suss them out, hoping to fit in. Now for once someone else was in that position, and Jonah found he enjoyed acting the all-knowing guru for her.

'I think Coldhardt liked you,' he said, following her up the soft-carpeted stairs. 'You impressed him.'

She had to wait for him at the door to the actual apartment so he could get them inside. 'You could have told me we were being watched. That's just creepy.'

'The kind of books you read, and you think *that's* creepy?' He pressed his fingerprint to the reader, and by the time he'd tapped in a seven-digit code Maya was reluctantly smiling.

'I guess Coldhardt has to be careful,' Maya conceded as they went inside, 'dealing with the people he does. But does he have hidden cameras everywhere here?'

'Uh-huh. Watch out for the one in the bog.' Jonah crossed to his bedroom and checked the computer was still processing his earlier commands. During her stay at Blackland's, Maya had whole tracts of the manuscript digitally transcribed, enabling him to check them against a private database of ancient languages he'd hacked into. 'And as for the camcorder hidden in the shower-head . . .'

'All right, very funny.' Maya joined him in the bedroom, looking a little happier. 'It makes sense that if his time is running out, he wouldn't waste it watching us getting dressed.'

'That's weird, we've lost power . . . the computer's off.' Jonah looked at her, distractedly. 'Anyway, what do you mean, "his time is running out"?'

'I mean, if Coldhardt is making contact with Nomen Oblitum, believe me . . .' She looked around the room as if addressing a multitude of hidden cameras. 'His time is running out.'

Suddenly Jonah heard a quiet, furtive noise outside in the hallway. Maya must've heard it too, but before she could open her mouth to speak, he held up a warning finger. 'Either one of Coldhardt's bugs just took offence and jumped off the wall to get us,' he murmured, 'or else –'

'Someone's inside,' Maya whispered. 'But how can they be?'

Jonah was thinking the same thing: the alarms

hadn't been triggered, and the security systems outside betrayed no sign of a break-in.

So when he went outside and saw a figure in black standing in the hallway, for a few moments he simply froze in confusion.

Then the fear pumped in as the figure turned and pulled off his balaclava. Familiar ice-blue eyes and a cruel smile widened together. 'Guess who, Jonah.'

'Uh . . .' *Stall for time*, thought Jonah. *Figure out an escape plan*. 'Sorrel, wasn't it?'

The smile didn't waver. 'Sorin.'

'And you're here about the cleaning job, right?'

Sorin threw the balaclava on the floor. 'I'm gonna clean up on you, bru.'

Jonah turned back to the bedroom. *No way out through there*. 'Maya, come and join the party,' called Jonah, trying to act like he wasn't bricking it. 'An old friend's come visiting.'

Maya emerged, arms folded tightly across her chest, looking as scared as Jonah felt. 'I don't know how you got in –'

'No. You *don't* know.' Sorin stared at her. 'You got an e-version of the manuscript. We want it.'

She looked away. 'I don't know what you're talking about.'

'I think you do.'

'Do you find people forget your name a lot, Sod'im, being the rubbish one of the group?' *If I can get him mad*, thought Jonah, *make him careless* . . . 'Where are the rest of Heidel's little helpers, anyway?'

'I don't need them to deal with a bookworm bitch and a pussy like you.'

'Oh, I get it. You've got stuff to prove, right?' Jonah took hold of Maya's hand and started to edge towards the living-room door. 'Coldhardt couldn't find so much as a surname for you, Sorin. There was loads of info on the others, but you've got no records, no rep.' *If we can get inside, hit the panic screens and shut him out* . . . 'What's your special skill anyway, Sorin – the ability to tan quickly in a dangerous situation?'

'You think tuning me grief's gonna save your ass?' Sorin hissed. 'Security's my thing, bru, and I'm better than you can believe.'

'Right.'

'Got inside here, didn't I? Like I got inside Blackland's little fortress.' He started walking towards them. 'And now I'm going to open *you* up.'

Jonah grabbed Maya and hauled her into the living room. '*Farewell glorious villains!*' he yelled, the trigger phrase for the panic screens to slam down and shield them, a quote from some mouldy old play Coldhardt loved. But nothing happened. Maya looked at Jonah helplessly.

'Oh, did the shutters not work?' Sorin strode through the doorway. 'Told you I was good. There's nothing gonna stop me taking your asses apart.'

'Not even hygiene worries?' Jonah kept backing away, keeping Maya close to his side. Then suddenly he threw himself at Sorin, hoping to catch him off guard. 'Run, Maya!'

Sorin fell backwards, but dragged Jonah with him, used his feet to propel him over his head. Jonah gasped as his back slammed against the wall, and he fell winded to the ground. He looked up and saw Maya hesitating in the doorway. '*Get help!*' he shouted.

'Aww, your girl won't duck and leave you! Sweet!' Sorin had pulled something from his pocket – a narrow tube he telescoped with a flick of his wrist and then put to his mouth.

Jonah heard the phut of the blowpipe, eclipsed an instant later by Maya's gasp. Her hand slapped to her neck, where her birthmark stained the skin. She fell to her knees, eyes turning glassy.

'What the hell –?' Jonah swung back to Sorin in mute accusation – in time to see a boot shooting towards his face. He ducked out of the way, heard the boom of foot-sole on plaster, pushed himself forward so he knocked Sorin off balance.

Got to end this quick if I'm going to stand a chance, he thought. As Sorin fell face first, Jonah brought one knee down hard on his opponent's spine and punched him in the back of the skull with all his strength. His knuckles jarred with the impact, sent shoots of hot pain through his whole hand. But Sorin stayed down.

'Who's the pussy now, "bru",' Jonah muttered, flexing his throbbing fingers as he ran over to where Maya was still kneeling in the doorway.

'Jonah?' Her eyelids were flickering, she held a tiny dart between thumb and forefinger. 'I'm OK. The bastard doped me. But I'll be OK.'

'We'll find a doctor,' he promised, taking Maya's arms and pulling her up. 'We need to get the hell out of –'

Phut. That sound again, and this time a scratch in his own neck. Jonah felt for the barb with scrabbling fingers, hooked it out. He saw Sorin, standing up, smiling again. Then his vision began to haze, and the ground seemed to tilt beneath his feet.

Oh no. Oh God. What's he done to me? Frantically, Jonah grabbed Maya and tried to make for the door. But his legs weren't playing that walking game now, they were buckling beneath him. Overcome with dizziness, he collapsed, and Maya fell with him. Jonah heard footfalls behind him, felt the vibrations in the floorboards as Sorin stamped out of the living room. Jonah tried to crawl away and drag Maya after him, but his strength was gone. The hallway began to distort like he was seeing through a fish-eye lens.

Then Sorin screamed out in pain.

The sound was sharp enough to score through the blackness encroaching, and Jonah turned.

I'm hallucinating, he thought, willing his eyes to focus.

Sorin was being held against the wall just a few metres away, by a man dressed in dark Arabic robes. The man wore a bronze face mask with three distorted circles for eyes and mouth, framed by a night-blue silk headdress that hid all but a swarthy glimpse of skin about the lips. There was a musty smell of age about him, almost overpowering. The light caught on a medallion of crimson glass hanging from a leather cord around his neck.

The man looked slight, but Sorin wasn't moving. And then Jonah heard movement behind, felt a shadow fall felt-soft over him. He looked up groggily to find another similar figure stooping over him, this time in blood-red robes.

Jonah felt a fresh chill of fear, enough to stir his tongue. 'Who're you?' he managed, as if knowing might help or matter as blackness tore away at the rest of his sight and coldness slipped through his veins like anaesthetic.

'We will take away your pain,' said a voice in halting English, and it was the last thing Jonah heard.

Tye had a map, but Motti refused to let her use it. 'You don't want anyone to think we're tourists,' he warned her. 'We'll look like easy marks.'

'Motti,' Patch complained, 'you're a bleedin' map fascist. This is Pentonville Road, not the Bronx.'

'He's right, though, we don't want to do anything that will draw attention,' said Con, 'from Heidel more than anyone else.'

'So how do you suggest we find this auction house if we can't check against the map?' asked Tye wearily.

'Shove it in a magazine or something,' said Motti. The handheld RFID receiver was wedged in his jacket pocket, similarly out of sight. 'Patch, go buy one from the news stand.'

'Back in my old manor after all these years,' Patch sighed, entering a grimy newsagent. 'Lovely, innit.'

Not very, thought Tye. King's Cross station sprawled behind them, trying hard to be presentable, but the surrounding neighbourhood had no such pretensions. The rubbish-strewn streets were busy with traffic and jammed-in shops, cafés and newsagents.

Shabby cut-price B&Bs huddled together in terraces, as if fearing the clientele they attracted. Huge warehouses – massive hunks of mouldering brickwork – dominated the blocky horizon, their stained or broken windows staring out blindly over the sprawl. Tower cranes loomed silently overhead like heroic statues, symbols of regeneration and better times coming. But for every new office block and trendy bar presenting polished glass and brushed metal fronts, another building close by was blackening further in the fumes.

Tye had flown Coldhardt's King Air 350 from Geneva to a small airport outside Oxford – just in case the more convenient airports were under obs. From Oxford they had travelled to London by train like tourists, their gear for the trip concealed in bulging rucksacks. While Patch and Motti made quiet plans on a laptop and Con slept, Tye had watched the greenery give way first to industrial yards, then to tottering houses set in sooty terraces and apartment blocks, where satellite dishes sat in their dozens like strange birds of prey, eyeing the trains rushing by.

Patch re-emerged a couple of minutes later engrossed in a copy of *Zoo*. Con tutted and snatched it from him, flicking through the flesh-filled pages until she found a sports article and framed the map around it.

'The auction house is about half a mile south,' she announced. 'And the bidding is not due to start for another hour and a half. Shall we get there early, survey the space, find a good place to spy on the bidders?'

Tye nodded. 'Sounds like we have a plan.' She followed Con and the boys along the busy street, breathing in its blend of bitumen and car exhaust.

'Uh, guys?' Motti suddenly stopped, looking gravely down at his jacket pocket. 'Our Spidey-sense just started tingling. We must be within two hundred metres of that manuscript tag.'

'Heidel could be coming our way!' Con realized.

Patch swore, looked around hurriedly. 'In here, quick.' He led them into a cramped tourist shop selling bad T-shirts and tacky gifts. While the others mixed and mingled with the customers, Tye cautiously looked out of the window from behind an inflatable Beefeater, searching for faces she'd hoped she'd never see again.

Motti came up behind her. 'No signs yet,' Tye reported.

'Figures.' He was checking the handheld. 'Signal's holding steady, hasn't moved. Which means the tag is sitting static some place, and we must've walked into range.'

Con had drifted back close enough to overhear. 'We'd better get closer and see who's minding it.'

'Hang on.' Patch started pulling and itching at his ribs through his Boxfresh hoodie. 'Just making sure my titanium blanket's in place. Saved my life last time.'

'What if this time she shoots you between the eyes?' Motti tapped him on the head and led the way out of the shop.

Patch turned pale. Tye steered him back out into the busy street after Motti, and Con trailed a little way behind them. The crowds were both a blessing and a blindspot; just because the tag was sitting pretty, that didn't mean Heidel's gang weren't circulating in the area. And while busy streets might mean that Bree and the others couldn't pull anything too homicidal, it also made them harder to spot.

The trail of Motti's tracker led down a quieter, smarter side street, where tarmac gave way to cobblestones. Apartment blocks lined the street in four-storey sweeps, but a large, ornate building, all stained plaster, colonnades and faded glamour, dominated the view. Tye was reminded of a wedding cake left out in the rain. The weathered sign outside the revolving doors proclaimed it to be the Irving Hotel in royal-blue letters.

'That's where our baby is,' Motti announced.

'It's a dead-end down here,' Con informed them, checking her map. 'Pedestrian access only through a narrow alleyway.'

'If they're watching out for us, they could pull something here,' Patch whispered, his face pale and sweaty. 'And who'd know?'

'The rest of you go back to the street,' said Motti. 'I'll check out the foyer alone, see if I can get more of a fix on the signal.'

Tye nodded. 'OK. You'll be less conspicuous on your own. Signal us with the two-way, tell us what you find.'

'We should have a codeword or phrase or something,' Patch suggested.

'OK,' said Motti seriously. 'If I say, "Patch is an ass", it means I found trouble. And if I say, "Patch is a needle-dick", it means all clear.' He paused. '*And* that Patch is a needle-dick.'

'Ha, ha,' said Patch. 'Can we just get on with it?'

As Motti disappeared inside, Tye, Con and Patch separated, each standing casually in a different direction, covering the compass for any fleeting glimpse of Sadie, Sorin, Heidel or Bree.

Tye kept her fingers on her radio. When it squawked into life, she jammed it quickly to her ear – and let out a huge relieved breath.

'Patch is a needle-dick!' she called triumphantly, and a crowd of passing tourists gave her funny looks, while Patch himself scowled and scuttled quickly away towards the hotel.

Looking about warily, Tye and Con followed him inside. The reception floor was tiled white and black, and the walls were lined with wood panels; thirty years ago they might have looked smart, but now both were scuffed and slightly tatty. The aging concierge looked as careworn as his surroundings, in crumpled blue uniform and faded braid. He eyed Motti suspiciously.

'Do your thing, Con,' Motti told her quietly.

Con put on a big smile and turned to the concierge. 'Excuse me, monsieur, can you help us?' she said charmingly in a strong French accent. 'We're looking for friends of ours.'

'The receptionist has gone to powder her nose,' the concierge informed her. 'She may be able to help you.'

Con nodded briefly at Tye. 'But I think you can help me, monsieur. Look at me. I think you *want* to help me, yes?' Her voice was getting lower, more sonorous and exotic. 'Yes, you will help me I am sure . . .'

The concierge's eyes were glazing over. 'I want to help you,' he agreed in a wondering whisper.

Seeing that Con's mesmerism had the man well under control – *her* control – Tye walked quickly to the ladies' toilet. A young woman with high cheekbones and a sallow complexion was washing her hands in the sink. Her staff name badge proclaimed she was Anna. Tye walked up beside her, pulled a phial from her pocket and shook a couple of drops into the tap water. Instantly a cloud of noxious fumes rose up into Anna's face, and Tye quickly retreated as the girl keeled over.

'Sorry,' Tye muttered, catching Anna smoothly before she could hit the ground. 'But you look like you could use a rest.'

The fumes from the knock-out drops soon dissipated into nothing more than a bad smell, and Tye towed the receptionist into a cubicle. She locked the door, propped Anna up on the seat, took out a fifty-pound note and tucked it into her hand. Then Tye pulled herself up and over the cubicle door and ran back to join the others.

She found Motti and Patch behind the reception desk and Con watching the doors while the concierge stood with his back to them, smiling into space. No one needed to ask her how she'd got on. It was a given.

'Penthouse was booked today,' Motti reported. 'Double occupancy. In the name of . . . how d'ya like that? Nathaniel Coldhardt.'

'He's a real comedian, that Heidel geezer.' Patch fished out two keys from a drawer beneath the desk. 'Looks like nobody's home. We got his key and the maid's, right here.'

'They might *want* us to think that their rooms are empty,' said Con, 'so we go breezing straight into an ambush.'

'Yes, the hotel they've chosen is hardly much of a challenge,' Tye agreed. 'I don't like it.'

'And I'm not even needed,' said Patch brightly. 'If you've got the keys to get in . . .'

'Unlucky, Cyclops, we need you all right,' said Motti. 'You're gonna break into the building opposite, scoot up to the top floor and scope out the inside of the penthouse from there. You see any signs of life, get on the radio.'

'You clever sod!' said Patch admiringly. He lifted the material covering his glass eyeball and plucked it out with a soft squelching noise.

Motti cringed. 'Jesus, Patch! Get out of here with your dumb "utility eye" crap!'

'Gets him every time,' said Patch happily, unscrewing the eyeball to reveal his extendible lock-picking tools hidden inside.

'I'll go with you,' Tye offered.

'We'll wait here for word,' said Con. 'My friend the concierge will turn away any visitors, but I'll tell him to make an exception for you two.'

'Make an exception,' the concierge agreed sleepily.

Tye and Patch squeezed past him and back outside. The street was still all but empty. A couple stood arguing outside one of the apartment blocks, too busy blazing at each other to notice much else. Patch pretended to reach in his pocket for keys, then set to work on the lock with pick and torque wrench. He had the door open so fast anyone would think he was legit, and Tye smiled to herself. In his own way, Patch was a little genius.

Once they were inside, Tye led the way up several flights of stairs to the top floor. 'That's the flat we want,' she said quietly, creeping over shiny tiles to the mustard-yellow door. 'Can't hear any signs of life.'

Patch put his ear to the wood for a second opinion, then frowned. ''Ere, look,' he whispered, and pointed to the door lock. 'Scratches and scoring round the entry point. Like someone's tried to break in and made a right pig's arse of it.'

Tye peered at the scratches and tutted. 'I guess you can't trust anyone these days.' She glanced around. 'Just get us inside, Patch. If anyone's home, we'll just say we saw the door wide open and wanted to check everything was OK.'

'That's us,' said Patch, tickling the lock with his picks. 'Friendly neighbourhood caring types . . .'

Moments later he pushed open the door. It gave on to a long, narrow entrance hall, studded with doors leading off on either side, and opening up into a large living room directly opposite. Tye noticed a rectangle of sunlight thrown down in there by an unseen window, warming the wooden floorboards. 'That'll be the view we want,' she murmured.

Then she saw a shadow shift in the hard block of yellow. The shadow of a woman –

'Patch, look out!' Tye yelled as Sadie burst into sight in the open doorway, all in black and wielding a hefty hunting knife. Coldhardt's gold ring glinted like the serrated blade as she lunged forward at Patch, slashing for his neck.

CHAPTER ELEVEN

Tye pushed Patch out of range of the blade but he overbalanced and fell against a doorframe, yelping with pain.

Sadie raised the knife to throw it down at him, aiming a kick at Tye as she did so. But Tye feinted backwards, grabbed a vase from the telephone table beside her and hurled it at Sadie's face. Sadie ducked, and kicked out again. Her metal heel cracked plaster from the wall; she would have shattered Tye's ribs if she'd been a fraction faster. As it was, Tye dodged the blow and now grabbed Sadie's calf, twisting with all her strength. Soundlessly, Sadie tumbled to the floor – only to execute a perfect backward roll into the living room before jumping to her feet.

Tye was already sprinting after her. *If I can reach that bitch before she's balanced, get the damn knife off of her . . .* As she ran, she glanced at the bay windows – and in an instant saw a sighted harpoon gun mounted there, aimed across the street at the penthouse with its open balcony doors. *Waiting for us to get inside and pick up the tag*, she realised. *It was a trap all right, but the trap was in here all along.*

Sadie swung the knife at Tye. She ducked beneath

the blow, used her momentum to pull off a tight somersault in midair, pivoted on one heel and high-kicked her attacker. The side of her foot connected with Sadie's wrist, knocked the knife from the girl's grasp. But with her other hand, Sadie reached forward and grabbed a thick handful of Tye's dreadlocks, twisting and yanking.

Tye gasped with pain as her roots started to tug through her scalp. She tried to struggle free. No good. Sadie's other arm was clamped round Tye's ribs with crushing force, and her head was being pulled back, exposing her neck.

Sadie hissed and opened her mouth wide in Tye's face. Tye saw the pale grey stump inside that had been the girl's tongue, flinched from the madness in the dark eyes. Growling like an animal, Sadie leaned in and started to sink her teeth into Tye's cheek.

Not gonna scream. Tye screwed up her eyes. *Not gonna scream –*

But then a whooping maniac came tearing into the living room. Tye's eyes opened.

It was Patch.

He was running full pelt, arms outstretched. He grabbed Sadie's head and yanked it back. Tye twisted free and fell to one side, clutching her burning cheek. But Patch was going too fast to stop – he and Sadie piled into a pine sideboard that collapsed under the impact.

Tye climbed shakily to her feet, tried to pin Sadie's arms to her side, but she was too slow. Sadie grabbed a length of wood and swung it wildly. Tye tried to turn from the blow but it caught her hard on the elbow. She staggered back and tripped over a low coffee table.

Meantime Sadie swung her ringed fist at Patch, who ducked just in time. She grunted as she bruised her knuckles on the wall, followed up with a second blow that whumped Patch in his good eye, sent his head smacking back against one of the sideboard drawers. He was too dazed to react as she hit him again with her ring hand, even harder, pounding blood from his split lip. Patch brought his arms up feebly over his face, but Sadie swatted them aside, raised her fist yet again ready to –

Tye brought a lead glass decanter down hard on Sadie's head.

With a low moan Sadie rolled back, eyes closed, fists still clenched. She collapsed in the splintered shell of the sideboard.

Patch tried to open his eye, the lid bruised and fat already like a dark flower blooming. 'Did we get her?' he slurred, dribbling blood.

'Yeah.' Tye sunk to her knees beside him, trying to calm her breathing. 'We got her.' She felt her tender cheek – if Patch had been a second later the flesh would have been scissored open. Roughly she tugged the bloodied ring from Sadie's finger and slipped it in her pocket, willing her hands to stop shaking. What was it she'd promised Jonah in the showers after his own fight? *It gets easier*.

'Yeah, right,' she muttered, pulling out the radio. 'Motti, it's Tye.'

'You mean it ain't the Queen of England?' he shot back.

'Be quiet.' Tye watched Sadie warily, convinced she was about to get right up again. 'We just ran into

Lady Bowfinger, waiting to take us out the second we went into that penthouse.'

'Shit.'

'No shit.' Patch coughed and wiped a string of bloody saliva from his chin. 'It's all been kicked out of me.'

'Tie her up, Patch,' Tye hissed urgently, and crossed to the window. 'Looks clear inside the penthouse. Guess they wouldn't want one of their own catching a stray harpoon.'

'Harpoon?' That was Con's voice. 'You're serious?'

'You don't want to know how serious.' Tye wiped cold sweat from her eyes. 'Just get inside that penthouse while you can. We'll watch from the window and warn you if we see any more company coming.'

'Perhaps you should simply shoot them first, no?' said Con softly. 'This is the second time they have tried to kill us. If not for blind luck this time . . .'

Con broke contact, and Tye sighed heavily. She glanced back at Patch, squinting through his swollen eye as he tied Sadie's hands behind her back with a leather belt.

'We're thieves, not killers,' said Patch firmly. 'Let's call the cops, tell 'em there's been a break-in. Should keep her tied up for a while.'

'I only hope your knots will,' Tye muttered, watching edgily from the window for any movement in the street below.

Jonah became aware of the world sliding back into solidity. His mouth was parched, and his whole body felt sick and hollow. He clenched his fists and fought against the feeling of nausea, tried to focus on his heartbeat, to drive it faster and faster, fast enough to drum out the poison and beat his other senses back into life.

As he rubbed his aching neck, his finger touched on the swollen mark where the dart had punctured the flesh; it stung fiercely, making him gasp, driving his eyes open. With the pain came sudden clarity, and he found he was sprawled on the sofa in the apartment's living room. The blinds had been drawn, and it was very cold. Maya was kneeling on the carpet beside him, awake and wary.

Jonah stirred groggily, grabbed hold of her. 'You OK? What happened to Sorin? Where did –'

Then he turned to his right and saw what she was looking at. Sorin was standing rigidly against the far wall in front of the two-way mirror, flanked by weird figures – one masked and wearing dark robes, the other an old man in a smock of flowing crimson silk. The ruby-glass medallion at his throat seemed to glow as it reflected the richness of the fabric.

'Welcome back, Jonah.'

Jonah turned quickly to his left at the sound of Coldhardt's voice; he had taken the same chair in which Maya had faced her questioning. 'How are you feeling now?'

'Like death,' Jonah muttered. 'What's going on, where'd you spring from?'

'I came here when my surveillance devices abruptly ceased operation,' Coldhardt explained, 'and found you had visitors.'

'They weren't exactly invited in.' Jonah turned back

to the figures, gritting his teeth. 'Sorin drugged me, I thought I dreamed these guys.'

'You were poisoned by a dart containing curare,' announced the elderly man in crimson, his voice deep and honeyed. 'Your neuromuscular junctions were swiftly affected. If left untreated, you would have died of asphyxiation.'

'It seems you and Maya owe your lives to the early arrival of my guests.' Coldhardt smiled. 'Allow me to introduce the Scribe and his man-at-arms – representatives of Nomen Oblitum.'

Jonah felt a jolt of apprehension, as the two robed figures touched their hands to their glass amulets in an almost defensive gesture. Each amulet resembled an ankh, the Egyptian symbol of life – but the arms were longer and curved down, and a stylised knot marked the point where the oval 'head' met the stem of the body.

'The Knot of Isis,' said Maya quietly, nodding to the amulets. 'The symbol of Nomen Oblitum.'

'Isis?' Jonah whispered.

'Yes, Isis,' said the Scribe. 'A most worthy patron. Egyptian goddess of love and destiny, who grew in significance to become a cosmic goddess over all the ancient world. In her ancient shrine in Sa el-Hagar, it was written, *I am all that hath been, and is, and shall be; and my veil no mortal has hitherto raised.*' The old man in the crimson robes stepped forward. 'We of the cult see through that veil. Our lives are dedicated to the assimilation of the ancient arts, just as Isis herself assimilated Semitic and Arabian gods, her power and influence growing over thousands of years . . .'

Now Jonah could see the Scribe's face more clearly. The features were vaguely Middle Eastern, lips pulled back in the rictus smile of an overeager salesman. But his eyes seemed sallow and dull, like he'd spent a lifetime studying things too close, too keenly; if the man really was a scribe, someone who spent his life writing out documents, perhaps that might explain it.

'The knot represents eternal life and resurrection,' the Scribe went on. 'Fitting for so long-lived an organisation as ours, do you not think?'

'Very fitting,' muttered Maya.

'If you saved us, then thank you.' Jonah was in no mood for a history lesson. 'But what's happened to Sorin? He's not moving.'

'The youth is held immobile,' the Scribe agreed. 'Just as we held and expelled the poison within you, so we can manipulate the meridians of the body.'

The Scribe nodded to his man-at-arms. The masked figure placed his fingers against the skin of Sorin's neck and flexed them into strange, gnarled designs. One moment Sorin held the same glazed and empty look in his eyes, the next he was screaming hoarsely and wildly as if wracked by the most incredible pain. And yet for all the anguish there in his face, his body barely moved – as if it were solid wax and fixed to the floor. Then the man-at-arms touched Sorin's wrist; the screams choked off and Sorin fell to the floor, shivering and panting for breath.

The Scribe himself now bent easily to press two fingers against the base of Sorin's neck. Sorin fell still again, his breathing growing more regular as if he were asleep.

'An interesting demonstration,' said Coldhardt finally.

'Horrible,' Jonah muttered.

The Scribe inclined his head. 'I merely demonstrate that our will works in perfect harmony with our physical form, to effect change in others. Do you wish to question this youth?'

'He's a hireling. I doubt he can tell me much.' Coldhardt stared hard at the Scribe. 'However, perhaps you could tell me why you saw fit to "effect" a forced entry into my premises. I arranged with you a time to meet here –'

'Come, Coldhardt.' The Scribe sounded amused. 'Our cult has not endured so long by accepting terms dictated to us. We wished to be certain we were not walking into a trap.' He glanced at the two-way mirror on the wall as if he could see beyond it. 'Mechanical defences are never adequate. And we have no wish to be spied upon as we discuss . . . business.' Now he fixed Jonah and Maya with his yellowish glare. 'So if you are satisfied that the children are unharmed, perhaps you can dismiss them?'

'There are two of you, with control over a homicidal criminal – and only one of me.' Coldhardt smiled without warmth. 'Forgive me if I prefer that Jonah and Maya remain.'

'If our enterprise is to succeed, we must trust each other fully. Without trust, we cannot give you the knowledge you seek, Coldhardt.' The Scribe took a step towards him. 'The knowledge of the Bloodline Cipher.'

'Ah, yes.' Coldhardt's voice was quiet and sharp as

flint. 'You claim to have cracked the code.'

The Scribe touched his amulet, then reached into his crimson robes and pulled out an ancient-looking volume, slim and bound in blackened hide. 'This is the master copy of the Guan Yin manuscript.' He came forward and offered it to Coldhardt. 'A treasure that has been in our possession for centuries.'

Coldhardt took the volume with the reverence of a priest and opened it with the casual expertise of a connoisseur. 'Fascinating,' he murmured, turning it in his hands. 'But I would prefer Maya to study it, if you don't mind. I understand she is something of an expert on this volume.'

The Scribe bowed his head. Maya rose and almost snatched the book from Coldhardt's fingers. She opened it, scrutinised the inside back and front, and then sat beside Jonah on the couch. It was definitely a different volume to the one they'd been studying; that much was obvious from the condition of the pages, which seemed a slightly different shape and stained near black in places. The size of the characters seemed to vary more too.

'How was the cipher encrypted? Jonah demanded.

'Only the truth of the text matters.' The Scribe reached out his hand for the book with long, yellowed fingernails like talons, and snatched it back. 'Naturally, it speaks of the cipher of the blood – the complex chemistry passed on from son to son. The strength, the sinew, the *will* of all our ancestors lies encoded there.'

'Is that a fact,' Maya muttered.

Coldhardt spared her the briefest glance. 'Are you

talking metaphorically or physically, Scribe?'

'Around eighty per cent of the human genome – the genetic information we each inherit from our ancestors – is thought of as junk DNA, a relic of evolution serving no purpose.' The Scribe smiled. 'With the cipher, we can unlock that purpose.'

Jonah snorted. 'Fourteenth-century genetics?'

'Science merely discovered late that which the old arts have always held – that the life is in the blood.' The Scribe's eyes seemed to shine darkly. 'Through our knowledge and skills we can manipulate the many bindings of the human body to protect and prolong the spark of the mind and the will of the flesh. We can halt the spread of time's corruption –'

But suddenly Sorin jumped up from the floor like someone snapping awake from a nightmare. Before Jonah could even react he was up on his feet. He shoved the Scribe into the mirror with a yell of anger, made for the door –

But the man-at-arms flashed out an arm and grabbed Sorin by the throat, stopping him mid-stride. The Scribe barked something in a language Jonah didn't understand.

Coldhardt rose from the chair, his voice ringing out, '*No* –'

But already the man-at-arms had jabbed a finger against Sorin's chest like a stiletto, then stabbed his thumb up behind Sorin's right ear. Sorin's eyes closed and his athletic body started twitching. Spittle frothed at his mouth. Jonah stared, sickened and appalled, as blood began to pump from Sorin's ear, flooding down the side of his face and neck.

'You're killing him!' Maya shouted.

'It is done,' the Scribe informed her.

With a final graphic convulsion, Sorin's body slumped lifeless to the ground as the man-at-arms released his grip.

'None may attempt violence against our order,' said the Scribe, his macabre grimace still in place. 'Whether pre-meditated, or in fear and agitation.'

Maya looked disgusted. 'That was just grandstanding, pure and simple. There was no call to –'

'Enough,' snapped Coldhardt. 'Scribe, his death was unnecessary.'

'Do not seek to judge us, Coldhardt.' Jonah saw the sneer in the Scribe's glinting eyes. 'Not if you wish to benefit from our instruction.'

A heavy silence settled over the bloody scene. Jonah put a hand on Maya's shoulder, both to try and calm her and to steady himself. It was like reliving the nightmare of when Budd and Clyde were slaughtered in front of him, that sudden, callous brutality as lives were ended in a handful of bloody seconds. Guts and head still spinning, he glanced back at Coldhardt with no idea what to do.

'Violence will always breed violence.' The Scribe stepped carefully over Sorin's corpse. 'But our ministrations – both physical and spiritual – can offer you that which you most darkly crave, Coldhardt. A long, long life . . .'

Maya opened her mouth as if to make some retort, but Jonah squeezed her shoulder. *No*, he mouthed, fearing the outcome of another interruption. Coldhardt had sat back down in his chair, looking suddenly much older. Jonah resumed his position on the couch, and Maya did too.

'We are not workers of miracles, of course.' The Scribe inclined his head humbly. 'We are technicians of the blood. Guardians of great secrets that take time to impart – perhaps years . . .'

Jonah stared at Coldhardt. *A long, long life,* he thought. *Is* that *why you've got involved with these people?*

'My old . . . associate – Anton Heidel.' Coldhardt shifted in his seat a little. 'He is the living proof of your technique – that's what you'd have me believe, isn't it? That you healed him, restored him . . . *nurtured* him for nigh on thirty years?'

The Scribe nodded. 'His body was very close to death. As a result, the work went slowly.'

And this is why you're getting proof that Heidel is who he claims to be, Jonah thought, wishing he were with Tye and the others right now, far from here.

'Coldhardt, are – are you saying you might be away for years?' In the quiet of the apartment, Jonah's voice came out more fragile than he would've liked. 'What happens to the rest of us?'

Coldhardt made no response.

Suddenly Maya pointed at Sorin's body. 'Did you know that Heidel employed *him*, Scribe?'

'Our work with Heidel is successfully completed. He holds no further interest for us. We seek fresh challenges.'

Maya wasn't to be put off. 'But doesn't it worry you that he was trying to stop Coldhardt using your services? You must know Heidel hates him.'

'How could we not?' The Scribe nodded. 'Heidel's mind fixates upon you, Coldhardt, just as when first he came to us, a dying man. It is understandable, of course. Those who work together in dangerous fields often forge close bonds. And when such men are betrayed . . .'

'Quite,' said Coldhardt softly, sending a tingle down Jonah's spine.

'It was this lasting obsession that led us to consider you as a likely patron. We are few, and may only dedicate ourselves to few, for the work is all-consuming . . . which is why it comes at so high a price.' The Scribe held out his hands like a priest offering benediction. 'We need funds to endure. And you are a wealthy man, Coldhardt.'

'I am aware of your terms. You drive quite a bargain.' Coldhardt gazed into space for a few moments, then leaned forward in his chair. 'Assuming I wish to pursue this path . . . what happens next?'

The Scribe placed his hands together, as if in prayer. 'The first step is to arrange a private consultation with the Mage. But before she can examine you, ritual decrees you must provide her with two things: a vial of your blood, and a gift of great wisdom . . . the gift to be specified by the Mage herself.'

Maya's face was sour as week-old milk as she sat there, shaking her head.

'You may contact us as you have before, should you choose to proceed. This interview is now ended.'

'And how am I to dispose of *that*?' Coldhardt inquired, stabbing a finger at Sorin's crumpled body.

The Scribe turned to him. 'Heidel would argue that disposal is your business.'

Without further ceremony, the Scribe swept towards the door, his crimson robes swirling about him like flowing blood, his masked man-at-arms following in his wake.

'They're going to stand out among the tourists dressed like that,' Jonah murmured, still feeling numb inside. *Don't look at the body. The blood. Don't even think of it.*

'A judge must wear his robes and regalia when practising, according to centuries-old tradition,' said Coldhardt, staring into space. 'Perhaps the officials of Nomen Oblitum are the same.'

'Or perhaps they were trying to add some substance to their act by trying to look the part – the spooky sorcerer and his acolyte.' Maya was looking at Coldhardt. 'Do you believe that stuff they told you?'

'Don't you?' Coldhardt barely seemed to hear her, studying the backs of his hands. 'They brought you back from near-death, as they claim to have done with Heidel.'

'"Claim" may be right,' said Maya. 'This is the dart Sorin put in me.' She produced it in her palm. 'You can have it analysed, see for yourself if it was as deadly as they claim – or if they're scamming.'

Coldhardt spared her a brief glance. 'I thought you were sympathetic to occult beliefs.'

'Not blindly so. I mean, so they had a copy of the Guan Yin manuscript. So what? So did Blackland, and he wasn't a sorcerer. There are at least three known to be in existence.'

'That man-at-arms guy killed Sorin with his fingers,' said Jonah slowly.

'A systemised attack on the weak centres of the body, performed with high precision and skill,' Maya agreed. 'Impressive, but not necessarily supernatural. Martial arts such as Dim Mak would provide the basics for –'

'Impressive?' Jonah stared at her. 'I wasn't remarking on how clever they were. I was reminding you that they murdered someone right in front of us!'

'The manner in which the execution was performed speaks for their skill.' Coldhardt had moved on to studying his fingernails. 'And the fact that they killed without hesitation in front of an audience speaks for their power.'

'They know you can't go to the police,' Maya retorted. 'They were trying to impress you and intimidate you both at once. They must feel you're desperate to know the cipher's secrets –'

'*What do you know of desperation?*' Coldhardt roared, standing up. Maya flinched and looked away. But Jonah kept watching a few seconds longer, and in that moment of naked anger he glimpsed something feral and inhuman in Coldhardt's eyes.

Heart bouncing off his ribs, he crossed quickly to the window. He wished he could turn his back on the body, on Coldhardt, everything; his own hypocrisy included. Because for all his supposed squeamishness, a piece of him was *glad* Sorin was dead now, glad that he would never get another chance to kill Jonah or his friends. And it sickened him.

It gets easier, Tye had told him in the locker room.

But do I want it to? he'd wondered.

He watched a large, dark car pull away from the

apartment block to dominate the narrow streets, its tinted windows hiding the sinister figures inside. It passed from sight but stayed in his memory, like a black fly crawling over his mind.

If Coldhardt does go, there'll be an end to it, he thought numbly.

And then . . . ?

'I will have Motti compile a report on how the security devices here were breached,' Coldhardt announced. 'It mustn't happen again.' Jonah heard his deliberate step as he crossed to the door. 'Prepare your things and join me in the car, both of you. It may not be safe to remain here. You will continue your work at the base.'

Jonah swallowed, turned back to him. 'What about Sorin's body?'

'As the Scribe said – I'm in the business of disposal.'

Maya didn't look up, perhaps stunned still by the force of his anger. A few moments later, the front door clicked shut as Coldhardt left the apartment.

A slow chill passed through Jonah. He put out his hand as if reaching for the real world outside. The bulletproof glass felt cold against his palm.

CHAPTER TWELVE

Tye wondered how long it would be before the van she was hiding in was reported as missing – and how quickly it would be found. Parked opposite a high-class auction house on a busy street off Chancery Lane, she couldn't imagine it would be long – then there was the matter of the black Saab Patch had broken into so she could park it round the corner and nick its place. She pictured herself apologising to the owner: *Sorry, but we're criminals trying to get video footage of a resurrected criminal mastermind and murderer for our shady employer back in Geneva – and your car was parked in the perfect spot for catching them as they go in and out*. That would go down well. *Oh, and by the way, you should've gone for the 9–5 estate over the saloon.*

She checked that Motti's MacBook was still picking up the audio signal from inside the auction room. Heidel had reserved seating for himself and Bree, front of hall – making it easy for Con to place a listening device under his chair. Now his softest whisper would be transmitted both to Motti's headphones and recorded for posterity, so Coldhardt could listen when they got back. *Speak on, sucker*.

Listlessly, she flipped open her mobile and re-read Jonah's last text. *Sorin out of picture. Not sure who that's a point to. All OK here. Watch yourself.* Coldhardt didn't like them stating too much over the phone – paranoid as always that they could be intercepted by others – but she wished Jonah wasn't quite so good at being cryptic sometimes.

'What d'you think Jonah's on about, then?' Patch had leaned forward from the back seat to read over her shoulder.

'How am I meant to know?' Tye closed the phone. 'Let's just be glad we don't have to worry about Sorin showing up here.'

'That's two down,' said Patch happily. 'Heidel's gonna be in for a surprise, innee?'

Tye glanced back to where Patch sat beside a black, stylish Henk suitcase. They'd stuffed it full of Heidel's personal belongings, stolen from his hotel room, everything from his fake passport to his black silk boxers. It turned out that the RFID tag that had lured them there had been removed from the Guan Yin manuscript after all; it was stuck inside a book of nursery rhymes. So they'd nicked that, too, along with a battered old leather briefcase which remained tantalisingly locked. Patch hadn't turned his talents to it yet; partly for fear of booby-traps, partly because he was busy pointing a camcorder discreetly through a gap in the van window. The viewfinder framed the brochure-wielding visitors as they swept up and down the steps of the proud old building.

'Con will radio us when Heidel and Bree head for the exit,' Tye reminded him; in her long dark wig and cool shades, sitting incognito in the back row, Con was barely recognisable. 'And Motti's watching the rear entrance with his listening gear in case they leave that way. You can relax.'

'Guess so,' Patch grunted, but didn't put down the camcorder.

'What are you doing?' she asked, suddenly suspicious.

'Just using the zoom.' He sighed. 'Getting close-ups of the best bums on the birds going by.'

'You'll go blind.'

'I was halfway there anyway, and now this!' He pointed to the swollen shiner Sadie had given him. 'I should get a T-shirt done – I went to London and all I got was this lousy black eye.'

'You need an ice pack on that,' said Tye.

'A lip transplant would be good, an' all.' He licked his fat lip and winced. 'I'm never gonna score, looking like this. A geezer like Sorin, bet he's always pulling. I bet girls chuck their pants at him.'

'Patch!' Tye grimaced. 'Anyway, you heard Jonah. Sorin's out the picture. One less big-shot male to compete with.'

'Thought this would be a good line of work to get laid in,' Patch went on morosely. 'You know, the glamour, the action, the intrigue . . .'

'The taping bums in a van . . .'

'All of that.' He looked at her. 'But I never meet no one, do I? No one who takes me seriously. I mean, Con's never gonna fall for me, is she? No one will. I'm just a dumb kid.' He put down the camcorder. 'A dumb kid with one eye.'

Tye reached out and squeezed his hand. 'It won't be this way for ever. One day we'll leave Coldhardt . . . and then we'll start proper lives.'

'Don't say that,' he muttered.

'But we *will*,' she told him. 'We'll have to. This isn't proper living, it's just . . . just a fantasy world. I mean, it's amazing, frightening, special – like nothing I ever dreamed could happen . . .' She stared out of the windscreen. 'But it can't last for ever. Think of the chances we take . . .'

He licked his lip again. 'I'm *feeling* them.'

'Exactly. Stay too long, our luck's going to run out.' She half smiled. 'Anyway, you must have enough cash put away by now to get that fancy new eye you're always on about.'

'It's an Intracortical Visual Prothesis, ta very much,' Patch corrected her grandly. 'They put these electrodes into your brain, linked to this little computer camera-eye, right? And you can *see*!' He beamed happily. 'You can really see things through it, for proper. Anyway, they're still testing it out. But I've been saving my cash and maybe I could fund them a bit, be their backer . . . We'd be able to help loads of people who can't see right. Starting with me, of course. Then I can find Mum and tell her – it's OK. She don't have to feel guilty 'bout what she did, I can see fine. Just fine. Maybe then she'll see *me* again.' He touched his eye patch. 'Say goodbye to this. No more Patch . . . Just plain Patrick Kendall.'

'Mr Patrick Kendall . . .' Tye smiled at him. 'Sounds quite sophisticated, actually!'

'D'you reckon?' He closed his swollen eye and

murmured the name over and over. 'Really?'

'I bet Patrick Kendall won't be able to move for hot girlfriends.'

Patch turned back to his viewfinder and put the lens back up to the crack between window and door. 'Well, that's all for the future, innit. Plenty of time, yeah? I mean, we ain't in no hurry to leave Coldhardt . . . I don't reckon we'll leave for ages. We're like a family.'

Tye hoped her bland smile would reassure him as she scanned the street once more for any signs of trouble. In truth, she had no idea what she felt right now.

Suddenly Motti's voice sounded from Tye's walkie-talkie. 'Heidel's telling Bree it's time to split. 'Bout the only interesting thing he's said since he got here. Brushstrokes this and cubism that . . .'

'Target on the way,' Con's voice confirmed over Patch's radio on the back seat. 'Bree's with him.'

'On it,' said Patch instantly, training the camcorder at the auction-house doors.

Tye sank down in her seat a little way, picked up Patch's magazine and pretended to read. A minute or so later she saw Heidel walk down the steps, Bree just a step behind him. Him in his dark Italian suit, her in a pale green summer dress and shades, they looked like any other well-off couple on their way home after a successful afternoon's bidding. *Have you ever got a surprise waiting back home*, thought Tye, watching Patch zoom in on Heidel's lined face. She wondered what emotions might show there when he realised Sadie was missing and Sorin out of the picture . . . that his plan had been shot all to hell and his hotel room stripped to its linen.

'Got some sweet footage here, Tye. Lovely.' Patch rested the camcorder on her shoulder, framing Heidel in the viewfinder while Bree hailed a black cab. He panned out as it pulled in beside him. Bree held open the door for Heidel, and the two of them climbed into the back.

'They spent five hundred grand in there,' drawled Motti over Patch's walkie-talkie. 'Think I should chuck a phosphor cap at the crap they bought? Can't make 'em any uglier.'

'Just get back here,' Tye told him, watching as the black cab pulled away into the bus lane and began creeping past the evening traffic.

Patch hit the pause button on the camcorder. 'So long, see ya, woudn't wanna be ya.'

Con jogged up and tapped on the window of the passenger door, her cheeks flushed. 'One microphone safely retrieved from the old fart's chair,' she bubbled, tossing the tiny bug at Patch. Tye closed up the MacBook, shifted it into the back and let her in. 'Now, let's get back to the airfield – stopping at McD's along the way, yes?'

'Mac attack!' Patch cheered, pocketing the mic. 'Although my quarter-cheese'll probably bite back, the way my luck's been running.'

'You should eat Filet o' Fish instead,' Con advised, settling happily in the front seat.

'Ready to roll, people?' Motti called as he opened the back of the van and scrambled inside alongside the bulging suitcase. 'I was checking the map while I waited out back, and I figure it's best that you drive us out of town to South Ruislip, Tye. We'll dump the van and pick up our train from there.'

Patch switched off his camcorder. 'Job done, money earned.'

She pulled the portable sat-nav from her bag, programmed it in, and then threaded her way into the traffic. 'Looks like we pulled it off again.'

'Of course we did,' said Con, sighing happily. 'We always do!'

Tye frowned, and for a superstitious moment wished she could touch something made of wood right then. Then she remembered the mahogany beads on the band holding her dreads back, and brushed against her bruised scalp as she reached for them. The pain made her wince so hard she stepped on the brake, and the van lurched violently.

'Hey,' grumped Motti. 'I know you must be missing Jonah, but there's no need to drive like him.'

Tye forced a laugh, accelerated smoothly away. 'Fair enough. Keep your eyes peeled for drive-throughs.' She felt a wash of fatigue numb her body. *Soon*, she told herself, *you'll be taking the plane back to Geneva, back home to Jonah and that safe, clean bed you're hanging out for. Really soon.*

But her fingers strayed to her cheek, and the bite-bruise that marked her dark skin like a brand, and she knew she would be seeing Sadie's eyes up close any time she closed her own.

There was nothing for Jonah to do but get back to cracking the Bloodline Cipher. He wanted to lose himself in the work, to jump from his bedroom down into that world in the screen and drive the blood and bodies far from his mind.

But he supposed it was more than that, too. The Cipher was no longer simply a challenge to be overcome; he was determined to strip away the mystery Nomen Oblitum had built up around themselves. He didn't like feeling he owed his life to a sect of black magic killers. It was as if that put him in their power somehow.

And the power they'd demonstrated was one of the most frightening things he'd ever seen. Maybe you could explain it away through Dim Mak and martial arts mastery . . . but that in itself was a kind of force and skill so way beyond the everyday it might as well be magic.

Jonah found himself praying the poison darts he and Maya had taken would test negative for curare, that he could prove the cipher *was* just a sophisticated hoax the NO men were trying to cash in on – something cooked up centuries back, maybe to con some European king into funding a would-be wizard . . . If he could prove that – and if only Tye and the others would bring back firm proof that Heidel was not who he claimed to be – Coldhardt would end his association with these people and that would be the end of that. Things would be back to how they were.

Let the freaks find some other rich shady type to work on. He rubbed his tired eyes. *Make it someone else's problem.*

Maya came into the room with two cappuccinos and sat beside him at the computer. They watched the stream of numbers playing across the screen. She'd been very quiet since they'd got back. He couldn't say he blamed her.

'You've got a lot of processing power here,' she observed suddenly.

He seized on the chance of distraction. 'I've tapped into an academic server farm,' he told her. 'I'm running the code on their massively parallel clusters of processors . . .'

'What happens if there's nothing to decode?'

'That would be perfect – it would mean these NO guys are hoaxing this stuff about junk DNA and holding back the years . . .'

'Out of interest, why do you find the idea of extending human lifespan hard to believe?' she asked, sounding genuinely curious. 'It is a legitimate area of modern scientific research.'

'Exactly – *modern* scientific research, not old stuff from when most people thought the world was flat.' Jonah paused and smiled. 'Hang on, though. What about a witch turning someone into a frog? That's got to be the result of some *serious* genetics research, right?'

'Actually, I'd say it was more a kind of "alchemy of organic matter",' Maya replied.

Jonah stared at her. 'Please be joking.'

'You didn't see my broomstick parked outside?' Maya suddenly showed her small, crooked teeth in a big grin. 'I'm just saying the old, arcane arts made progress into the mysteries of life far faster than science did. I've seen so much evidence –'

He shot her a look. 'From translating those creepy old texts for your little occult group in Moscow?'

Maya nodded. 'I've studied a great deal.'

'And you think Nomen Oblitum is for real?'

'The cult exists,' she said flatly. 'And the Scribe had done his homework. I've come across all that stuff about the significance of Isis to Nomen Oblitum. But as for whether that Scribe was on the level about the cipher . . .' She looked away. 'In any case, when I said there may be nothing to decode in the Guan Yin manuscript, I wasn't implying it's a hoax. But what if the scripts are simply a written-down version of some polyglot tongue – a hotchpotch of languages that people of the time would have understood in that written form – bits of old German, bits of Flemish, you know . . .'

Jonah smiled. 'I'm running a word and character match too through Yale's antique languages database too for pattern similarity. You never know, it might just bring something to light.'

Maya smiled back. 'Think you're clever, don't you?'

'Yep.' He put a hand on her arm, squeezed it. 'Look, I'm sorry for what you had to go through today.'

'Not exactly your fault.'

'Motti will suss out how everyone got past the defences, and Coldhardt will check out the drug on those darts and a doctor's going to check us out.' Jonah's fingers strayed to the tender lump on his neck. 'Don't worry about Coldhardt. He's flared up at me too, I know how scary it can be.'

'I'm fine,' she said, but the way her body stiffened suggested otherwise. 'He's your boss, not mine. I mean, I can leave any time I want to . . . right?'

'Do you want to leave?'

Maya stared broodingly at the computer screen. 'I

don't like unsolved mysteries,' she said at last.

Jonah smiled. 'Me neither. So how about you tell me more about these exotic symbols you say you can spot in the cipher.'

'OK.' Her face softened as she reached out for the mouse and called up a file. 'Here's a composite scan I did. All the symbols I think I see, together: *rou*, *ji*, *jin*, *gu*, *xue*, *mai*, *qi* . . .'

'*Flesh* and *temple/sacrifice* I know, but the others . . .?'

'*Sinew, bone, blood, vein, breath*.'

'Sure we're not translating a biology textbook?'

'Ha, ha.' Maya shook her head. 'What you might not know is that those are also the terms Chinese scholars used to describe the art and character of someone's handwriting.'

Jonah frowned. 'That can't just be coincidence.'

'I know. The symbols, once they've been decrypted, are sort of referring to themselves.'

'Self-reflexive . . .' Jonah frowned. 'Hmm. Sounds like the coder may be having a little joke. A joke at our expense.'

'What?'

'It might be a way of telling us that there's no actual code to crack – that the whole manuscript is nothing more than a lot of nice handwriting.' Jonah felt a surge of relief. 'A plaintext language, like you speculated – but a made-up one. Gibberish that means nothing at all.' He sank back in his chair and grinned. 'Which is proof that those weirdos in the robes *were* making up all that stuff and Coldhardt can tell them to go to hell.'

'I told you,' said Maya. 'The cipher exists.'

'How d'you know for sure?' Jonah sighed. 'Look, I'm sorry, Maya, I know you've spent a long time working on the translation of this thing –'

'It's not a hoax, Jonah. End of story.' She turned back to the screen. 'So. Here's the trickiest of the decrypted pictograms, placed right at the end of the first section . . .' She scanned the list of filenames and double-clicked to bring it up. 'There, see? It's known as *Xin*.'

'And why is *Xin* the trickiest?'

'It's a pictograph of the physical heart, but in ancient Chinese writings it's used to refer to the mind as well as the emotions. Sort of a *heart/mind*. That can make translations difficult.'

'Hearts and minds being one and the same . . .' Jonah sighed. 'That would make a lot of things easier.'

She looked at him, her grey eyes penetrating. 'Like when your head knows you're in a life that's bad for you, but your heart tells you to stay put?'

He couldn't hold her gaze and looked away, bristling. 'Or when *your* head accepts that some fourteenth-century cipherpunk might have taken you in, but your heart can't bring itself to admit you've wasted your . . .' He frowned, focusing on the characters. 'Hang on . . .'

'What?'

'That part of the text you showed me where the symbols had been overwritten – where is it?'

Maya called up the relevant file.

'There.' Jonah pointed. 'Look at the way that downward stroke has been gone over in darker ink . . .'

'You can see, the ink underneath is really faded.'

'Yeah, it looks faded now we're coming to it seven hundred years later,' Jonah agreed. 'It probably didn't look so faded back then. And if the re-toucher was only correcting certain words, why use an ink that's so much darker than the original? It looks like soot or something has been added to the tempera mix . . .'

'Mmm.' She raised her eyebrows. 'Tell me again why Motti calls you a geek?'

'I just noticed that the downstroke touched up on this symbol here . . .' He started rearranging the various files side by side on the screen. 'Looks a bit like *this* part of your inverted, rotated pictograph for "sinew".'

Maya peered in to check, scrunching up her eyes the way she did. 'You're right.'

'Probably just coincidence.' Jonah sighed. 'It's easy to see patterns where there aren't any . . .'

She smiled. 'Head doesn't want to believe, but the heart's got other ideas, right?'

'Maybe those self-referencing Chinese characters aren't a joke,' said Jonah. 'Maybe they're telling us not to look for the meaning in the words . . . but in the actual *handwriting*.'

'Whoa,' Maya breathed. 'You mean the lines and strokes of the characters where they've been retouched?'

'Might be worth checking those sections of the text,' he agreed. 'Don't you think?'

She didn't answer, already busy calling them up on to the screen, fingers tapping impatiently on the mouse as she waited for each image to load.

CHAPTER THIRTEEN

The plane stood ready to go on the crumbling airstrip, and as dusk darkened the rural sweep about them, Tye stared at it longingly. She was standing in the doorway of a barn built alongside, keeping watch. Motti had given the usual forged papers and paid off the owner for use of the airstrip. But this time he'd thrown in a bit extra to be allowed to use the site's X-ray security systems. All kinds of stuff must pass through this secret strip.

'Last time we came here, we'd just sprung Jonah and were taking him back to Geneva,' she remembered.

'Yeah, that day's tattooed on my heart,' said Motti gruffly from inside the barn.

'It's tattooed on my *fart*!' Patch blew a raspberry by way of demonstration, and Tye rolled her eyes.

'C'mon, Cyclops, would you get going?'

'You wanna fly tonight or *fry* tonight?' Tye glanced back at Patch as he placed Heidel's well-worn leather briefcase on a small conveyor belt in front of the X-ray camera. 'If there *is* a booby trap inside this thing, let's hope it ain't triggered by X-rays.'

Con wriggled off her hay bale and hid behind it instead. 'Not funny.'

'Not meant to be.' The scanner hummed into noisy life. 'But there can't be anything too dodgy inside this case. I mean, why would Heidel risk taking it past Heathrow security?'

'Yeah. Like, nothing gets past those airport guys,' Motti deadpanned. 'Anyways, could be he didn't risk nothing. Could be a back-up booby trap he made over here and left in the room in case we got past the bitch with the bow.'

'We can't underestimate these people,' Con agreed.

As if on cue, Tye felt a whole storm of pain as something cold and solid chopped into the side of her neck. *Looking the wrong damned way*, she realised. With an exaggerated scream of pain to warn the others, she collapsed to the ground with her eyes shut; pretending she was out cold until she knew what they were up against.

'None of you move!' she heard a man bellow in a fierce Scottish accent. From the sound of things, no one was arguing. And now she saw a second man emerge from behind the barn, striding up to join his friend in the doorway. He was wearing a balaclava and holding a sawn-off shotgun, and Tye guessed the first man was packing the same – he'd probably hit her with the stock.

Two of you, Tye thought, trying to ignore the numbness in her neck. *Any more?*

'Who are you?' she heard Motti drawl. 'The cops?'

'Shut your mouth,' the second one said, a Londoner by the sound of it. 'Dunno who you are or what your game is, but the boss don't like being snooped on.'

'You are working for Heidel?' Con enquired.

'Who the hell is Heidel?' said the Scottish man. 'Just hand over the camcorder.'

Someone saw us filming outside the auction house, Tye realised, *must've followed us here*. But the Scot's tone of voice and speed with which he answered suggested he really *didn't* know who Heidel was. Perhaps they only called their boss by a codename?

'Camcorder, now!' The Londoner was skittering about in the doorway like the ground was burning his shoes, cranked up on adrenaline. 'Or I'll waste the lot of you.'

'All right, take it easy!' Patch's voice sounded high and strained. 'You can have it.'

'Throw it here.' Tye heard a faint slap and shuffle as the Londoner caught the camcorder and jammed it into his jacket pocket. 'What's this other stuff you got here? What're you doing with it?'

Tye swore in Creole under her breath. If these gorillas made off with the rest of their evidence, their mission here would have been a complete washout. She braced herself to move.

'It is only our luggage,' said Con languidly. 'We're going on holiday.'

'Don't get clever,' the Scot warned her.

'I won't get clever. But you are getting tired, I think, yes?'

'Shut up.' He lowered his voice to a whisper, but Tye still caught it: 'Street only told us to get the camcorder, Fin. It's sorted. Come on.'

'Yeah, but what's this other stuff?' the man called Fin persisted.

'Look at me, both of you,' Con tried again. 'You

need to look at me, *listen* to me –'

'I warned you, bitch!' Fin shouted, his voice wilder, breath quickening, psyching himself up to fire. 'I'm gonna split you in two!'

His finger twitched on the trigger of the sawn-off.

Tye lashed out with her foot and knocked Fin's legs from under him. The man fell backwards – firing the sawn-off as he went down. The Scottish man screamed as the top of his shoulder was scattered over the barn wall, the impact knocking him backwards. He dropped his own gun, crashed into a hay bale.

Stomach churning, Tye threw herself towards Fin, but he recovered quicker than she expected and rolled clear, knelt up. She hit the ground, looked up and found herself staring into the barrel of the shotgun.

Single selective trigger, she realised, recognising the model in a long, frozen moment of shock. *No need to reload, he's going to –*

Then Motti's boot smacked into the barrel and knocked it clear even as the cartridge discharged. Tye flinched from the thunder of the blast, felt the heat on her face from the fierce spit of shot, smelt the over-powering reek of cordite. Forcing her eyes back open, she lunged towards Fin and punched him in the face. But the blow was stiff and weak, he rolled with the impact and she lost her balance, falling forward. She heard Fin scrambling up, but Motti jumped over her and kicked him in the balls. Fin's whoop of pain was silenced by a punch to the jaw that left him reeling. He shambled away without another word. Motti made to follow, but then –

'The other one!' Con shouted.

Tye turned in horror to find the Scottish bloke gripping his sawn-off in one bloody hand. His eyes were wild and staring behind the black mask, his breath coming in ragged snatches.

'Back off!' he screamed, aiming straight at Tye's head.

Motti put up his hands and did as he was told. Still on all fours, praying fervently to any gods that might listen, Tye crawled slowly backwards. Too frightened to speak, she knew she had to keep eye contact, had to keep some kind of connection between them. If she lowered her head it might be all the excuse he needed to blow it off. *Don't do this*, she thought, as a tear teased down her cheek. *Please don't. Don't.*

'Know why they call them "wristbreakers", pal?' she heard Motti say softly. 'Use a sawn-off one-handed, recoil's gonna jar it right out of your fingers. You might kill our girl . . . but then how're you gonna stop the rest of us from killing you?'

'Your friend has run away.' Con's voice was as hard as her stare. 'Run after him, and you might even make it to a hospital before you pass out from blood loss . . . yes?'

Grunting and moaning with pain, the man turned abruptly and fled into the darkening night.

Tye let out a long, long shaky breath and lowered her head to the ground, fighting the nausea rising inside her. A moment later, she felt Motti's arms around her, hauling her up, holding her close. She held him back for a few seconds, staring numbly at the bloodstained straw on the floor.

'I'm OK,' she mumbled, straightening up. 'Everybody else?'

'Alive, at least,' said Con, hugging herself tightly. 'Thank you, Tye. I'm sorry – I nearly got us killed.'

'You tried,' Motti told her. 'He was too wired, too strung out for you to –'

'I appreciate the kindness, Motti.' Con closed her eyes. 'But don't.'

Then Tye saw Patch's pale face peeping out from behind the X-ray machine. 'Thought they'd never go,' he joked weakly. 'Whoever they were.'

'I heard them say they were working for someone called Street,' said Tye, wiping sweat from her face with her sleeve. 'Someone who must have seen us filming Heidel and come after us.'

'Weren't you checking for tails?' Motti asked.

'Weren't you?' she retorted, her voice rising without her meaning it to. She bit her lip, willed herself to keep calm. 'I didn't see anyone following us. Sorry.'

'Oh, and you were great too, Cyclops.' Motti glared at Patch. 'You gave those psychos the camcorder just like that.'

'Fair play, I gave 'em the camcorder,' Patch agreed, holding up a small back rectangle. 'But I never gave 'em the tape, did I?'

Motti was shut up for once, and Tye forced a little smile. 'Good work, Patch.'

'Not only that, but while you kept them tosspots busy, I was getting Heidel's case open.' He stooped behind the X-ray machine. 'Just as everything kicked off, I saw on the scanner there's an incendiary device inside hooked up to the combination locks. Put in the wrong numbers and – phtt! – everything goes up in smoke.' He held up a small firework-sized device attached to a length of wire. 'Couldn't keep *me* out, of course. I was about to lob it over there and start a distraction when you persuaded him to scoot.' He frowned. 'They *have* gone, haven't they?'

'They might be fetching back-up,' said Motti moodily. 'This Street character could be on his way –'

'Or *her* way,' said Con.

He nodded. 'The 'strip owner might even be in on it.'

'We should clear out,' Tye decided.

'We're all loaded up,' Motti said, turning back to Patch. 'Except for that case.'

'You opened it, Patch,' said Con, acting composed again, smoothing her fingers through her hair. 'What's inside it?'

Patch blew out a long breath. He looked like he didn't know quite where to start. 'Later,' he said. 'Just you wait . . .'

They cleared out of the barn, quietly and efficiently, leaving the bloodstains and the sawn-off behind them. Soon Tye was taking the plane up into the moonless sky, relief thumping in her chest like a second heartbeat.

She flew low over fields and cities, hugging the landscape to avoid radar detection. Then the plane struck out across the Channel. The churning darkness of the ocean below was mirrored in the black, scudding clouds above. As if the night could know no peace.

Tye felt just the same. She put the controls on to autopilot and sank back in her seat. She was tired, an aching tiredness that seemed to groan through her whole body. Over the rushing whoosh of the turbines, she heard nervous laughter and chatter from the cabin, as if from a million miles away. She looked at the seat beside her, where Jonah usually sat.

'Nearly never saw you again,' she murmured, pretending he was here. 'Twice in one day.'

Suddenly Patch came up behind her, made her jump. 'Sorry, mate . . . just wanted to show you a little picture we found in Heidel's briefcase.' He perched a battered photograph on top of the altimeter. 'Thought it might brighten up the flight deck.'

He ducked back to join the others and Tye stared at the creased, faded picture, at two men with slicked back hair and sideburns. They were sitting on a spotless white terrace, in sunlight and sharp grey suits, drinking champagne. One of the men was young, in his twenties, maybe, dark and lean, smiling like a shark. The other was older, grey-haired. His eyes held shadows and his smile was strained, as if he felt he'd been left posing for the picture too long.

Tye could almost sense the resentment still lingering as he stared out at her across the years. And she felt the thump of her heart in her throat.

The smiling shark was a youthful Coldhardt, and he was pallying up to Heidel. But now Coldhardt was old himself, while the man she'd seen getting into a black cab that afternoon had barely aged a day since the picture was taken.

CHAPTER FOURTEEN

Jonah sprawled on his bed, rubbing his gritty eyes. The clock said it was gone four in the morning. Grimacing, he turned its face to the wall. He'd been up all night with Maya, looking for patterns in the overwrites. But now he was starting to flag, while she was looking as fresh as when they'd started, studying the screen up close while he rested his eyes.

'The next retouched characters,' she announced, 'are another circle . . . followed by a downstroke.'

'Flip and rotate by . . .' He frowned. 'What are we up to now?'

'Should be seventy degrees.' She turned to her pad of paper, arranging the various retouched strokes into different combinations, concocting new pictograms. They were following the same process of 'rotate and reverse' she'd used on the standalone symbols, in the same order. But the results weren't encouraging. The symbols Maya arrived at were typically an exotic mess, only bearing the faintest resemblance to real Chinese pictograms.

Jonah scratched the lump on his neck. It was itching like hell. Coldhardt's doctor – a wiry, mysterious man named Draith who would turn up, patch up then disappear again – had given him and Maya a full physical this evening and pronounced them fit and well. The wounds would soon go down, he said – the itching was down to the way skin tightened as it healed.

All the more remarkable considering those darts had contained a blend of curare just as the Scribe said. Draith's report explained in overly clinical terms how the darts contained enough poison to kill an adult inside of thirty minutes.

Jonah had crumpled the report into the tightest ever ball and chucked it in the bin. It lay buried now, out of sight if not out of mind, beneath hundreds of pieces of scribbled-on paper. He watched as another scrunched-up sheet sailed over from the desk to add to the pile.

'There are too many circles,' Maya noted sullenly. 'Chinese writing uses angular strokes. I don't see how the circles fit.'

'Maybe we should skip them,' said Jonah. 'I mean, a circle's a circle however much you flip it or turn it around.'

'So why did the phantom author retouch them?'

'To piss us off?' He sighed. 'It's working.'

Maya nodded. 'I'll try this page again but missing out the circles . . .'

He picked up his mobile. The last text from Tye had come through hours ago – she should be back by now. But Coldhardt had sent no word, and the hang-out was quiet. He read her words for the thirtieth time. *On way home. Bad time. Not get easier. Do I want it to.*

Jonah felt his tiredness grip him all the more. Sounded like she was feeling the same way he was. Her strength had always made him feel stronger – she'd always been there to help prop him up, to persuade him he could actually make it through this freaky life. He wished he could hold her right now. That would certainly wake him up . . .

'These lines aren't making a new pictogram.' Maya put down her pencil. 'Just another doodle from hell.'

'You're sure you've followed the same pattern of rotation and inversion –?'

'Of course I am.' She shot him a vexed look. 'It doesn't work. I really thought you were on to something . . .' Distractedly, she traced her fingertips round the edge of her birthmark, as it seemed she often did when thinking. 'There are no touched-up characters in the appendix. That *must* mean that the ones we find in the bulk of the manuscript are some kind of key.'

'There you go again,' said Jonah, 'wanting to read the end of the book first.'

She ignored him, chewing on the end of the pencil. 'I think we're missing something with the circles.'

'Missing a point to the bloody things . . .' Jonah took a gulp of stone-cold coffee. In the sample of five hundred random touched-up words they'd collated, it seemed that certain characters had been traced over more than others – particularly the circular shapes.

'They must be key,' Maya persisted. 'In the old rituals, a summoning circle is used to conjure demons, and the symbols drawn around the outside of the circle can protect the mage who summons . . .'

'Maybe the circles act like spacers,' he suggested.

'Telling us to ignore the characters beside them.'

'Or maybe the circles might make up a numerical system by themselves. You know, first one for tens, next one for units . . .' Maya looked at the sample in front of her. 'In which case, maybe the character *following* each circle is a part of the number.'

'Could be a binary code,' said Jonah suddenly, sitting up on the bed. 'That's all zeros and ones – could be read as circles and downstrokes?'

'Except the zeros are followed by all kind of characters,' said Maya. 'Could be *coded* binary, I guess . . .' Her shoulders slumped. 'Truth is, it could be *any* counting system. How are we supposed to tell?'

'Maybe it was obvious to the other members of the cell,' said Jonah. 'A significant number.' He turned the clock away from the wall again. 'Maya, I don't know about you but my last sleep was drug-induced and not exactly refreshing. Maybe we should think about turning in.'

'There's three hundred and sixty degrees in a circle,' she muttered, not taking the hint. 'And each degree is made up of sixty minutes, and each minute made up of sixty seconds . . .'

'That's time, not angles.'

'It's both! I'm talking about minutes and seconds of *arc*.'

Jonah rolled his blurry eyes. 'That's just showing off.'

'Blame the ancient Sumerians. They worked out time and geometry back in ancient Mesopotamia – and here we are still using their systems four thousand years later.' Maya looked at him with that strange crooked smile. 'Incredible how some things endure . . .'

'It seems sort of overcomplicated, though, when you think about it,' Jonah reflected hazily, 'dividing time and circles up in lumps of twelve and sixty.'

'Not complicated to the Sumerians or the Babylonians. They did all their calculations in base sixty.' Her eyes widened and she suddenly gasped. 'The Chinese calendar has the same mathematical basis. And it's *circular* – the years are counted and named in cycles of sixty . . .' Maya's pale, freckled face was growing more flushed by the moment. 'Jonah, we're on the right track, we've got to be!'

'You're jumping to some pretty wild conclusions here,' Jonah warned her.

'I'm jumping on your bed!' she warned him back, leaping over his lap and bouncing up and down in an ecstasy of release, her grin wide and red hair catching in the light. 'If we find some kind of cyclical pattern in the re-inked characters then it might mean –'

There was a muffled knock at the door. Maya stopped bouncing as Jonah crossed to open it.

'Jonah,' breathed Tye, pushing through the doorway and into his arms, making him stagger back inside the room. 'I thought . . . I mean, I . . .'

'Er . . .' He returned the hug, self-consciously. 'Coldhardt never said you were back.'

'We haven't told him, yet. There's stuff we need to –'

Tye must have sensed his awkwardness, looked up – and now saw Maya sitting down on the edge of the bed. Even with tired eyes, he caught the emotions moving through Tye's eyes – surprise, confusion. Hurt.

And then he saw the livid bruise on her cheek. 'Hey, what happened to your –'

'Sorry,' said Tye briskly, heading back towards the door. 'I thought you'd be alone.'

'Had to kill the time till you were back somehow, didn't I?' Jonah grabbed hold of her hand. 'Uh, working, I mean.'

'Yes, we were just working on the cipher,' Maya agreed.

Tye looked at her. 'On the bed?'

'I was just kind of bouncing on it. I was happy.' Maya grinned sheepishly. 'Your boyfriend's smart, and I think we could be close to a breakthrough with the cipher.'

'He's not my boyfriend,' Tye began automatically, 'we –'

'Don't worry, I won't tell,' Maya interrupted. 'It's clear that something is between you, but there is nothing between him and me.'

'Of course there isn't,' said Jonah hastily, his cheeks flushing.

'You read body language, you can tell.' Maya shrugged. 'I'm not lying.'

Tye stared at her, then glanced back at Jonah. She looked away, put a hand to her forehead. 'You know, whatever. This is, like, nothing. Nothing on a day like today.'

'What happened?' asked Jonah, going to her.

'Come down and you'll see,' she said wearily. 'If you can tear yourself away, I mean.'

She left the room. Jonah started after her, then hesitated, looked back at Maya.

'You should go,' Maya said, but her sympathetic smile faltered as she pointed to the computer. 'Just hurry back, OK?'

He mock saluted. 'Do my best.' *And hope that one day that's enough*, he thought, as he crossed the wood-floored landing after Tye.

Tye knew that Maya was telling the truth about not being interested in Jonah, and that Jonah wasn't really into Maya. But as she took the spiral steps down to the hangout, two at a time, she knew also that Jonah could never share himself with her the way he had with that red-haired stranger tonight. He'd often lose himself for days at a time in the world on his screen; that capacity baffled Tye, but she'd found it kind of cute. She loved his quietness, the way he made her feel she could tell him anything.

But that's not how you make him *feel, is it?* she thought darkly. There he was sat with some red-haired stranger who could lose a night with him in just the same way, who talked the same hacker-speak he did. She pictured him laughing with Maya yesterday morning over their early days with water-coolers, or whatever. All it meant to Tye was a cold drink from a plastic cup.

Because I'm stupid, and they're smart, she thought unhappily. *Because I was smuggling dope while they were taking classes. And though the choices we made and the crowds we hung with all led us here to Coldhardt just the same, where are they going to lead us next?*

Today it felt like the world was raining down around her ears.

She rejoined Motti, Con and Patch, gathered round the snooker table, laying out the haul from Heidel's briefcase.

'Is the geek coming, Tye?' asked Motti.

Patch sniggered. 'Give her a chance, Mot, she was only with him twenty seconds.'

All we ever manage is snatched moments here and there, she thought as she wearily put on the smile expected of her.

'What'd I miss?' Jonah called, hurrying down the staircase. 'D'you get the stuff?'

'We almost *got* stuffed,' said Patch, showing off his purple eye.

Tye let the others speak for her, watching Jonah as he listened tensely to all that had happened. She could see the concern large in his eyes as he looked at her. 'I'm fine,' she said patiently as Patch reached the bloody conclusion of events. 'Really.'

'She's *super*fine,' Motti added, reaching into his pocket. 'Look what she got back from the bitch with the bow . . .'

'Coldhardt's ring!' Jonah grinned and snatched it. 'Fantastic, Tye. God, when she was waving it in my face at Blackland's like a trophy, I wished . . .'

You're always wishing, thought Tye. She didn't want to enjoy his praise just yet. 'Yeah, well . . . I just hope the British police can handle her now.'

'Coldhardt should let you keep that ring,' said Motti. 'You earned it.'

'Maybe you shouldn't even tell him you got it back,' Jonah suggested.

'You can't do that!' said Con, snatching the ring

away and gazing at it herself. 'That would be immoral!'

Tye couldn't help but laugh at that, and the others joined in.

'What's immoral is that you weren't there in that barn with us, geek,' said Motti, his smile fading. 'Getting a shotgun rammed up your ass.'

'Well, you know it wasn't all plain sailing this end, either,' Jonah told them, itching a livid red spot on his neck.

Con raised her eyebrows. 'You got acne?'

'What happened with Sorin?' Patch asked eagerly.

Jonah took a deep breath. 'He broke into the safe house, poisoned me and Maya, then he was killed by a pair of freaks from Nomen Oblitum, right in front of our eyes.'

'What the hell . . . ?' Tye's fears and anxieties slunk off to the back burner. 'Are *you* OK?'

He used the phrase she had used a minute before, and meant it about as much as she did. 'I'm fine. Really.'

'Wanna fill in some of the details here?' Motti pressed him.

Tye and the others listened to Jonah in silence. No light relief or laughter now.

'. . . and Coldhardt took care of the clean-up and the corpse this afternoon,' Jonah concluded. 'Sorin's dead, me and Maya are alive, and we've got the same people to thank.'

'They sound like blokes you don't mess with,' said Patch with feeling.

Con looked troubled. 'And you really think Coldhardt's going to deal with them?'

Jonah shrugged. 'Depends if you've come back with hard proof that Heidel's back from the dead, only thirty years older.'

'Thirty years older?' Patch handed Jonah the same battered photograph he'd shown to Tye on the plane. 'Uh-uh. Check *this* out.'

Tye watched the frown etch itself into Jonah's face as he stared at the young man and the old, together.

'Mental, innit?' Patch murmured. 'You think of Coldhardt and you think he's been old all his life . . .'

Con nodded. 'And there's Heidel proving it's an option!'

Jonah laid the photo down flat on the baize, clearly weirded out. 'If this picture's for real, then surely the Heidel we met has *got* to be just a lookalike.'

'Maybe he *is* the genuine geezer,' Patch argued. 'If these NO men are as tasty with their fingers as you say . . .'

Jonah looked at him. 'You really think some freaks in fancy dress can magically program your DNA to make you live longer?'

'Doesn't really matter what we think,' said Tye. 'We've got plenty of evidence now for Coldhardt to decide what's real. He's the only one who'll know for sure . . .'

'About any of it,' Motti agreed, picking up a snooker cue. 'Still, it looks like your geeky Russian girlfriend was right about one thing.'

'She's not my girlfriend,' Jonah snapped, as Tye shifted uncomfortably. 'What thing?'

'Coldhardt stole the idea of employing a hip, young taskforce to help him out in his twilight years from his old boss, all right,' Motti went on. 'But what he forgot to tell us, was that the boss man in question just happened to be Heidel.'

'So Coldhardt turned on his boss . . . ?' Jonah stared down at the rest of the briefcase booty laid out on the table, and Tye watched as his discomfort became confusion. 'What is all this stuff?'

'The crap Heidel was carrying round in his briefcase,' said Motti. 'Rigged to go up in smoke if anyone forced open the case.'

'Any un-mega-talented person, anyway,' Patch chipped in proudly.

Jonah made to rifle through a small pile of manila wallets. 'OK, so what're these?'

'Uh-uh.' Con slapped his fingers lightly. 'We need to preserve fingerprints, yes?'

'They're Heidel's personnel files,' said Tye. 'Past and present.'

'And they make pretty good reading.' Motti looked at Jonah. 'D'you remember Coldhardt namechecking Karl Saitou when we got back from LA?'

'He was the competition, wasn't he?' Jonah nodded. 'Morell was all set to give Saitou the job of stealing the manuscript.'

'Let's flashback a little further . . . to the time that style forgot.' Motti flicked open the cover of the top file with the tip of the cue to reveal a photograph. It showed a young Asian man in his mid-twenties, with neat, straight features and a mop of dark hair. The collars on his blue shirt looked long and sharp enough to stab his navel.

'Here's Saitou as he used to be,' said Con.

'Weapons and security expert, former prizefighter and authority on ancient civilisations.'

Jonah nodded. 'Your typical combination.'

'"*A competent if unimaginative criminal*", Coldhardt called him – but he must have worked alongside him as part of Heidel's team in the seventies.'

'Saitou joined the outfit in 1971,' Tye added. 'There's no file on Coldhardt, so we don't know when he came in . . . But judging by the freaky outfits in that photo of Coldhardt and Heidel together, it has to be around the same time.'

'So Heidel was to Coldhardt what Coldhardt is to us . . .' Jonah looked lost in thought. 'But did Coldhardt turn on his friends as well as the boss, or were they all in on it?'

'If only we'd known this sooner, we could've asked someone who was there – then *and* now.' Motti slid Saitou's file from the top of the pile and used the cue to flip open the next. '*This* is a guy called David Street, another gang member from the class of seventy-one.' The photo showed a tall, aristocratic-looking dark-haired man with a bad moustache. 'He was their expert on electronics and computer systems, as well as an old-style cat burglar and safecracker. Meant to have been best in the business.'

'And it turns out our mate Davy was in London yesterday, keeping an eye on Heidel like we were.' Patch produced the camcorder tape. 'Seems we accidentally got him on tape – he saw us, and sent his boys round.'

'They must've found you pretty quickly,' said Jonah, as Patch led the way over to the TV room.

'I reckon Street must have followed us himself and arranged back-up in transit,' said Tye, falling into step beside Jonah. It felt good just to push away the love stuff for a bit; at least they could still function professionally, and –

Love?

Oh shit.

'Question is,' said Jonah, oblivious beside her, 'did Street realise you were working for Coldhardt?'

'I don't think so,' said Con. 'Surely he would take more than just a camcorder tape if he did?'

Patch quickly loaded up the mini-DV player, and soon was fast-forwarding past his little butt montage to tuts from Con and Motti. Tye sat by herself, trying to get her thoughts on track. *Later*, she told herself. *Deal with it later when you're alone.*

She glanced at Jonah. He chanced a smile, and she pretended not to see.

Or maybe just run and hide.

She forced her eyes to focus on the screen, on Heidel and Bree hailing their black cab – and in the background, stood behind a vintage Merc, was a better-dressed, clean-shaven but still recognisable David Street. He stood watching Heidel as he entered the cab, his face unreadable. Then he glanced towards the camera, frowned and turned back to watch the cab pull away.

Patch sighed. 'If the viewfinder was home-cinema-sized I might've spotted him.'

'If it was home-cinema-sized *and* if he'd been wearing a short skirt,' Motti corrected him.

Street took out a phone from his pocket. Then the

camera swung off him, favouring Heidel and Bree as their taxi turned the corner and out of sight.

Patch sighed. 'For *that* he nearly kills us.'

'Maybe he's got a big heist in the offing,' Jonah reasoned. 'Might've thought you'd been following him for weeks . . .'

'Maybe.' Motti flicked off the TV. 'What the hell was he was doing there at the auction house, anyway?'

'Checking out his former boss the same way we were?' Con suggested. 'If Coldhardt knew that the auction would be a draw for Heidel, Street would too.'

Jonah agreed. 'And when your old boss comes back from the dead and starts pulling jobs, you're going to be curious . . .'

'Not to mention head-buggered,' Patch added.

Motti threw a cushion at him. 'Who the hell would *ever* mention "head-buggered" 'cept you, dumb freak?'

Tye hugged herself as the swapping of insults, clues and ideas went on. Private thoughts aside, she felt a weird mix of unease and excitement, discussing this stuff without even telling Coldhardt what they'd found. It felt wrong, but kind of a rush; like finding out your parents kept a secret diary, and sneaking a read before they could –

'You're back.'

– catch you.

Pale and grave as a vampire, Coldhardt was watching them from the doorway, his stony glare sweeping over each of them in turn.

'It appears we have things to discuss,' he said.

CHAPTER FIFTEEN

Tye, Con, Motti and Patch sat beside Jonah on the sofas, like they had done a thousand times before. Only now the atmosphere wasn't so much the kind you could cut with a knife, but one you might smash to bits with a sledgehammer. As the post-dawn skies began to blush blue through the windows of the hangout, Jonah found he had to keep pinching himself – to be sure he wasn't hallucinating.

It was the sight of Coldhardt, here in the hangout.

In the usual chic austerity of the hub the boss seemed completely at home, the big spider in his brushed-steel web. But there in the TV room, watching the Heidel footage on a squashy sofa in a sea of beer cans and sweet wrappers, he was more of a fish out of water. In a whole year, Jonah had never known him come here once. It was a special space for his 'children' alone, and now suddenly it was as if Dad had come to visit the playhouse. None of them knew quite how to react.

He wished Tye would catch his eye. How angry could she be with him? Maybe she was just tired . . .

God knows I *am*, he thought, scratching at his sore neck.

'This is totally freaking me out,' Patch whispered.

'Gee, really, Cyclops?' Motti glowered at him. 'We're taking it all in our stride.'

Con sighed. 'We should have told Coldhardt what we'd found straight away.'

'And let the old bastard keep us in the dark?' Motti shook his head. 'No way. Not this time.'

'You will tell him that, yes?'

'Watch me.'

Patch scoffed quietly. 'I'm watching your trousers turn brown, mate.'

Jonah wondered why Coldhardt hadn't blown his top at them, railed and raged at them for going through Heidel's stuff without him. Perhaps because he had seen the photographs from the briefcase, and the files lying open. A window had been opened on to his past, and he was still staring into it, right now, watching Heidel large as life on the huge TV screen.

'Would anyone like coffee?'

Maya's voice rang out from the top of the staircase, and everyone jumped about half a mile.

'Sod the coffee, I need a man's drink after a scare like that,' said Patch weakly.

Motti snorted. 'Maybe Red will go fix you some Sunny D.'

'What's going on?' asked Maya, running lightly down the stairs. 'Jonah?'

Jonah pointed to the TV room and held a finger to his lips. He heard the traffic noise cut out suddenly as if the tape had been stopped, braced himself for Coldhardt to reappear. But then the long, timeless moment passed and the noises resumed as the old man started to watch the footage over again.

'How many more times?' Tye muttered, curled up with her eyes closed in the corner of the sofa.

'You found proof, didn't you?' Maya asked slowly. 'Proof that Heidel's who he says he is.'

Patch brought her up to speed on all they had been through and all they had gained. 'Coldhardt didn't say much, just flicked through the stuff from the case and went in to watch the footage we got. Now we're just waiting for him to come out and give us a bollocking.'

Maya looked puzzled. 'For bringing him what he wanted?'

'For sticking our noses in,' said Motti. 'For acting like we're more than just his personal slaves.'

'But you are much more than that.' Maya looked at them. 'You are his family. The course he is set upon may involve him leaving you for many years; naturally you want to be sure of what he is getting into.' She paused. 'You do not wish him to walk into a trap.'

'And we do not wish to find ourselves unemployed,' said Con. 'Very good, Maya. When put like that, our case sounds quite reasonable, no?'

'That mushy crap might work if Coldhardt weren't so big on living up to his name,' Motti rumbled.

'Then maybe it's time we broke the ice.' Jonah stood up. 'Maya's making coffee. I'm going to ask Coldhardt if he wants one. Seems only fair, since he paid for the coffee bar.'

Turning his back on their frowns and surprised looks, and before he could change his mind, Jonah walked quickly and quietly over to the TV room. He hovered in the doorway, opened his mouth to speak, to break the silence so that –

'It could be him,' Coldhardt said softly as he watched, in a voice half wondering, half afraid; a voice surely not meant for others to overhear. 'It really could be him.'

And Jonah realised: *That's why he hasn't lost his rag with us. We're the last things on his mind right now.*

We don't matter.

He left Coldhardt mumbling on the sofa and rejoined the others. It felt as though he was kicking his heart a little further on with every step.

'I don't think the boss wants a coffee,' Jonah said.

Con was pointing past him discreetly, mouthing: 'Behind you.'

Jonah turned to find Coldhardt suddenly recovered and standing in the doorway of the TV room, watching them. Maya left them to it, heading for the countertop.

'I'll summon you all when I need you,' said Coldhardt stiffly. He turned to Heidel's belongings on the tabletop and the suitcase beside it. 'Box up these and take them to the gate. They will be couriered for fingerprint matching and DNA analysis later this morning. Motti, the audio data . . . ?'

Motti practically jumped to attention. 'The MacBook's there by the phone. The recording's all loaded up, just hit play.'

Coldhardt nodded vaguely. Then he turned, collected the laptop and left the hangout.

'No, really, it was no trouble,' Tye called after him – very quietly.

'We were well-paid, weren't we?' said Con, making out she wasn't bothered.

Tye shot her a look. 'And who's going to pay you when he's gone?'

'He ain't gone yet,' said Motti.

'Only 'cause he got off on you kissing his arse so nicely,' Patch retorted. He put on a camp American accent: "Recording's all loaded up, big boy, just hit play!"'

'How about I hit a dumb mutant buttwipe?'

'Ow!'

But Jonah was only half-listening. He could still hear Coldhardt's voice, so grave and frail. '*It could be him. It really could be him . . .*'

Heidel's belongings were soon crated up and dumped by the main gates. Then, after grabbing some cereal while the others trooped off to bed, Jonah decided to catch up on some sleep himself. Maya was impatient to get on with cracking the cipher and needed his computer, so he let her take over his bedroom while he crashed in one of the guest rooms.

Good cover story, he thought, as he had to pass Tye's room to get to them.

And as he did so, Jonah knocked on her door.

She opened it in her dressing gown. Her skin hid bruises well but he could see indigo-black smudges on the skin around her collarbone. She looked tired. 'Hey,' she said.

Jonah smiled. 'Nice opening gambit. I just wanted to check we were friends?'

Tye gave a smile that looked like it tasted bitter.

'What else could we be?'

'I don't know . . . These last days, ever since I first heard about that bloody grimoire . . .' He shrugged, itched the lump on his neck. 'Nothing seems right.'

'Maybe after tonight it'll seem straighter. One way or another.'

The two of them stood there. Jonah wondered if Tye was waiting for him to say what surely had to be on both their minds.

'Can I come in and lie down with you?'

She smiled but looked away again. 'I know what your "lie downs" are like. I want to, but I really am killer tired . . .'

'Me too. We could *really* just lie down and –'

'I need a little time right now, 'K?'

Jonah shrugged. 'And a little space? Fine. You got it.' He stomped away down the corridor. *That was sensitive, you doofus*, he told himself. He paused, turned back round – in time to hear the quiet click of Tye's door closing.

He lay on the unmade bed in the first room he came to, turning and fidgeting till sleep reluctantly came and tugged him under.

Jonah woke feeling like crap and looking about as good. The rest of the day passed slowly and fitfully.

He played video games with Patch. Patch kept winning, so he went to the gym to work out. Con was there, beating the hell out of a punchbag. He didn't fancy taking her on in that kind of mood, and so left her to it and took a walk to the main gates. The crates were gone.

'Great,' he muttered. He wondered how long the results would take, how much cash Coldhardt would splash to speed things along.

He walked around the grounds, brooding till he bored himself to death. Coming back to the hangout he found Motti was back from checking out the security systems at the safe house; checks Motti had made himself in the absence of orders from Coldhardt. He still saw it as his responsibility.

'That Sorin was smarter than he looked,' Motti explained. 'Took out the whole system and every bug in the place with something . . . Some kind of EMP, maybe, I dunno.'

'Electromagnetic pulse?' Jonah frowned. 'I thought that knocked out all electronics in the area? The retina and fingerprint scanners, the entry coder, they were all still working.'

'He put down enough juice to cripple the main chip and blow every bug in the building – and then somehow he reset the external barriers.' Motti shook his head in grudging admiration. 'Perfect for an ambush. Those scanners were set to welcome any eyeball, any thumb and any seven-digit code – so you wouldn't be tipped off anything was wrong till you got inside.'

Jonah nodded. 'So the NO guys didn't break in, they just *strolled* in.'

'Shame Sorin bought it,' said Motti. 'Who knew? The guy was a talent. Won't ever make his name now.'

'Was there any . . .' Jonah shrugged, 'any mess from the killing left behind in the safe house?'

Motti looked at him levelly. 'What do you think?'

The hangout slowly filled up again. Con came

back, put on some music. Patch returned to his computer games. Motti went off to his bedroom studio to mess around with some tracks, and Tye was still keeping to herself.

Let her stew, thought Jonah, and slouched off to see how Maya was doing. Because it was his bedroom, he didn't think to knock – and so walked in and found her asleep on his bed. She was curled up in just her black vest top and knickers, her red hair spilling over the pillow. Must have been too trashed to go looking for the guest rooms – or maybe she just couldn't sleep away from her precious cipher files.

His gaze lingered a few seconds. He noticed again the dark tip of the tattoo beneath her collarbone, the welt on her neck like a red star above it. From skinny thigh to pencil-ankles, Maya's skin was smothered in the same grey-brown freckles that dusted her elfin face.

This is when Tye comes in and decides I'm a total perv, he thought. Quickly he took a jacket and laid it over Maya's lower half. Then he checked his computer for any progress on decrypting the manuscript.

No character matches. No words thrown up by the translators. All that processing power, and for what? He noted the pile of screwed-up paper around the bin had grown larger too.

Did Coldhardt even need them to crack the Bloodline Cipher now? All this work they were doing seemed more for Maya's benefit than the boss's.

Pretty soon Coldhardt would be choosing between his regular life as it was now and the services of Nomen Oblitum. Jonah felt a tightness in his stomach; the same pains he got as a kid, when he'd overhear his foster parents discussing him, talking about sending him back. He shut his eyes, still feeling so tired. But Maya was lying in his bed, like a cuckoo.

Since he had nowhere else to go, Jonah returned to the guest room and lay on the unmade bed, waiting for the call from Coldhardt.

He went on waiting.

Shadows stole in, as the light through the window ebbed to grey.

When Jonah woke again, it was close to six the next morning. And the phone started trilling just a half-hour later.

He listened to it, a sick feeling building in his stomach.

Time to go, he thought.

Jonah was the last to arrive in the hub. Even Maya had made it there ahead of him. He felt a moment's resentment at her intrusion: *You just got here. This isn't about you.*

It's about us.

Coldhardt looked in control again, sitting at the head of the table in his usual gaunt splendour. His fingers toyed with the gold ring Tye had snatched back from Sadie, and he seemed relaxed and calm – unlike most everyone else round the table.

'I can appreciate you may be concerned by recent developments,' he began abruptly. 'Not to mention intrigued.'

'One word for it,' Patch muttered.

'Did the tests you had done on Heidel's stuff check out?' asked Motti bluntly.

Coldhardt put down the ring and regarded him. 'All belongings – including the most recent personnel files – are covered in Heidel's fingerprints. Genetic detritus recovered from the clothes – hairs, dried skin and so on – has been DNA tested and matches positively. And the voice . . .' He smiled suddenly, a smile that clearly had no intention of ever reaching his eyes. 'Its tone has deepened a little over the years . . . but it could be Heidel's voice.'

Jonah took in all this over the hammering of his pulse in his temples. 'So Heidel's really alive?'

'And he hasn't aged . . .' Tye shook her head. 'Could he have had surgery, be made up to look younger?'

'Perhaps you could catch up with David Street,' Con added, 'see what he thinks?'

'He is no longer an ally,' said Coldhardt. 'And before you ask, neither is Karl Saitou.'

'But surely if –'

'The matter is settled.' The scrape of Coldhardt's chair interrupted her. 'There is something you missed when you rifled busily through Heidel's belongings.' He stood up and raised the old leather briefcase in one gnarled hand. Then he produced a large knife from his pocket. Jonah swapped a look of alarm with Tye.

But Coldhardt only used the blade to tease open an invisible seam in the leather at the base of the case.

'A secret compartment,' Patch realised. 'Never saw it on the X-ray with everything going on.'

'A favourite trick of the old man's,' Coldhardt murmured, carefully reaching inside. 'A small place to store secrets, sealed for over thirty years.' His face remained impassive as he reached in and removed a small handful of glittering stones. Diamonds, or –

'Smokestones,' Con breathed.

Coldhardt had given one to each of them, a badge of belonging, but they were not the first owners, it seemed. Scattering the gems carelessly on the table, Coldhardt reached in again. And this time he pulled out a small piece of stiff card, marked with a familiar crimson symbol.

'Oh my God,' said Jonah, and the others turned to look at him – all save Maya, whose eyes were as riveted to the find as his own.

Motti kicked Jonah under the table. 'Wanna let the rest of us in on the thrill, geek?'

'That's the Knot of Isis,' Jonah said.

'The symbol co-opted by Nomen Oblitum,' Maya added. 'And that is their card of contract.'

Tye looked at her sharply. 'You've seen it before?'

'Yes.' She looked at Coldhardt. 'The card of contract is given only to one whose body and consciousness the Mage has agreed to aid with her teachings,' Maya explained. 'It confirms the Mage has accepted the subject's gift.'

'I'm guessing that's not a box of chocs,' Patch murmured.

'It is chosen according to the means and circumstances of the subject,' Maya explained. 'It may be a million gold pieces in one case, or a single rare plant in another.'

'Why did Heidel want to go to Nomen Oblitum in the first place?' Tye asked Coldhardt.

Scooping up the smokestones, Coldhardt slipped

them into his breast pocket. 'He didn't discuss his weaknesses.'

'Well, whatever was up, sounds like you did your best to cure him.' Motti mimed a gun to the side of Patch's head and pulled the trigger.

The casual assurance seemed to force its way back into Coldhardt's voice. 'Do not make the mistake of equating knowledge with understanding, Motti.'

'Maybe none of us understand 'cause you never explain.' Motti stood up and slammed his hand down on the tabletop. 'You know what? Keep your secrets, Coldhardt – who cares? Go off with your friends in the robes to have a thirty-year makeover, whatever. Just tell us straight – what happens to *us* while you're gone?'

'I have not yet had my first consultation,' said Coldhardt calmly. 'Until I acquire the Mage's prize, I'm as in the dark as you are about how long the process will take, and of what I can and can't do in the meantime.'

'Motti is talking about *us*,' said Con. Her voice sounded cold but Jonah could see the pleading in her eyes. 'Our future.'

'I must address my own future first.' Coldhardt gestured to Motti to sit back down. Motti sighed and did so, and Coldhardt looked at each of them in turn. 'I ask you to trust in me, my children.'

No one answered.

He smiled. 'At the very least, trust in the fact that I have invested in you all, quite heavily. You are prized highly, and always shall be.'

Jonah turned to Tye to gauge her reaction, to see if

Coldhardt was telling the truth. Motti, Patch and Con were staring at her too.

Looking uneasy, Tye nodded. 'I think he means it.'

'So what is the great gift you need us to acquire for you?' Jonah demanded.

Coldhardt pressed a button on his remote and the screens on the wall illumined. All heads turned to see a map of various islands, none of which Jonah recognised. 'All I know,' said Coldhardt, 'is that my gift will be found in the hold of a particular cargo ship, the *Aswang*, sailing in the Illana Bay region of the Moro Gulf.'

'A cargo ship?' Jonah frowned. 'What can Nomen Oblitum want from a cargo ship?'

'This hasn't been a regular craft for many years,' Coldhardt explained. 'The *Aswang* is a "phantom" vessel – stolen years ago, repainted and registered under a different name and flag. It's now owned by a multi-millionaire with a particular interest in Philippine mythology. He uses it to store a repository of mostly stolen artefacts dating back three thousand years – the *Aswang* has become his personal shrine to the pantheon of Philippine gods. Usually it is moored off one of the many islands he owns, but he moves it periodically for security reasons.'

Motti nodded. 'Guess both sides of the law would be after a haul like that.'

'I have precise coordinates on board the ship for where the treasure will be found,' said Coldhardt. 'You must make your way to that point.'

'Stealing from ancient crypts and crumbling old temples is one thing,' said Jonah. 'But won't there be a whole crew on board this crate?'

'A skeleton crew, ill-equipped to defend a ship that is over 150 metres long. And since the owner has the local pirates in his pay, they will not be expecting trouble.'

'And what about Heidel and Bree?' asked Tye. 'Sorin may be dead and Sadie may be arrested, but they'll still be coming after you. Heidel seems to know your plans before you do.'

'Yeah,' said Patch, 'Nomen Oblitum might be working with Heidel to stitch you up!'

'By killing Sorin and saving Jonah and Maya?' Con looked dubious. 'That's a strange way of stitching up, no?'

'They could have taken care of me at the safe house,' Coldhardt agreed, 'if that was their intention.' He looked round at his 'children' gravely. 'There are always risks; that is what I pay you for. But on this occasion . . . I will furnish you with the information you need – and you will organise between yourselves how best to achieve the goal. Don't share your plans with anyone. Not even me.'

Motti looked taken aback. 'You mean . . . you trust us to do it?'

'I *pay* you to do it.' Coldhardt half smiled. 'Now, the ship is old, it moves slowly – but it will have reached its destination at Balimbing within four days. I suggest you make your plans with all speed.' He turned to Maya. 'Meantime, I would like you to remain here under my personal supervision and continue your work.'

'All right.' Maya shrugged. 'I have nowhere else to go.'

'You still want the grimoire decrypted?' Jonah raised his eyebrows. 'Why? Their translation of the sample text matched ours – and whatever "magic" they need to do, they'll be working from their own copy of the manuscript.'

'I always prefer to read a book myself than to be told stories.' Coldhardt smiled, turning the ring between his fingertips. 'Now. You must begin.'

Jonah slowly rose to go. The others did the same. They followed him over to the concealed lift that would take them from the underworld back out to the light.

'I will see you again,' Coldhardt told them.

Jonah glanced at Tye, and saw she looked troubled. 'He means what he's told us,' she said quietly 'But there's something going unsaid . . . I'm sure of it.'

'He's just found out that the friend he thought he'd killed is still alive after all,' Jonah reminded her. 'That's going to shake him up, right?'

She nodded, and Jonah should have felt better. But he too had the feeling that Coldhardt was keeping something from them. Something waiting in the darkest shadows of the winding road ahead.

CHAPTER SIXTEEN

'Well, she's out there somewhere,' Motti drawled, gazing out over the waters of the South China Seas. 'Thirty-five thousand deadweight tons of rust, crap and Filipino treasure.'

Tye was too busy revelling in the feel of white sand between her toes to frown too hard at him. 'I was trying to see nice things on the horizon, thank you.'

'Not in this line of work,' quipped Jonah, sat in a deckchair beside them with his laptop. In shorts and a Chunk T-shirt, a straw hat perched on his head, he was still trying to crack the cipher. No doubt he'd be back in touch with Maya again before long.

Why did he have to be so smart? *Opposites attract*, thought Tye. That was the easy bit. *But what do they do then?* She felt the afternoon breeze on her face and legs, closed her eyes and dreamed. *They rob a thirty-five-year-old cargo ship out in the Sulu Sea and live happily ever after. What else?*

Tye had flown out the Talent last night to Zamboanga, in western Mindanao in the Philippines; it seemed a good base from which to intercept the slow-moving bulk carrier, which would have to pass by this peninsula. She had sailed these waters a couple of times way back, with smuggling crews when she was fourteen. She'd never dreamed that some day she'd be flying high above them in air-conditioned luxury, staring down at the intense blue. The ocean was like a vast plain of lapis lazuli, its glittering surface littered with powder-white islands, like the droppings of some great celestial bird. Fishing boats left sharp trails across the smooth sea, spreading in any and all directions.

It was hard to imagine something so beautiful could be so dangerous. But the waters were crawling with modern-day pirates, many of whom would kill as casually as they looted. This job would be no breeze . . . But with the gentle sea-blown gusts soothing her skin, she determined to try and stay in the moment and enjoy her surroundings.

Zamboanga City was surrounded by water, which made for great beaches as well as seafood. Once, so Con informed them, it had been a Spanish colony, and the busy streets still held traces of that old splendour in crumbling adobe walls and red terracotta roofs. The shops all advertised in English, but Tye heard the locals bandy words in Spanish Creole. The talk got rowdier when the motorised trike-cabs that thronged the roads reached their destinations, and passengers were hit up by the drivers for a few more pesos.

'We should do all our job-planning on beaches,' Con declared, lying on a beach towel and sipping a Sea Breeze cocktail as red as her bikini.

'I'm up for it,' said Patch. He'd taken off his top, his scrawny body as white as the sand he sat on and the piles of paper they'd been poring over. 'D'you think we should have a beach party later?'

Motti shook his head despairingly. 'We should start scouting this evening.'

'Dib, dib, dib.' Patch saluted.

'Jonah's calculated three likely routes the ship could be taking, so we know roughly where to search,' said Tye, ignoring him. 'But there's no guarantee we'll find the *Aswang* tonight.'

'That'd be a shame.' Patch sniggered. ''Ere. Reckon *Aswang* is short for *Ass-Wanger*?'

'Reckon "Patch" is?' Motti shot back.

'D'you know what an aswang is, Patch?' Con looked at him. 'It's a flesh-eating ghoul that roams these islands at night, eating small children. Like you.'

'I'm all man!' Patch protested. 'Even so, maybe a night spent scouting the seas wouldn't be so bad.'

'Except for the pirates,' Motti noted.

'They'll be active mainly after dark,' Tye noted. 'We'll scout in daylight.'

Con nodded. 'But we must pull the job at night, no?'

'Less chance of detection,' Motti agreed.

'I'll fool 'em into thinking I'm one of their own,' said Patch. 'I've got the eye patch already, I'll just pretend I've got a wooden leg. Ha-harrr!'

'Not that kind of pirate, numbnuts. They don't got swords and parrots now, they got M60s and rocket launchers and they're organised real slick.'

Tye nodded. 'And then you've got the Filipino navy patrols, Chinese crack smugglers . . .'

'I wanna go home,' said Patch miserably.

'And I'm going to *call* home,' Jonah announced,

slamming his laptop shut like an oversized book. Tye saw a familiar spark in his eyes; could tell he wanted to grin and jump about but was scared of jinxing his possible breakthrough.

'You've made some progress on the cipher?' Tye asked.

'I think so.' He looked over to the promenade at the edge of the beach, fidgeting like a dog itching to chase a stick. 'Well, better get on to Maya . . .'

'Guess you had,' said Tye, watching him go and telling herself it was fine. 'While we'd better jump in a couple of speedboats and get searching.'

Jonah soon found an internet café not far from the grand, colonial-style City Hall. It smelled of fish, and the chairs were sticky, but the PCs were fair spec and the only staff member seemed engrossed in the TV.

He bought ten minutes of time. Then he quickly bypassed the no-uploads protocol, hacked into the timer so it didn't count down and loaded some heavy-weight security software to make sure his trail through the web couldn't be traced. Finally he loaded up Instant Messenger; Maya had suggested he message her instead of calling if anything came up, insisting it would be more secure. She'd had that spooky look in her eye that suggested she saw so much more than he did. And with stuff this big going down, he was taking no chances.

Jonah searched for her status and found she was online.

Hey maya, he typed, and waited impatiently for a reply.

He sent a prod.

U asleep?

Then the little yellow envelope appeared by the Messenger icon. He clicked on the window.

I'm here, her message read. *How do I know it's you?*

Look in second drawer to your left u will find pants

There was a pause. Then she wrote again:

Ugh! What else will I find?

Jonah suddenly realised and swore. *Er . . . grotty magazine that isn't mine and I never saw before?*

Next time let's agree a password. What's up?

What's ROUND u mean. :-) He paused, smiling like the emoticon he'd typed. *Want to get excited?*

Is it the circles?

Yeah some of the overwritten ones are perfect, u cant see where pen stroke begins. But then on others, u can. Check it out

He waited, drumming his fingers on the desk. After so much time spent staring at those bloody overwritten characters, he felt he was finally getting somewhere. And once again, the clue was in the *drawing* of the letters rather than any inherent meaning they might carry – an almost entirely self-reflexive cipher. Jonah found himself wondering about the guy who'd encrypted this. 'You were a clever old bastard,' Jonah murmured. 'But maybe not quite clever enough.'

A few minutes passed before Maya wrote back:

The start positions are all in different places!!!!!

Jonah smiled and typed again: *Yep. So we know DEF not normal handwriting. The author cycles through the different start points. It's a carefully assembled pattern. And that makes me wonder if this really is a ciphertext – v convenient that random encoding allowed for such a pattern.*

There was a pause. Jonah waited impatiently for a response.

OK . . . you're far enough away over there that you can't come back and hit me.

He frowned. *Wot u on about?*

Promise you tell no one. Not Coldhardt, not Tye, not anybody. Swear it

He shrugged. *I swear.* And pretty soon he really was swearing, as her block of text blinked into being.

*Remember I said before the manuscript *might* be plaintext – a written-down version of a hotchpotch of languages? Actually I know damn well it is. It is the written form of an obscure language system derived from a thirteenth-century Sino-Vietnamese dialect – with some other stuff thrown in. My tutor in Russia, the one who disappeared, member of that occult group I do translations for – he spoke a little.*

A few seconds later a fresh message appeared.

Hate me?

Jonah felt so angry he almost killed the exchange then and there. But that would let Maya off the hook too easily. He started tapping hard on the keys.

No wonder u weren't interested in main part of the manuscript. U already knew wot the bloody thing said. Bet u only went to Blackland cos he had a copy of manuscript with appendix.

That's right . . . Sorry.

Then you know what the Bloodline Cipher is!

No.

Don't dick me around.

A minute or so passed while Jonah fumed in the corner of the café. Then Maya wrote again.

Tutor thought the Bloodline Cipher was in the appendix only, with the key concealed throughout the bulk of the book. The key to something very powerful. That's why so many have tried to steal or destroy each copy of the manuscript. Blackland's is only copy with appendix intact.

Why are you so bothered about it? Jonah typed.

Told you. Don't like unsolved mysteries.

So what does the main bit say, he typed crossly. *Or can't u tell me?*

I trust you, came the instant response. Then a lengthy pause. Jonah imagined her, sitting at his desk, picking the right words to put in and leave out. He glanced nervously at the café proprietor – his ten purchased minutes were long since over – but the man was still absorbed in the TV.

Finally, Maya's response came through.

Manuscript gives higher understanding of the meridians of energy about the body. Depending on point of view it is either ultimate medical handbook – or DIY manual on How to Destroy a Human Body. Incredible knowledge.

Jonah sighed. *And now we find it has an added mysterious pattern*, he typed.

But what does pattern MEAN? she shot back.

Jonah sighed, feeling the nerves clench in his stomach. *May have to leave that to u to work out. Think gonna be busy*

There was a pause. Then she wrote back:

Doing job tonight?

Jonah began to type: *If we find ship before sunset.*

Then he thought twice and deleted the line of text, tried again:

Could tell u. But then I'd have to kill u. See u (I hope)

He logged off and removed all trace of his uploads, then left the café. He stepped out into the bright sunshine, looked down the hill towards the wooded promenade and the indigo swell of the sea. And Jonah wished and wished that it would never get dark that night, while wishing too that this whole business was over.

If Maya was right about what the manuscript contained . . . then what further powers did the Bloodline Cipher promise?

Maya waited for another message from Jonah, just in case. It didn't come.

Sensing a presence behind her, she turned and started. Coldhardt was standing there, watching her from the doorway.

'I think it's time we talked frankly,' he said.

CHAPTER SEVENTEEN

Jonah wedged himself into an uncomfortable flip-down seat in the boat's cabin beside the door, the hot stink of diesel in his nostrils, the roar of twin engines deafening in his ears. Whoever thought that taking a trip out on a moonlit sea was romantic had clearly never gone for a three-a.m. jaunt in a 'tora-tora'.

They'd secured it from a man in one of Zamboanga's sleazier bars, who claimed to be a gun-runner. Some soft, compelling words from Con in Tagalog had him eating out of her hand – the same hand that was clutching his ignition keys just five minutes later.

'*I've sent him home to sleep with orders to say nothing*,' Con told them. '*No one will be able to tell what craft we're using*.'

The souped-up fishing boat was maybe sixteen metres long from prow to stern. The cabin was compact and crowded – particularly with a radar set built in as an optional extra. Tye was at the wheel. Motti sat at a table behind her with a stack of maps, marking out their course. But it was Con working the hardest, practically swinging from a handgrip in the low ceiling as she turned between Motti, the maps and the radar screen, feeding through instructions to Tye, trying to keep her balance as the boat ploughed across the choppy sea. A bright red bulb glared down on the scene; red light didn't mess with your night vision, so your pupils didn't have to readjust to the dark. Out at sea in the seamless, shifting shadows, Jonah supposed losing that advantage could cost you big time.

Feeling about as much use as a fifth wheel, he gathered his black poncho around him and stole outside to see how Patch was doing. Since the boy was hanging over the rail at the side of the boat looking like death, Jonah figured the answer was 'not so good'.

'Seasickness or nerves?' Jonah asked.

Patch groaned, then threw up noisily over the side of the boat.

'Enigmatic answer. Like it.' Jonah patted Patch's back sympathetically and crossed to the prow of the boat.

The night was hot, and the gibbous moon looked paper thin, shining eerily through a black mist of clouds. A few stars glimmered fitfully. The only other light came from distant fishing boats, parked out for the night, their decks lit by coloured strings of globe-sized bulbs hanging overhead.

In contrast, Tye had left their boat's lights switched off because it made them harder to spot, especially at speeds of sixty miles per hour. The bad news was, they would look suspicious if picked up by other ships' radar. There was no good reason for a boat to be speeding at night, only a dozen dodgy ones. Pirates would most probably leave them alone, but the Filipino navy had at least ten ships patrolling the area.

If their paths crossed just one of them, it would be Game Over.

Jonah itched the stupid lump on his neck, and sighed. They were eight miles from shore. It didn't sound like much. But Jonah watched the cresting waves swell and crash over the prow, and imagined floundering through that churning darkness, knowing you had no chance of reaching safety . . .

Not that safety was waiting ahead of them at the end of this little trip.

Tye and Con had sighted the *Aswang* just a few miles north of where Jonah had predicted after calculating the ship's average cruising time, course to date and final destination. So here they were, ready to sweep in and start marauding like good'uns – without even knowing what treasure they'd be taking away with them . . .

A wind was whipping up, and the boat lurched. The sound of Patch's heaving carried across the deck, and Jonah decided to go back inside. He skidded starboard to the cabin door, and opened it against the wind. He wasn't feeling brilliant himself.

'Hope Patch is going to be OK,' said Jonah, joining Tye beside the wheel. 'Can't see him opening much in that state.'

'He'll get it together,' said Tye. She gave him an encouraging smile. This used to be her world, he supposed, night after night. It was just routine stuff for a smuggler, but it was going to take more than a smile to make Jonah feel confident.

'We're getting closer,' Con reported, tapping her screen. 'This dot is twenty-two miles away, towards the limits of the radar. But if it stays on this course, and we catch it up no trouble, then it's definitely the target.'

Jonah felt a hard frisson of nerves. 'What if the navy intercept us?'

'There's over seven thousand islands in the Philippines, geek, with over half of 'em uninhabited.' Motti didn't look up from his maps. 'We'll find someplace to hide.'

'And if *pirates* intercept us?'

'We mess our pants.'

All too soon, Jonah saw the cargo ship's silhouette loom ahead of them beneath the purple-black contusions of cloud. Their little ship was lurking off the starboard bow, and Jonah stood watching from the deck with Patch and Motti.

Patch looked up at Jonah, pasty-faced. 'Bet now you're wishing we'd gone for the beach party.'

'Just a bit. We are sure that's the *Aswang*, right?' But even as Jonah spoke, the clouds parted enough for him to read the plain white legend near the prow. The walls of the ship were thick with great dark continents of rust; the moonlight made them look like old bloodstains.

'That's what we gotta climb. Maybe thirty metres.' Motti pointed to six rugged-looking launchers he'd laid out on the deck. 'US navy issue. They use compressed air to send up a titanium grappling hook on a Kevlar line. Noiseless and accurate – and 'cause we all know Patch could only throw his hook about a metre.'

'Shut your hole,' said Patch. 'Why's the thing so dark?'

'Ship that size, if they light up the deck, they can't

see pirates coming alongside,' said Motti. 'But they're bound to have –'

A massive beam of white light arced out from the side of the ship, raking over the choppy surface. It scanned first one way, then another. Jonah heard the engines stir, felt the ship lurch as Tye turned the tora-tora, taking them out of range of the searchlights. As they circled round, he saw a spooky, eldritch glow from the port side of the ship, as similar spotlights skimmed the waves.

'D'you think they heard us?' Patch fretted.

'Not over the sound of their own engines,' said Motti. 'Nah, that looked like a routine sweep, more a deterrent than anything else. We're dark and we're small and we're too close for their radar to work properly.'

'Then they don't know we're here,' said Jonah, hoping it was true.

'But now *we* know the range of those lights, and that there's someone port and starboard manning those things.' Motti nodded thoughtfully. 'There'll be a chief mate on board with responsibilities to watch everything for the captain, who'll probably be sat on his ass someplace snoring. As for the rest of the crew . . . got no idea. A full crew complement could be as many as thirty if this was a working ship. Reckon we'll only find a handful, but they'll have radios and most likely be armed . . .'

Suddenly, the spotlights cut off. 'Missed us,' Patch hissed triumphantly. The darkness grew absolute, and Jonah found it hard to tell where sea stopped and sky began.

'Now's the time to get going,' Motti announced. 'Where the hell's Con?'

'Here.' She pushed open the door, dressed now in a black jumpsuit with her hair stuffed inside a black beanie. She was wearing fingerless leather gloves, and passed round three more sets. Tye eased off on the engines, holding them maybe two hundred metres off the port bow.

Con watched Jonah, Motti and Patch put on their own gloves. 'We run through the plan once more now, yes?'

Motti nodded and drew them closer for their final briefing. 'Me and Jonah shoot the hook and line and go up first. We take the deck. Any crew, we subdue.' Motti pulled out a large wooden baton from a locker. 'Found this. Oughtta help.'

'Any spares?' Patch asked.

'Nope. But you can bet your ass the crew will be armed. We can always take their weapons.' Motti gripped hold of it as if for comfort. 'So, once we've secured the area, me and Jonah signal for you two to come up. While you're climbing, we scout around for someone Con can put the 'fluence on to decoy the rest of the crew.'

Con nodded. 'Got it.'

'With everyone distracted, Patch gets us below decks. We locate Coldhardt's little gift, hope it ain't too big to carry, and radio Tye for pick-up. Then we keep going down till we reach the bilge pump at the base of the hold. Patch's exploding eyeball makes us a hole in the hull we can jump through, Tye pulls alongside in the tora-tora and gets us the hell out. Any questions?'

Patch put his hand up in the air. 'Please can I go to the toilet?'

Motti cuffed him round the shoulder and turned to Jonah. 'Geek, you can go tell Tye to take us in.' He paused, gave a tiny, knowing smile. 'But be back out here inside sixty seconds, OK?'

Jonah nodded and ran to the cabin door. Tye was at the wheel. She turned as he entered. He ran straight over, put his arms round her waist. She grabbed him back and held him tightly.

'I'm sorry I was a bitch,' she whispered.

'You weren't!' he protested. 'I was stupid.'

'You're never stupid. I wish you *were* stupid.' She looked at him. 'But don't be stupid up on that ship, 'K?'

'I'll be totally sensible,' he promised. 'As sensible as you can be scaling thirty metres of rust, anyway.'

'You scared?'

'God, yeah.'

She kissed him. 'Me too.'

He glanced back at the door. 'Motti says to take us in. Wish I didn't have to –'

'Go,' she whispered, smiling. 'It's OK. We'll pick up later. Promise.'

'That's what I call an incentive.' Jonah pressed a clumsy kiss to her lips and ran out through the door, a swell of adrenaline rising through him. *Yeah. We're going to do this*, he thought, snatching up his grappling hook launcher.

He looked back at the closed cabin door.

We've got *to do this.*

He heard the note of the engines change as Tye

opened the throttle and they rode the black waves, nudging closer and closer to the rusting stretch of the ship until it towered over them like a dark cliff. Motti shoved the baton through his belt and checked it was secure. Then he aimed his launcher up in the air and motioned Jonah to do the same.

At his nod, Jonah braced himself for the recoil and fired. With a click and a hiss the line disappeared up into the darkness. 'Please, please, please,' Jonah murmured, bracing himself for the hook to come tumbling down on his head.

It didn't. He pulled down cautiously on the line and felt it grow tauter.

Motti yanked a lot harder on his. 'If this comes loose while we're halfway up, it ain't gonna be pretty.' He gave one more tug then grunted satisfaction. 'OK, then. Last one up kisses Patch's ass. Move.'

Jonah gripped the line, glad of his cushioning gloves, and launched himself into the air. His feet clunked loudly against the throbbing hull as he pulled himself up, one hand after the other. The grate of the huge ship engines, the hiss and churn of the swirling sea beneath him, his muttered prayers and swearing and the drum of his panicking heart all seemed to crowd in his ears. He kept looking up, dreading the sight of a Filipino face and a gun muzzle peering down at him. How long would it take to fall? Jonah drew comfort from the sight of Motti, a gangly shadow-spider matching him for pace as they scaled the side together.

His arms were shaking and he was hoarse for breath as he reached the top. With a final effort he hauled himself through a gap in the safety railings enclosing the deck perimeter and dropped to the rusty floor. It was trembling harder than he was with the force of the engines.

Jonah got up stealthily, his eyes now fully adjusted to the darkness. The long deck was a rusty jumble of boom chains, vents, backhoes and huge spools of wire. There was no sign of any crew – but now Motti was clambering quietly through the railings.

'No one around,' Jonah murmured, helping him up.

'Let's be sure it stays that way,' Motti murmured. He leaned over the railing and signalled to Con and Patch. 'You wanna scout ahead?'

Jonah nodded, and padded away through the muggy gloom, staying close to the rails so he could swing himself overboard if worse came to worst. He doubted the sea could make him any wetter – beneath the black linen shirt he was sweating like hell.

Suddenly, maybe ten metres ahead, he saw a tiny flare of yellow and froze. It was the flame from a cigarette lighter. Someone was having a smoke on deck. Jonah caught the dull gleam of moonlight on metal and realised a machine gun hung from a strap on the man's shoulder.

Cautiously, he turned and made his way back to the stern. But suddenly someone jumped out from behind one of the vents to his left. A man, little, black and agile, blocking his way and wielding a machete. Jonah barely had time to react before the man was swinging at him, babbling in an excited voice.

Willing himself to stay cool and focus, Jonah blocked the man's swinging arm and punched him in the jaw. It shut him up but didn't floor him, so Jonah kicked his attacker in the balls and wrestled the machete from his grip. The man staggered back and tripped over a cable. But by now, the man with the cigarette was rushing towards him, swinging up his machine gun while reaching for the radio in his belt. Rather than run away and make a target, Jonah charged towards the man and brought the machete down on his gun, knocking it aside. Then he thumped the man in the stomach and shoved him against a lifebelt holder. Thinking fast, he grabbed the lifebelt and pulled it down over the man's head and shoulders. Now the man couldn't use his arms or reach his radio, so Jonah cracked him on the side of the head with the hilt of the machete. Silently, the man crumpled – the cigarette, improbably, still clamped in his lips.

Motti came running up. 'Good work.'

'There's another one back there,' Jonah told him. 'Took your time, didn't you?'

'Sorry. Had one of my own to take out.' Motti mimed hitting someone with his borrowed baton. 'Patch found your man and dragged him off to Con. He should be nicely under by now.' He reached down and snatched the cigarette from the sleeping man's lips. 'We better hide this sucker and regroup in case someone heard the fighting.' He took a deep drag on the cigarette then threw it overboard, while Jonah hauled the man across the deck, laid him down beneath an old rusted winch and draped some heavy plastic sheeting over him. The man's silver lighter had fallen out; Jonah scooped it up for a keepsake and headed after Motti.

Jonah and Motti found Patch and Con crouched in the shadows with a very docile guard.

'Don't know his native language,' said Con crossly. 'But at least he speaks some English – says there are ten men aboard.'

'Three down, seven to go,' Patch muttered.

'Have this guy tell his buddies to come running,' said Motti. 'That he's found a grappling hook and someone jumping overboard. We'll hide him out of sight, let them scoot by and then get going.'

'We hope.' Jonah looked over the side, scratching nervously at his neck. There was no sign of the boat – Tye had retreated out of sight again.

'While the crew are looking for him, we should be able to get what we came for.'

Con looked into the little man's eyes and started speaking in some weird mixture of English and Tagalog. The man was nodding, so he must've understood some of it. He picked up the radio and started gabbling into it. Then he jumped up and hid inside one of the big coils of wire.

'Like a self-basting turkey,' Motti remarked. 'Pretty smooth sweet-talking, Con.'

She prowled away across the rusty deck. 'Now we're here we should move, no?'

Jonah followed her lead, sticking to the thickest shadows and moving cautiously. If the crew really were to come running, they would make enough noise to be heard a fair way off. But so far, nothing.

Then suddenly, they heard the pound of footsteps approaching from out of the darkness, and low, urgent voices. Jonah ducked behind the vast square lid of a cargo hatch, and the others joined him as five men hurtled past, each clutching an iron bar or an automatic.

'That's most of 'em,' breathed Motti, and the second they'd gone by, he was edging out on to the deck walkway again. 'So far, so good.'

Jonah followed close behind as they made their way towards the prow of the ship, where the front decks would be found, a stack of state rooms, bridge and wheelhouse above and with stairway access to all decks below. He wondered how long they would have before the angry crewmen discovered their hypnotised buddy and went raging in search of the intruders. The thought made him quicken his step and edge past Motti, taking the lead as they rounded a large storehouse.

Which meant it was him who first saw the two guards blocking the entrance to the front decks.

And him who became the target for their M16s a split second later.

'Two, armed!' Jonah yelled, throwing himself to the deck as the Filipinos raised their guns to fire. But forewarned, Patch had produced one of the spare grapnel launchers and fired it now – sending the miniature anchor smacking into the chest of the nearest guard. The metal missile slammed the man back into the doorway and the gun flew from his flailing arms.

Even as he fell, Con was circling round behind his startled companion. By the time the man glimpsed her foot flying towards the side of his face, it was lights-out time.

'Nice decoy, geek,' said Motti, offering Jonah a hand up which he gratefully took. 'Patch, do your stuff.'

Patch had already pulled out his torch, shining it over the locking mechanism on the bulkhead door just to the left of the main entrance. 'Looks like a time-delay mechanism twinned with digi-combination lock . . .'

'Lemme see.' Motti took a look himself, ready to assist. 'Jonah, Con, get up to the bridge and take care of the captain. Could be a useful guy to have on our side – or a useful hostage, whatever's easier.'

Cranked up on adrenaline, Jonah pushed open the door to the bridge complex and flew up the stairs with Con. The wheelhouse was on the third floor – Jonah guessed as much when a wiry Filpino man in a stained white vest and a peaked captain's hat jumped out from inside. He had a revolver in his sweaty hand, pointing right at Jonah. He barked at them, his face twisted with fear and rage.

But Jonah wasn't stopping. By the time his brain kicked in with a yell of *This is a really dumb idea* he was scaling the final staircase, closing on the captain fast – racing towards a loaded gun aiming at his face. He saw the man's finger twitch on the trigger, twisted aside desperately even as he threw himself up the last steps. He wound up headbutting the captain in the groin. The man yelled and the gun went off harmlessly at the ceiling. Jonah rolled clear, as Con arrived. She kicked the captain clear out of consciousness.

'Prop him up,' she murmured. 'I must mesmerise him.'

'He won't be awake for ages, you nearly took his head off.'

'He nearly took off yours.' She smiled as the

captain started to moan softly. 'Ah! You recover already. What a strong specimen you are, Captain. I think we could use such a man on our side. You hear me . . . ?'

The captain stared at her, too dazed to struggle.

'You *are* on our side, the side of the intruders,' Con went on. 'Listen to me, my ally. Anyone you do not recognise on this ship – why, these persons are your greatest friends, no? And you will do all in your power to aid and protect them. Yes, listen to me . . .'

As Con's voice grew deeper and softer and strayed into other languages, Jonah staggered inside the wheelhouse, his whole body trembling. The room reeked of stale BO and cigarettes. He gazed out over the shadows of the sea. The skinny moonlight in the water glittered like some precious treasure was just beneath the surface. 'What the hell am I doing here?' he whispered. Then he pulled out his walkie-talkie and radioed Tye. 'It's Jonah.'

Her voice crackled back at him, terse and urgent. 'D'you need me?'

Yes I do, he thought, as the giant ship thundered on into the widest, darkest night, with no one at the helm now. Out of control.

Back on the tora-tora, Tye shook the radio. 'Jonah? Please copy, are you –'

'I'm here. It's OK.' Even through the crackle of the radio set, Tye could hear something in his voice that suggested it wasn't. 'Con is brainwashing the captain and Patch is breaking in downstairs.'

She bit her lip. 'We need to keep this frequency

clear, Jonah. Give me the word when you're ready and I'll move into range. The blast will give me visual of where you are. Just jump and I'll catch you.'

'Sounds good.'

'Soon,' she told him. 'Out.'

Tye looked out of the cabin window at the hulking silhouette of the *Aswang* against the purple sky. It looked just as ghoulish as its namesake.

Suddenly she heard something outside. A quiet rattle. The wind knocking something? An uneasy feeling took hold. She'd been distracted when Jonah called in – just for a few seconds, but it could've been enough for someone to get past their radar, just as she'd sneaked under the *Aswang*'s.

There was a flare gun in the cabin, and Tye picked it up, cradled it in both hands. The night was warm but she felt cold and clammy as she edged out of the red-lit cabin and into the dark, trying to tell what was real and what was shadow.

Suddenly a hand clubbed down on her wrist and the flare gun clattered from her grip. Immediately, she spun round and jabbed with her other hand at face level; her knuckles cracked against bone. Her attacker was a man in a wetsuit, and a knife blade glinted in the moonlight. She kicked him in the stomach, danced back as he doubled up and smashed the knife from his grip. Then she delivered a high kick to his chest that propelled him overboard. Warm spray arched over her, but she knew from the sound of the splash her attacker had hit the water well, twisted in the air and dived. Which meant he would most likely come back for more.

Instinctively she stooped to snatch up the flare gun – without first checking the deck was clear. Another attacker came up from behind and grabbed her in a crushing bearhug. Tye felt the air driven from her lungs as struggled to free herself.

Then, she heard a quiet *phut*, and a sharp stab at her neck.

Her eyes widened as she saw a small fishing boat bobbing out of the dark towards her. Two people were rowing, and another figure stood behind them, but the night hid their features, and Tye's vision was already blurring. *Curare,* she thought fearfully, *maybe it's Sorin, he wasn't dead, he's come back –*

Desperately she tore the dart from her throat. Then she grabbed hold of one of the arms round her chest and heaved her body forward; using her attacker's weight and momentum against him she flipped him over her shoulder and he crashed down on his back.

She swore. Heidel's face was looking up at her. 'You've let everybody down, Tye Chery,' he said, smiling. 'Whatever would Coldhardt say?'

Tye stamped down hard on Heidel's sternum, stunning him. 'For that he'd probably say "thanks",' Tye hissed.

'Just you wait, little girl,' Heidel said through gritted teeth.

Tye staggered backwards, almost overbalanced. She could feel the drug taking hold. It felt like a crowd of drowsy flies had flown inside her head. She straightened and saw how close the approaching rowboat was now as she blundered back to the cabin. She had to outrun them, had to fight off the drug.

But it's curare and it's going to kill you. Tye felt a shard of terror knife through her insides. *How* can *you fight?*

It seemed there were two cabin doors. She clutched for one and missed. Maybe this was best, though – the red light inside was burning blinding bright as hellfire now, and Tye didn't want to go to hell. Although she kind of doubted there was space in heaven for someone like her.

'*Think of the chances we take*,' she'd told Patch. '*Our luck's going to run out.*'

She had to reach the radio, warn Jonah and the others. Couldn't let them down. Couldn't let *him* down. But a big wave bumped the boat and she stumbled, fell on her side. She rolled on to her back but couldn't get up again.

Tye looked up at the stars that had dared peep through the dark and terrible sky. They started to spin about, chasing their tails like Catherine wheels before erupting into comets, the original bad omens. As her eyes flickered shut, as the people came aboard and rough hands held her down, *I'll miss you, Jonah*, was the last thought to slip away.

CHAPTER EIGHTEEN

Jonah watched the captain, back at his controls, smile over his shoulder at them as they headed down the steps. He called something after them.

'That is sweet, no?' Con smiled demurely. 'He wished us luck.'

'We could use it,' said Jonah.

By the time they got back to the main deck, Patch had cracked the bulkhead door. Motti was holding one of the guards' M16s in one hand and a bunch of what looked to be slim lipsticks in the other.

'The weapons have been converted to fire simulated ammo,' said Motti. 'Wax bullets. Without protective clothing they'd hurt us bad but wouldn't kill us.'

'Comforting,' said Jonah. 'The captain might only have maimed me just now.'

'They must want any intruders taken alive for questioning,' said Motti.

'Interrogation?' Patch shuddered and held the door open. 'Think I'd rather take the bullet. You lot coming?'

'He's right, we should split,' said Motti, dropping the wax cartridges. 'The crew ain't gonna need three guesses to work out where we're headed.'

Beyond the bulkhead was fetid, salty blackness with

a metallic reek. The floor beneath them was pooled with puddles and rust. Patch's torch cut slices from the dark, revealed the stairwell in pieces as he searched for a light switch. Then dim, low-watt light hummed into life, hardly enough to see by.

Motti jammed the M16 through the door handle, wedging the muzzle behind a pipe running vertically beside the frame. 'Should slow 'em down anyway,' he muttered, facing the staircase. He was first down the steps, and Jonah brought up the rear. Their footprints echoed in slippery cascades, as they went down one level . . . two levels . . .

'Vault's the other side of this bulkhead,' Motti whispered. He studied the door built into it and nodded as if it was familiar. 'Three-part steel frame, internal rock-wool insulation. Not bad.'

'Lucky we don't need to blow it open, then.' Patch had a couple of small tools in his hand and was setting about the entry-coder beside the door. 'Just a bit of friendly persuasion . . .'

With an echoing clunk, the deadlocks keeping the door closed retracted. Patch grinned at the others – but Motti shoved him aside, carefully opening the door in case of other traps. It was dark inside, with a stench of dead fish.

'How could anyone call this a shrine?' Con was breathing through her sleeve. 'It stinks.'

'Whoa,' said Patch, training his torch inside. 'Tripwire there. See it?'

Jonah jostled with Motti to see. A gleaming thread of silver was pulled taut across a narrow access corridor.

'Probably gas,' Motti noted. 'Wouldn't want an explosion in here in case his collection went up in smoke.'

'So do we just step over the wire?' Jonah asked. 'Keep our eyes peeled?'

'That would make sense. Too much sense.' Motti pulled a pair of weird-looking goggles with crimson lenses from inside his jacket and wore them carefully over his spectacles. 'Uh-huh. We got us some infrared tripwires here too. You can bet the silver wire's just a dummy to get us to step over it and wade right through the real thing.'

He took off the goggles and offered them to Jonah. He could see a crazy criss-cross of red light beams stretching beyond the tripwire.

'If any one beam's interrupted for more than a second,' said Motti, 'game over.'

'How do we get past them?' said Con tersely.

'Defeat the trigger mechanism.' Motti snatched Patch's torch and played the beam on a black box with a dull metal capsule wired on top. A cable connected the box to a computer keyboard with built-in LCD, just inside the doorway at ankle height. 'Being controlled from this thing. Know the type, geek?'

Jonah pulled off the goggles, squeezed into the narrow space and checked out the screen in the torchlight. His nerves were too frayed already to feel any extra apprehension. 'Password override will be in Filipino,' he muttered. 'But if I can hack into the clock mechanism and freeze it, we'll have the world's longest second. Then we can trip the beams as much as we like and the processor won't register a thing . . .'

Con smiled. 'Amazing how something so clever can be so dumb.'

'Don't talk about the geek like that,' Motti mock-chided.

Jonah concentrated. It didn't take long to hack in, isolate the code and disable it. 'OK, fingers crossed we're clear.'

Motti pulled his baton from his belt and warily waved it into the invisible beams. Nothing happened.

'Mate, you're a genius,' said Patch, as Jonah led the way through the access tunnel to the next door. There was seemingly nothing attached – no clever locks, no scanners. Nothing. Only a sign which Jonah couldn't read, except the number 'one'.

'This is the right cargo hold,' Con breathed.

'Motti?' Jonah called back down the corridor. 'What's keeping you?'

The torch beam showed him crouching beside the disabled computer, holding still. 'It's OK, I just . . .' Motti straightened up. 'Thought I heard something up above.'

'Let's get going,' said Con. 'At least we don't have to get out the same way.'

Patch tapped his eye patch. 'Not when I can give you the best bang of your life,' he joked nervously.

Motti stalked towards them. 'OK, open it up, Patch.'

Patch cautiously tried the handle. The door opened outwards a little. 'It ain't even locked. They must never have thought anyone would get this far.'

'Or there's a trap the other side,' Motti reasoned. 'Stand clear.'

Jonah stood aside from the entrance, as Motti carefully opened the door.

Nothing happened. Jonah peered inside the cargo hold. The smell of salt and rust was even stronger, the darkness thicker still. He heard Patch fumble for a light switch.

'Let there be light,' Patch proclaimed, as the dim orange lighting flickered into life, illuminating the vault, 'and there was . . .'

'Nothing,' Jonah whispered. He stared around in disbelief. It was just a dark, stained shell of a place. 'There's nothing here at all. But Coldhardt gave us the exact details –'

'Yeah,' said Motti, 'the details he was given by the NO men.' A horrible silence fell, heavy as the dark around them. 'It's a trap, guys. A goddamn frickin' trap.'

'I said this was a stitch-up!' Patch shouted.

'But all those barriers we passed,' Con protested. 'Why put them in place if there's nothing to guard?'

Sudden fear scrabbled at Jonah's guts. 'To keep us below decks while they spring something?'

'OK, let's get down to the bilge pumps beneath this hunk o' crap,' Motti ordered, leading the way over to an open hatchway in one corner. 'Jonah, radio Tye to come get us as arranged. Patch, get ready with the eye.'

'Ten-second fuse,' said Patch, running after him. 'Then BOOM.'

Jonah pulled out the radio. 'Tye? We need pick-up.' Only static answered him. 'Tye? Come on . . .'

'Motti, Patch, come back,' Con shouted. Jonah saw

she was peering through a small rusty hole in the wall of the hold. 'There's a boat outside but it's not Tye. Looks to be an assault craft.'

Motti hesitated by the hatch. 'Navy?'

'Unmarked. And it's waiting right where we're supposed to come out.'

'How'd they know?' Patch wailed.

Motti swore and looked accusingly at Jonah. 'You told Maya?'

'No!' he protested. 'I said nothing about the job.'

'We gotta get out of here.' Motti was striding for the door, clutching his baton. 'Where the hell is Tye?'

'I can't reach her,' Jonah snapped, running to catch up.

'Tye knew just where we were coming out,' said Con, bundling after them with Patch. 'What if she –'

'Tye would never sell us out,' said Jonah.

'See if we can raise her above decks.' Motti started running through the access corridor, wet rust crunching beneath his feet. 'If a boat's waiting out on the port side for us, maybe we can get away to starboard.'

Maybe. The word jeered at Jonah as he scrambled back up the dimly lit stairwell in Motti's wake. He felt sick. His clothes and hair were soaked with sweat. Why wasn't Tye answering the radio? 'Come on,' he hissed, banging his palm against the casing in frustration. 'Come on!'

The rifle was still wedging the door shut. Motti strained to pull it out, but it was stuck tight. He swore, snatched off his glasses to wipe the condensation from them. Jonah took hold of the rifle handle and managed to yank it free. Con and Patch stood back as he cautiously opened the door a crack. He saw two bodies lying on the deck outside just as they'd been left.

'OK,' Jonah whispered to the others. 'Looks like no one's figured we're here yet –'

They stole outside on to the moonlit deck, but then suddenly Con stopped. 'The sound of the engine,' she whispered. 'It's changed tone, it's –'

The air seemed suddenly torn apart by noise as a giant grey helicopter swung up over the side of the cargo ship like a huge and vengeful beast. Jonah was nearly knocked off his feet by the gale of the rotors beating down on him, by the sheer, deafening din. Bright search beams snapped on from the copter's belly, bleaching Jonah's view of the decks like floodlighting. Patch clutched hold of Jonah's arm, while Con stood behind Motti as if he could shield her as the helicopter came roaring down as if to crush them underneath. Jonah felt like a rabbit facing down a juggernaut.

'Run under!' Motti bellowed in Jonah's face. '*Move!*'

Shocked out of his daze, Jonah ran, dragging Patch with him. The lights grew blinding as the howling metal continued its inexorable descent, and as he emerged the other side the rotor wash almost blasted him to his knees. He and Patch staggered and stumbled away, running for the cover of the storehouse. Con had already reached it. Seconds later Motti joined them, his hair whipped loose from its ponytail, as wild as his eyes. 'I told you! This whole thing was a set-up!'

'Who are they?' Con shouted.

‘What do we do?’ Patch looked terrified. ‘Mot, what the hell do we do?’

Jonah jammed the radio up against his ear. ‘Tye! Tye, for God’s sake, come in!’ But he knew that even if she were there he wouldn’t be able to hear her now.

‘They got us, big time,’ said Motti bitterly. ‘They got boats, they got a chopper –’

Patch flipped up his eye patch and pointed to his glass eyeball. ‘And I got this. A socket full of BANG. Maybe we can take ’em out!’

But then a second sleek copter swept up into sight beyond the railings and hovered alongside. It looked to Jonah like a Blackhawk or something, flown in from some hi-octane blockbuster. Only this was real – this was right here and now, on some godforsaken speck in an ocean of blackness, and Jonah wanted to bury his head and scream. Spotlights and rotors combined into a near-solid force, a hurricane of dust and whiteness pinning him to the wall. Then someone was grabbing his wrist and pulling him away.

It was Motti. Jonah saw Con and Patch ahead of him, pelting over the tangled deck for the stern. No chance of escape, no hope of safety. Just running into the dark like animals, the howling of the rotors like a monster’s hunting roar close behind. Too close. And growing louder.

As he ran, Jonah chanced a couple of backward looks. Squinting through the glare he saw a door in the side of the copter slide open. There were figures inside. Soldiers? The copter banked towards them. And beyond it, Jonah saw the first helicopter was rising up into the dark, swooping overhead, heading astern as if to try and cut them off.

He opened his mouth to warn the others, as if there was anything they could do. Then he heard a fresh hubbub ahead over the maelstrom of noise, saw fleet shadows rushing over the deck towards them and felt his heart bang fit to burst. The crew of the cargo ship was coming for them now, shrieking threats in broken English, still wielding their clubs and machetes.

'Take 'em!' Motti hollered, first to meet the mass of nimble bodies. He clubbed one aside with his baton, kicked another. Con dealt with one more, tossing him to the deck, using his chest as a springboard to leap on to a further two. One man got past her – the same man Jonah had fought before, a steel bar in one hand and hate in his eyes.

Already panting for breath, Jonah dodged a swing and landed a punch himself; throwing his whole body into the blow, he floored his opponent. 'Mot, maybe we can take them hostage!' he yelled wildly. 'Maybe we can deal?'

But Motti was looking past him. 'Patch!'

Jonah swung round. The Blackhawk was getting closer, hovering port side just above the safety rails – five or six men in gas masks and black jumpsuits jostling in the wide doorway, armed with automatics. Were they loaded with simulated ammo or the real deal?

But something looked to have snapped in Patch. He was screaming at the soldiers, his words lost in the gale as he reached under elastic and velvet and yanked out his glass eyeball. Jonah's heart caught in his throat: *He's going to do it, he's going to blow them out of the sky*. Patch drew his arm back to hurl his customised grenade –

But then he stumbled, lost his balance and fell on his side. The jolt of his landing knocked the eye bomb from his fingers. It rolled away towards the middle of the deck, vanishing from view amid a pile of rusting debris and oil drums barely fifteen metres away from where Jonah was standing.

'*Down!*' shouted Motti. Further aft there was a large cargo hatch, the cover of which protruded a half-metre from the deck. He grabbed Con and dragged her towards it.

Jonah started to run too, took a couple of steps and glanced back to check Patch was behind him. But Patch wasn't getting up. Jonah froze – how long was the timer, ten seconds? How many of those had passed already? Was the bomb even primed? Should he risk trying to find it and throw it overboard?

While the questions kept firing uselessly in his mind, Jonah sprinted back to where Patch lay between copter and bomb, flat on his back, clutching his leg. Now he saw the blood on Patch's hands, black as tar but flowing like milk from his shin.

'Shot!' Patch hissed through gritted teeth. 'Wax or not, they bloody hurt. Sorry, mate.'

Jonah said nothing, hauled Patch up by the armpits, started to drag him away. Rust kicked up around his ankles as the deck beside him was raked with gunfire. The men in the copter were still shouting, maybe warnings, maybe threats. Fresh adrenaline kicked in as Jonah quickened his step. But then the other copter overhead trained its lights on him, blinding him. It felt like bullets were whizzing everywhere. For a moment Jonah was disoriented, his thoughts racing faster than the gunfire. Was he staggering towards the bomb? How much time could there be left now?

'Quick, Jonah!' Patch yelled.

'We're gonna do this,' Jonah promised him.

But then Patch was jerked out of his arms by the impact of another bullet. The boy screamed as he slammed against the deck. Jonah stooped automatically to lift him up again.

'Can't make it,' sobbed Patch, tears streaking down his cheek as he looked up at Jonah. 'Sorry, mate.'

'I said, we're doing this!' Jonah shouted back at him.

'Come on, Jonah!' Motti's hoarse cry sounded close. Jonah looked behind him to his right and saw Motti crouched behind the cover of the hatch, just a few metres away.

Jonah hauled Patch to his feet. 'Lean on me,' he gasped. The light shifted and the drone of the copters upped urgently in pitch as they lifted into the air. The firing stopped. *They're getting out of range.* Patch slipped and stumbled again, fell to his knees. Jonah saw fresh blood on his friend's thigh and hip, felt his insides turn.

'Can't,' Patch panted. 'Can't . . .'

Jonah looked back, saw Motti scrambling up to help them. 'Jesus, geek, it's gonna –'

'*Go!*' Patch shoved Jonah hard in the chest.

Caught by surprise, Jonah staggered back and knocked into Motti. Both fell sprawling on to the hatch. Con reached up from hiding and grabbed for them. 'Patch!' shouted Jonah, as Con's fingers scrunched up skin and shirt and she heaved him over the lip of the hatch out of range of –

The explosion was colossal. Blood-red flames roiled up from the pile of oil drums and a wave of fierce heat beat across the deck. Jonah felt it searing his back. But inside he was frozen. *Patch?* Over the thunder of the blast and the heavy thrum of the copters above, he heard Con scream Patch's name as loudly as he was shouting it inside his head.

She started out from behind the hatch cover, choking as thick black fumes blew over her. The smoke and ash diffused the fierce white searchlights above, lent an unreal haze to the scene. *This isn't happening*, thought Jonah as he stumbled after Con to where a small, ragged figure lay sprawled and still on the deck. *We win. We always win.* The noise of the copters seemed hushed by the smoke, the light was growing fainter. Jonah realised dimly that one of the craft must be touching down. *Maybe we can still slip away in the smoke, if Patch isn't hurt so bad. Maybe –*

'You were too slow, man!' Motti seized Jonah by the shoulder and spun him round, furious. 'Why were you so damn slow!'

'You could've helped me sooner!' Jonah bawled back. 'You saw, he pushed me away, I couldn't help –'

'Shut up, both of you,' Con snapped. She was kneeling beside Patch, holding his gory hand. His tattered clothes had been black to begin with and hid most of the blood, but there was no hiding the burned mess of his face. He'd lost his eye patch along with most of his skin. He was shaking. His good eye flickered open and he tried to smile.

'You're OK?' Patch whispered.

'You're gonna be OK too,' Jonah insisted, crouching beside him.

'Flames again . . .' Patch coughed, and his face twisted with pain. '*Told* you that bloody grimoire thing was cursed. Bad luck . . .'

'We gotta get that leg elevated. Help stop the bleeding.' Motti jumped up, staring round frantically through the smoke, then pulled off his jacket, and tossed it at Jonah. 'I – I'll find something. You make a tourniquet. Con, you could maybe slip away before –'

She shook her head, kept hold of Patch's hand. 'I'd never make it.'

Jonah was pulling frantically at one of the filthy denim sleeves, trying to tear it into a bandage. 'Patch? Patch, listen, don't go to sleep. Stay with us.'

'Stay?' Patch was shaking harder. ''Course. Not gonna leave you.' His eye started to flicker shut. 'Not ever . . .'

'Come on, Patch,' Jonah begged him. 'Please, just –'

'*Look!*' With her free hand, Con frantically wrestled with her top. 'I'm going to take my bra off! Are you going to miss that? Well?' She sobbed, tears pouring down her face. 'Look at me!'

Patch tried to focus. 'Bloody hell, Con!' he breathed. But his gaze quickly flicked from her chest to her eyes and lingered there as he managed to smile. 'Now I know . . . I died and gone to heaven.'

His head rolled back.

'No, Patch!' Jonah shouted, leaning forward and

shaking him by the shoulders. 'Wake up! You can't –'

He broke off as Motti shouted out in pain somewhere close by. He stared into the smoke, trying to see – but then suddenly two dark figures in gas masks were looming over him. Another was already dragging Con away into the smoke.

'Get off me, you bastards!' she yelled. 'You did this! You did this!'

'Our friend needs help,' Jonah added, gasping with pain as his captors yanked his arms behind his back and cuffed his wrists. 'You've got to help him!'

'Oh, I think he's beyond help now, Jonah.' Another man breezed up to him out of the thick smoke like he was taking a stroll on a fine day. 'Pity. But at least we've secured the rest of you.'

'Wait . . .' Jonah stared in horror. This man wore no gas mask. He was wearing a *face* mask, brass with three twisted circles at the eyes and mouth. It was the man who had killed Sorin. The man from Nomen Oblitum. Jonah struggled desperately to break free. The man reached out with finger and thumb and pressed them carefully against Jonah's neck.

'Dim Mak,' the man explained, a slight Germanic edge to his voice. 'Sensationalists call it the black martial art of the "Death Touch" . . . but a more accurate translation might be "Touch Point".'

Jonah tried to speak, tried to move, but he could do neither. He couldn't even cry any more.

This isn't happening. Jonah could hear and see and fear, but he was trapped – a prisoner in his own body.

'Please, you must pardon my rudeness. This mask

doubles as a respirator, as well as providing a necessary disguise.' He pulled off the mask to reveal thinning black hair and a gaunt face; once-neat Asian features losing definition with age. Jonah had seen the man before in a photograph, taken long ago.

'I'm Karl Saitou,' said the man, smiling. 'Thanks to Coldhardt, I own you *and* your friends.' He was still smiling as he jabbed a knuckle into Jonah's wrist.

Then, like a plug had been pulled in Jonah's head, Saitou and everyone else were lost in blackness.

CHAPTER NINETEEN

I should be dead, thought Tye, waking up to find she couldn't move. For a moment she almost panicked; then realised she was in some kind of stretcher that held head and body rigid, the kind they used to lift people out of war zones. That would maybe fit with her hazy memories of a helicopter, carrying her through the darkness.

With her limited vision, Tye could see she was in some kind of cave. A hole in the rock wall was letting in daylight through thick metal bars. Outside she could hear the surge and hiss of the sea hammering the shore. The warm moistness in the air matched that in Zamboagna, so she didn't imagine she'd travelled far.

But Tye was imagining all kinds of other things as she lay there, wondering why she was still alive. She heaved out a sigh.

'Who's that?' came a sudden voice from the other side of the cave. 'Tye, is that –'

'Jonah?' Tye could've cried with relief. 'You're OK?'

'I think so.' There was a deadness to his voice that suggested otherwise. 'Where are we?'

'I don't know. I was attacked on the boat, Heidel got me. What happened to you – are the others here?'

'Coldhardt's been tricked,' said Jonah hoarsely. 'That can't be the real Heidel we met, whatever he thinks – and Nomen Oblitum's a fraud. The *Aswang* was empty, a lure to reel us in. Karl Saitou arranged the whole thing.'

'Saitou?' Tye tried to process the rush of information, as a cold sense of foreboding built inside her. 'Jonah, where are the others?'

'I – I don't know.' Emotion edged into his dull tones. 'There were helicopters, smoke . . . Con and Motti were taken away by men in masks, but Patch . . .'

'Patch?' Tye swallowed hard. 'What is it, Jonah?'

'Kendall is dead,' came a woman's voice as cold as the metallic echo that tinged it. Bree's voice. 'He bore the brunt of the blast of his own explosive.'

'No,' Tye whispered, as a key turned noisily and a metal door clanked open. 'No, he can't be. Jonah, tell her –'

'He . . . he was in a bad way,' said Jonah hoarsely. 'But if he's dead it's because her friends just left him there.'

Tye closed her eyes tight. God knew, she was no stranger to death, but . . . Patch? 'We were talking about the future, about his new eye, so many plans . . .' A sob wrenched its way past her twisting mouth. 'He was only fifteen,' she whispered. 'He *can't* be dead . . .'

'I'll give you a few minutes,' Bree muttered, stalking to the other side of the cell.

A few minutes? And then I'll be fine? Tye felt a pit of grief opening up in her chest, but as the minutes crawled she resolved to fill it instead with anger, with hate. She would keep her feelings from this bitch even if nothing else was within her power.

Bree walked up to Tye, peering down like a well-heeled doctor looking in on a patient. Her dyed blonde hair was scraped back, her composure studied and assured. *A formidable planner and analyst*, Coldhardt had called her.

'Your friend was talented, but the least important of your group,' Bree said coldly. 'I should point out that for all our posturing back at Blackland's fort, for all Sadie's runaway enthusiasm, we didn't want many of you dead. You're too valuable to us. Which is why, Tye, you were shot with a tranquilliser dart last night and nothing stronger.'

'Yeah, you wanted us alive.' Jonah snorted. 'That's why the crew came at us with clubs and machetes. Why Saitou shot the hell out of that cargo ship –'

'And Street, too. They are still working together, you know.' Bree walked out of Tye's field of vision towards Jonah. 'But our men fired plastic bullets, and the crew were ordered to take you alive if they could.' She paused. 'You were being covertly filmed from the moment you scaled the *Aswang*'s hull by night-vision fibre-optic cameras, threaded throughout the superstructure of the ship. I supervised the recording myself.' Tye could hear the leer in Bree's voice. 'And I must say, you all performed beautifully, overcoming the various obstacles we placed in your way.'

'Why record us?'

'Your talents are to be auctioned. Naturally prospective buyers will wish to view you in action.'

She crossed back to Tye. 'Don't feel left out. We'll be making a special presentation of your own talents.'

Tye's mind felt like mud, trampled by thoughts and fears and fresh revelations. 'Where are Con and Motti?' she demanded.

'Safe and snug in a cell of their own. We're on one of Saitou's islands in the Philippines, his private retreat, well away from the prying eyes of the world . . .' Bree looked back towards Jonah. 'I thought you two might enjoy a little time alone together. I know how the two of you pine for each other, even when under the same roof.'

Tye looked away, fighting to control her reactions – not to the pathetic jibes, what the hell did they matter? But she kept morbidly picturing poor Patch's body, lying all alone on that godforsaken deck. Tears were prickling the backs of her eyes but they were going to damn well *stay* there.

'Young love is so painful, isn't it?' Bree persisted.

'You don't know a thing,' breathed Tye.

Jonah sounded exhausted. 'Yes, she does. And there's only one way she *can* know. The same way she knew when we were boarding the *Aswang*, and where we planned to exit the hull.' His voice dropped lower. 'The dart Sorin shot me with didn't contain curare, did it?'

'No. Like Tye's, it was merely a tranquilliser,' she said matter-of-factly. 'While you slept, Saitou inserted a microtransmitter into you and that Maya girl, just beneath the skin. Then he performed in our staged little Nomen Oblitum drama as the Scribe's man-at-arms.' She smiled. 'We've been listening in to you regularly ever since. The implants convert speech into a digital signal that is recorded and then uploaded to an online decoder whenever a Wi-Fi system comes into range.'

Tye stared up at Bree. 'But . . . Coldhardt's doctor checked Jonah's and Maya's wounds. Said they were healing fine even though the darts *did* hold curare –'

'Dr Draith is working for me. For twice Coldhardt's fee, he will say whatever I want him to.' Bree sounded now like a teacher explaining something simple to a stupid child. 'You see, Saitou and Street have formed a consortium. A group of very different people all with something in common – the desire to put Coldhardt out of business permanently, and his empire into liquidation. They recruited me to work out the perfect way to do it.'

Tye should've felt outraged, but she just felt more numbness.

'So you hit upon using a Heidel lookalike?'

Bree smiled down at Tye, who stared rigidly back. 'We scoured half the world to find a man who was suitable in both looks and the right temperament for the part.'

'Someone who was a psychopath, you mean.'

Bree shrugged. 'Surgery enhanced his similarity to Heidel. Street and Saitou were on hand to coach him in the old man's little ways and mannerisms. And a professional voice coach worked wonders with the accent . . .'

'What about the hotel room? The stuff we took had Heidel's DNA all over it, how come your actor didn't leave bits of himself anywhere? The only other fingerprints on any of the stuff Coldhardt found were –'

'Hers,' said Jonah heavily.

'Our fake was never inside that hotel room.' Bree's eyes shone in the golden daylight from outside. 'I placed the material there myself. Dr Draith treated Heidel in the aftermath of Coldhardt's attack, you see, and inherited one or two personal belongings . . .'

'You knew Coldhardt would be after evidence that Heidel was for real,' Jonah reasoned. 'So you took the radio tag from the Guan Yin manuscript to draw Tye and the others to that hotel room.' He sounded so unengaged, as if his usual zeal to know the truth had died, as if this ordering of the information was purely down to force of habit. 'You knew they'd suspect a trap, so you gave them one – you put Sadie in the flat opposite.'

Bree smiled and nodded. 'Distracting you from the possibility of a far greater trap, waiting in the wings . . .'

Tye barely heard, still clinging on to her cold façade while swallowing back a knot of tears.

'You let Sorin be killed, you left Sadie to the police . . .' Jonah exhaled heavily. 'You don't give a damn who or what you sacrifice, do you?'

'It was imperative you believed yourselves to be ahead of the game,' Bree said calmly. 'When poor, talented young Sorin was killed, it sent a powerful message that Nomen Oblitum was not in league with Heidel. When you beat Sadie in London, there had to be visible consequences or you may have suspected a trick. When Heidel burnt a priceless original copy of the Guan Yin manuscript, you and Coldhardt took him and his agenda all the more seriously.' She gave that sickening smirk of triumph. 'And before you ask, yes of course we knew there were scans of the cipher backed up in Blackland's library. Heidel beat the knowledge out of him.'

'I suppose you would hardly have burnt the book without leaving us a lead to follow,' Jonah realised.

'Not after we already killed Professor Morell and blamed it on bungling kids, purely so his laptop could surface for sale on the open market,' Bree agreed. 'It was bait we knew Coldhardt could not refuse. Naturally Saitou knew the location of Blackland's manuscript would be contained in the laptop – Morell had emailed him the precise details the very night he died . . .'

'Clever.' Jonah sighed. 'But why kill Budd and Clyde in Los Angeles? To make Coldhardt think there were others after the manuscript, to rush him into sending us to Texas?'

'That's right,' Bree agreed. 'And Coldhardt's enthusiasm was much appreciated. It meant we didn't have to endlessly monitor Texan airfields for your arrival, ready to break into Blackland's fort ahead of you to present Heidel's premier performance.'

'You must have been so proud,' Tye muttered.

'Street and Saitou certainly were. Only five months of surgery and rehearsal and Heidel was ready to live again . . .'

Tye glared up at Bree. 'Except Street almost blew it when he wound up in our surveillance footage.'

'That was careless of me,' said a man in the doorway with a low, quiet Scottish accent. He joined Bree in standing beside Tye. She recognised him at once from the surveillance footage in London. Street waggled his fingers at her in a creepy little wave. 'I couldn't risk going after you myself to get the tape back, and the only alternative was to send a couple of try-outs hoping to get on my payroll.'

Tye nodded. 'And they messed up totally.'

'Happily, it made little difference to the way Coldhardt acted,' said Street coldly. 'If anything, the thought that his old partners might be banding together to attack made him pitch in with Nomen Oblitum sooner rather than later.'

'You see, Tye, I haven't been explaining all this to you and Jonah because I like the sound of my own voice,' said Bree, 'or because I need you to see how clever I am. I want you to grasp the situation entirely, so you know . . . so there can be no doubt at all . . . that it is not only we who have manipulated you.'

Tye found she was holding her breath as charged seconds passed, like the pause between thunder and lightning.

'Coldhardt knew that the *Aswang* was empty. He was sending you into a trap – because the Mage of Nomen Oblitum demanded he hand over his operatives as a gift.'

'No,' said Tye simply. 'He wouldn't.'

'The cost of consultation is three-fifths of his fortune, and the five of you were to be given as a gesture of faith,' Street stated. 'A down payment.'

Tye's mind darkened as she remembered Coldhardt's words in his last briefing: *'You are prized highly, and always shall be . . .' 'My gift will be found in the hold of a particular cargo ship . . .'* She closed her eyes. *I knew he was holding something back.*

'And Coldhardt is on his way here now. He thinks he'll be meeting with the real Nomen Oblitum . . .' Bree gave a smile of pure pleasure. 'Looks like you just can't trust anyone these days – doesn't it?'

CHAPTER TWENTY

Jonah, strapped tightly into his stretcher and gazing up at the ceiling, suddenly heard the metal door squeal open, wheels on the rocky floor, and the sudden stab of Tye's voice: 'Where are you taking me?'

'Tye!' Jonah shouted. *I'm not losing you too*. 'Tye, I'll find you.'

Street crossed to him, still all smiles and soft-spoken. 'That's very sweet. But you don't need to worry about her just yet. We want her input for the big moment – Coldhardt's momentous meeting with the members of Nomen Oblitum.'

'You mean Saitou in his fright mask and a bunch of actors?'

Street tutted. 'I'll have you know, my friend, that the Scribe was once a venerable man. He's a fallen priest from an occult Egyptian society.'

'I'd like to see him fall a lot further.'

'You don't believe much in magic, do you, Jonah?' Street leaned in closer. 'Not like your friend Maya. You know, she's gone very quiet since her cipherpunk partner upped sticks. She's just pottering about in Geneva.' His voice hardened a touch. 'You said in Zamboanga you were nearing a breakthrough with translating the Bloodline Cipher. What did you tell Maya in that internet café?'

Jonah looked up into Street's lined face and dark eyes. 'Of course, you heard the keys clicking but you don't know what we said . . .'

Street ignored him. 'My own experts have studied a secret copy of that manuscript for years and come up with nothing.'

'So the manuscript that the Scribe showed us was yours?'

'An inferior version to the one in Blackland's collection. It contains no appendix . . .'

Jonah tutted. 'So you can't even translate the first bit. Your experts are a bit useless, aren't they?'

'That's why I've had to recruit others.' Street smiled. 'This year we found a Russian occult specialist who gave us a bit of background detail on the Guan Yin manuscript. He blabbed that Nomen Oblitum possessed a copy, but he died before he could tell us much more.'

Maya's old tutor, Jonah realised dully. *The one who disappeared, never to be seen again.*

Street paused. 'You know, we spent a long time wondering how best to bait the Heidel trap. And when Morell let it be known that Blackland possessed the only other copy of the Guan Yin manuscript in existence, I knew it was the perfect lure.'

'You posed as NO men and used your knowledge of the manuscript to make Coldhardt believe you knew all its secrets.' Jonah smiled. 'But you never got beyond the title page that was cracked already, did you? Why not ask the real Nomen Oblitum? They exist – Maya knows of them. And the real Heidel was dealing with them thirty years ago . . .'

'No one can contact them,' Street murmured. 'They come to their potential subjects – just as our oh-so-venerable Scribe came to Coldhardt. Now come on, my friend, tell me what you've found out about the cipher. We'll get hold of the scans of the appendix and crack the code ourselves eventually, but why duplicate your own work? If the secret is worth something, maybe we could trade . . . ?'

'I'm making no deals with you.'

'Still loyal to your boss, eh? Still think we're the enemy?'

Jonah snorted softly. 'Why do you hate Coldhardt so much?'

Street's gaze drifted, as if he were seeing into the past. 'We were like brothers,' he said simply, 'with Heidel the big man guiding us, the head of the organisation. It was a good life back then, you know. Like a family, but bigger and better . . . stronger than any family I've ever known. We made a pact of blood, uniting us, come what may . . .' He smiled thinly, focused again. 'Well. Old laws or new, Coldhardt figured nothing was strong enough to bind him to a contract. Nothing was ever good enough. He turned on us all – killed Heidel, stole his fortune, destroyed his files, tried to take everything away from us. All that was ours by rights, all that we'd been promised for the future –'

'Oh, boo-hoo,' said Jonah.

'Coldhardt ran before we could kill him and he's been running ever since. Building up his empire, using the likes of you to do it. Making you feel like family. Exploiting you. But now we're taking back what's ours by rights.'

No guesses who wrote the speeches for the Heidel impersonator, Jonah thought.

Street looked down at him with compassion. 'I'm sorry things have to be this way, kid. I know how you must be hurting.'

'Maybe you could ease the pain by adopting me,' suggested Jonah. 'I'm sure that after I've forgiven you and your consortium for killing Patch we could be really close.'

'Nah, you'll have to go to the highest bidder. We have costs to recover.'

'I'm not for sale.'

'Coldhardt bought you with a single smokestone.' Street glared down at him. 'At least it's honest this way, Jonah. No dressing up the relationship as something it's not. You'll slave and steal for some rich son of a bitch and he'll see you all right.'

'And if I don't cooperate?'

'There are all kinds of implants.' His smile was chilling. 'Some can be made to hurt.'

Jonah looked away. 'I don't care what you do to me.'

'Which is why we're looking to auction you in twos – so the safety of one hinges on the good behaviour of the other. You and Tye could be together, doing what you do best for somebody new. Or you can sulk and say you won't, and Tye gets to learn what pain really means. Just think about it a wee while.' Street turned and walked away. 'Con and Motti are thinking about it already. They send you their regards.'

Jonah said nothing. The door in the wall slammed shut and the key turned behind him but he kept on struggling in the stretcher. He knew he couldn't afford to stop.

He and his friends were captured. Patch was dead. Coldhardt had sold them out. But no one was going to profit from today. No one would be scoring any victories.

He'd see these bastards burn first.

Tye was wheeled along in her stretcher by Bree, through an exquisite series of landscaped tunnels. It felt as though she were inside some enormous open-air temple, sculpted rather than built. The weather blew in through splits and holes in the tunnels, warm and fresh against the stone cool of the place. The crash of the sea, or a bright glimpse of shimmering blue, was never far away, and Tye supposed their path was following the coastline of the island.

She felt weirdly empty, but quite calm. It was like the scale of her grief had scared off her emotions, sent them all into hiding. Instead, in that numb inner landscape, the little things seemed magnified. She had an itch on her thigh she was desperate to scratch. She could smell her own sweat. Her mouth tasted sour, and she longed for the Tic-Tacs back in her hotel room at Zamboanga. Tye thought of her meagre belongings there. The staff would think they'd done a runner to get out of paying. They'd never know she could have bought that whole hotel if she'd wanted . . .

It was only then that her thoughts turned to all the things she had back in Geneva – the car, the yacht, the breathtaking view from her window. Stuff she would never see again.

And right now all she wanted was some mouth-wash and Jonah's hand to hold.

That and Patch back.

Her thoughts shied from Coldhardt.

It was because of him Patch was dead.

And yet Patch had stayed with Coldhardt because of Tye, and Jonah, and Motti and Con – because of family. So maybe they all shared in the guilt. Each of them had faced death so many times; it came with the job, they each went into it with their eyes open. *Like soldiers*, she supposed. *You just never, ever really think it will happen to you . . .*

Like when you love someone and think it will last for ever. But then it doesn't, and your whole world splits apart.

'I will see you again,' Coldhardt had told them, so definite as they left. She'd actually found it comforting at the time. But all the time he'd meant he'd see them here, locked up and ready for auction.

'Ah. Here is our living lie detector.'

Tye recognised the voice of Heidel – the impostor. Bree stopped pushing and a moment later the old man's head appeared, looming over her. She saw his eyes were no longer rheumy, they were clear. Trick contact lenses, she supposed, to make him seem way older than he could've been.

When Heidel spoke again, the voice was a little higher and softer – his real voice, presumably. 'You know, you hurt me when you threw me over your shoulder on the boat.'

Just leave me alone, thought Tye, wishing she could itch, trying to concentrate on the smash of the sea on the rocks outside. Such a beautiful, fresh sound.

'Perhaps I should exact some recompense for your actions now,' Heidel persisted, 'while you're so very helpless.'

'If it's any consolation, I've beaten myself up already,' said Tye languidly. 'I should have seen sooner who was the boss and who was the lackey. When we faced off at Blackland's, it was Bree who took all the real decisions, Bree who refused to hand over the gun . . . It was even Bree that you looked to when you said it was time to go – like you were getting approval.'

'Not so stupid, are you, Tye?' Bree smiled. 'It's one thing to find an impostor who not only resembles your chosen subject, but who can take on their character . . . it's quite another to find one prepared to threaten, maim and kill for money. I think we can forgive our Heidel a slight lack of leadership qualities. And I think your people-watching talents make you the most dangerous of your little gang by far.'

'You know, it's very liberating, committing acts of violence in character,' said Heidel. 'You can just walk away and tell yourself someone else did it.'

You're not going to just walk away from this, Tye thought. *Just give me one tiny chance to get even . . .* 'I suppose you didn't need to stay in character by the time you got on our boat,' Tye noted. 'The real boss would never have come out to the front lines.'

'Your ex-boss is on his way to the front lines right now,' Bree reminded her. 'Which is why we need that keen eye of yours.'

'Are you taking her to the inner sanctum now?' Heidel asked.

'Tag along, if you like,' Bree offered. 'Prepare for your big entrance.'

With a lurch, Tye was off again, wheeled through the labyrinth of rock. Primitive paintings had been daubed on the ceilings, showing curly waves outlined in red, huge crimson sunflowers and figures with spears. They looked ancient, but were probably as fake as everything else in this set-up.

Then suddenly dark rock gave way to piercingly blue sky as the latest tunnel gave on to an outdoor arena, as large as a tennis court but with high, circular walls. A kind of balcony ran around the perimeter, ten metres or so above ground level, gouged from the solid rock, affording onlookers a better view than the one Tye had, pinioned and flat on her back.

She craned her neck to take in her surroundings. A wicker throne had been constructed at the rear of the arena, flanked by a smaller seat on either side. Water had collected in a natural sinkhole in the middle of the floor, where petals and lily pads floated serenely. Three smaller tunnels branched away from the arena, roughly aligned with each of the three seats. The place had the calm and gentleness of a temple about it.

Tye wondered how long that would last.

'Where will you put her?' asked Heidel.

'Saitou will decide,' said Bree. 'It's his show. I'm just the one who makes it happen.'

There were some people milling about by the sheer walls, dressing certain cracks and crannies with festoons of flowers bound into Knots of Isis, like they were adding detail to a movie set for filming.

Suddenly, Tye heard Street's voice from some way off, calling Bree over. She strained to hear their conversation.

'. . . they say the *Aswang*'s cameras picked up a man moving about the wreckage there, on deck,' Street reported.

'Pirate scout, most probably,' Bree responded. 'Or a looter.'

'The captain had gathered up the bodies of the dead and injured, but this bandit boarded and . . .'

Heidel came to stand beside Tye. 'I wonder who'll bid for you?' he said. 'Wonder where you'll end up?'

Shut up, she thought, trying to listen to Bree.

'. . . Coldhardt shows, he'll be scanned for weapons,' the bitch was saying, 'and once he's escorted here . . .'

But Heidel kept speaking over her. 'Do you suppose your new employers will keep you chained up like a dog on a leash, hmm?'

Impatiently, Tye turned on him. 'I hope the real Heidel was better at intimidation than you are,' she said. 'You're the kind of thug who kills an old man with a baseball bat. That doesn't make me afraid. Just makes me want to kick your ass.'

Heidel sneered down at her and patted her tightly bound ankle. 'That I'd like to see.'

So would I, thought Tye dismally.

'Ah, so the players begin to arrive.'

The voice was deep and close by, and sounded faintly

German. Tye heard sandals slap on the rock, heard a gull clatter away from a high perch in the wall. Then an aging Asian man with windblown dark hair in a black tracksuit came into her line of vision. She recognised Karl Saitou from the photograph back in the hangout, but he had definitely gone to seed. He looked at Bree and his smile seemed a little too big for his face; a face that had grown gaunt and sunken, like someone had stuck a straw up beneath his chin and sucked hard.

'Is she behaving?' he asked. 'Will she do it?'

'I thought I'd let you explain what we want,' Bree demurred.

'Well, Tye, it's pretty simple . . .' He looked down at her with the kind of smile a company boss might give the mail worker. 'Coldhardt's coming here shortly for what he believes will be his first full consultation with Nomen Oblitum . . . his first steps towards extending his lifespan.'

'Oh, the irony,' chimed Bree.

Saitou nodded happily. 'He's bought into the whole deal; he's already delivered you as a down payment. But naturally the cost of treating him will be far higher. You remember that enamelled gold ring of Coldhardt's that you stole from Sadie's finger and took back home?'

She didn't bother to reply.

'Well, we were kind of hoping you would do that.' His grin almost split open his face, and Tye wished she could give it a hand. 'That ring now contains another of our miniaturised chip-implants – one that uses wireless tech to invisibly splice itself into a local computer network. Being inside the hub, it can bypass all firewalls and external security, and we can access it remotely to get to anything stored on Coldhardt's network – his bank accounts, property deals, contacts worldwide . . .' He slapped a jovial hand down on her shoulder. 'And all thanks to you, girl! You took the bait . . . and placed it right where I wanted it.'

'She's a bloody liability.' Heidel chuckled. 'No wonder Coldhardt wanted rid of her.'

Tye refused to react, looking past their stupid laughing faces to the epic circle of blue sky above, the scrapes of white cloud blowing across it.

'OK, Tye, now here's the deal,' Saitou went on. 'You should know that we're going to play a little joke here today. It's beautiful. We've gathered together everyone who's been a part of this, everyone who's put up funds to take Coldhardt down . . .' He gestured to the balcony. 'And, suitably disguised, they're going to watch his downfall, here in my temple.'

'You see, Coldhardt believes it's Nomen Oblitum's headquarters,' Bree put in. 'He will be escorted in and presented to the Scribe, his man-at-arms –'

'That's me by the way,' said Saitou.

'– and the Mage . . . who will turn out to be none other than Heidel.'

'Can you imagine the look on Coldhardt's face?' Saitou guffawed. 'The humiliation?'

Now Tye looked at him. 'You've been waiting, like, thirty years to play a schoolboy prank?'

'To destroy Coldhardt.' Saitou's face had suddenly drained of humour. 'Same way he destroyed our organisation, our way of life. He killed the boss, siphoned off the funds for himself, and disappeared.'

He towered over her, dark eyes narrowing, spittle flecking his lips as his speech got hoarser. 'I've waited so long to get back at him. Spent decades studying the highest martial arts, made myself better and stronger than he could ever be. I've spent years tracking his activities, gathering allies from the people he's trampled over, waiting for the perfect opportunity to reel him in, and now I've finally got him.' He mimed gripping something with both hands, a throat maybe. 'Got him to dispose of as I choose.'

Tye stared up at Saitou and was surprised to feel a trace of pity. *Could that be me in thirty years*, she thought, *eaten away by the life I've led, nothing left but the need to hate?* She thought of Patch, who would stay young in her mind now, unchanging, for ever. The tears lumped up in her throat again.

'I want you to watch the whole thing, Tye,' Saitou snapped fiercely, 'because when I'm finished humbling Coldhardt, when I've brought him down as far as he can go, I'm going to ask him if he's sorry – if he's truly ashamed for all that he's done. And you will know if he's telling the truth, and you will tell me.' He put his hand to the side of her neck. 'If you don't . . . if I think you're lying to try to protect him . . . this is a taste of the kind of pain I can give you and your friends.'

He flicked the skin of her neck with one finger, and twisted his thumb against the basc of her skull. Tye gasped as a wave of crippling cramp seemed to sear through her entire body. She started to convulse, unable to control the pain, unable to do anything, even find breath to scream. *This is why I'm strapped down so tight*, she realised. *So they can do this.*

The ordeal screamed on, and Tye realised she must have blacked out for a few moments. When she came to, she felt like someone had stuffed her skin full of tinder and set fire to it. Her cheeks were wet with tears, and her lip was gashed where she must have bitten it. But Saitou was still hovering over her. He smiled and leaned in, whispering like a doting father to his swaddled baby.

'Just a taste,' he said.

CHAPTER TWENTY-ONE

Jonah had managed to worm his hand into his jeans pocket, and his fingers closed around the cigarette lighter he'd collected from the Filipino guard on the *Aswang*. He manoeuvred it out again, and held the head of the lighter against the swaddling straps. He felt for the flints, trying to move his thumb enough to strike a flame.

As escape attempts went, he reflected, this one was stupidly unsafe. He knew he might be horribly injured in the process, or even die. But after what he'd been through, and the promise of what lay ahead, life wasn't something he was fussed about clinging to that tightly.

What about Tye? What will she do if you're gone?

But it was because of her – and Motti and Con – that he had to take the chance. Sooner rather than later.

The flints scraped under his thumb tip, but didn't catch. He tried again. This time, he felt the heat of a flame. Almost immediately it became unbearable, burning his fingers. He gasped, tried to wriggle them away, down to the underside of the lighter, but in the enclosed space, the flame was forced down by the fabric, singeing the back of Jonah's hand and his hip. He wanted to scream out in pain – but knew any noise would bring the guards running and end things there and then.

He saw smoke start to curl from the stretcher fabric, and a point of smouldering brown grow slowly wider. But he wasn't sure how much longer he could keep his mouth clamped shut. His thigh was being flame-grilled. He gritted his teeth, breathed in shallow puffs. He smelled fabric burning.

It's the stretcher. It's not my jeans, no way. Please, God, this will work, oh Christ, oh Jesus –

A moan escaped his lips as the pain grew sharper, fiercer. Tears leaked from his screwed-up eyes. It was like the bones in his hip and thighs had trapped the scorching heat inside them.

Then full flames crackled up from the stretcher material, orange and smoky. Jonah tried to stifle his moaning scream, bucking with his body, frantically trying to bring up his arm, praying he could tear through the burning fabric before the flames could spread any further. He swore and sobbed, eyes wide with terror, until the fabric ripped and he freed his lower arm. He flapped it about, trying to put out the flame, straining every muscle to tear free.

Finally the burning fabric ripped again, enough for him to wriggle most of his arm out. From there he feverishly hauled himself from out of the fiery shroud and tumbled off the trolley, falling to the rocky ground. Then he saw that his jeans *had* caught fire, and he rolled over and over, trying to extinguish the flames. He splashed into a puddle of stagnant rainwater that had collected beneath the open window. The shock of the cold water felt even worse for a moment, but at least the flames were put out. He tugged off his smoking jeans, losing his Nikes in the process, and used them to beat at the flames on the stretcher until they were dead too. Then he slumped back to the shallow puddle and lay in it, the stench of burned flesh, hair and fabric hanging in the air with the thick smoke, like the big question – *what now?*

It was tempting to lie just where he was, but Jonah realised the grille in the cell door had no glass, and that the smoke would soon seep out to alert a guard. He checked his leg. A large patch of skin was sticky red and blistered and incredibly painful. He thought of Patch, and he thought of the flames that followed the Guan Yin manuscript.

But this time the fire had actually brought good luck. *Maybe things are on the up*, Jonah thought without much enthusiasm.

Gingerly he pulled his jeans back on with blistered hands, ripping a hole in the charred denim so it didn't chafe his burns so badly, then pulled on his shoes and crossed to the grille in the door. The smoke was hanging in a thick pall – he only hoped that it was thick enough for what came next.

'Help!' he yelled, jumping on the stretcher and pulling the fabric over him. 'Fire! There's a fire!'

A startled Filipino man appeared at the grille, then bent to unlock the door. As he did so, Jonah rolled off, got behind the trolley and charged forward. The door was pushed open – and the guard took a high-velocity trolley to the chest, crying out as he flew backwards and cracked his head against the bare rock wall behind him.

Jonah pushed the trolley aside and grabbed the guard, dragging him inside the cell. If this were a movie, he thought, the guard's outfit would make the perfect disguise. But even if Jonah hadn't been blond and pale-skinned, this guy was a foot shorter and skinnier all over. 'Suppose they'll just have to take me as I am,' he muttered.

Once he'd tied the guard's wrists with his leather belt and gagged him with his socks, Jonah hefted him on to the trolley and took his keys. So far, so good. He hadn't injured himself too badly, and was now at large in some weird open-air prison complex, trapped on an island someplace with no way off.

It's a start, he thought. Cautiously he went off to find his friends.

Forgotten for now beneath the balcony of stone, Tye lay helpless, tired and sore on her stretcher trolley. The place was beginning to fill up, and there was a definite air of anticipation. Saitou was talking to Bree, who was wielding a clipboard, presumably ironing out any last-minute hitches while managing to flutter her eyelids. Yeah, Bree was definitely a bit sweet on Saitou, Tye decided.

The aging Scribe was smoking a fag, kicking his feet on the intricate main throne. Heidel was handing crimson cloaks to those who wished to view from the gallery as supposed members of Nomen Oblitum. Those who did not appreciate such frivolity, or who did not wish to mix with others, were invited to view the spectacle from a TV suite elsewhere in the complex – Bree was televising the event as she recorded it for posterity. There would most probably be a special DVD of the day's events for guests to buy on their way out – or thrown in for free if they bid for one of Coldhardt's children at auction.

Bree walked over to Tye, and clicked her tongue, mock sympathetic. 'You must be very uncomfortable, trussed up like that.'

Tye was getting good at not reacting. She stared straight ahead.

'My dilemma is this, Tye. I can't have you watching Coldhardt on that trolley. You would be seen. All our careful planning would be wrecked. And yet if I let you stand unrestrained, you may attempt to disrupt the stage-management of our little event.' She sighed. 'So what am I to do with you?'

Again, Tye made no response – but when Bree produced a knife and slashed along the length of her surgical shroud, she couldn't help but flinch. The movement caused her pain, she felt sluggish and stiff; as if her circulation had given up and the blood congealed in her veins. But Bree was motioning her to get off the trolley.

'You will stand on the balcony with the others,' Bree explained, 'disguised in an acolyte's cowl. And you will study Coldhardt's sincerity.'

'I was studying Saitou earlier.' Tye put on a smirk. 'Doesn't know you're alive, does he, Bree?'

Bree shook her head, apparently amused. 'You think a gutter girl like you can manipulate *me*?'

She shrugged. 'I think a gutter girl like me would

make Saitou hotter than a prissy bitch like you ever will.'

There was just the tiniest flicker of annoyance in Bree's eyes, but it was worth silver and gold to Tye. 'You're tolerated, because you're worth cash to this enterprise,' Bree said coldly. 'But don't feel too smug. Because we value our investments, you'll be the sole charge of one of my special security people. I can rely on her not to tolerate indiscipline . . . and so can you.'

Bree turned towards the mouth of one of the tunnels, and nodded. Tye felt her heart cannon as she saw the familiar figure striding towards her. Black, spiky hair, a porcelain-pale face darkened with bruises and make-up, staring brown eyes . . .

'Sadie,' Tye breathed.

'Would you believe she only killed one person while breaking out of police custody?' Bree lowered her voice confidentially. 'And while she always knew she had to throw that fight with you in the flat, I believe it's left her feeling slightly resentful. You will be careful, Tye . . . won't you?'

Tye didn't answer. Sadie snapped her teeth at her, and gave a smile as tight as an executioner's noose.

'There's not long to go now,' said Bree. 'And then show time can begin.'

Jonah couldn't decide whether to celebrate or curse his luck, as he limped through the tunnels. He couldn't see any security cameras anywhere – but then, he hadn't seen any on the *Aswang* either. Whatever, it seemed inevitable he would get caught. And so far he hadn't found Motti and Con – or Tye.

One room showed promise. It was locked, and looked empty besides some shelves with food and drinks supplies. But he had to be sure the people he cared for weren't in there.

Quickly finding the right key on the ring he'd taken from the guard, Jonah crept inside. No one was here, but he did clock a discarded stretcher trolley in the corner. From the dirt and bloodstains, it had seen use recently. Perhaps he was on the right track – perhaps Tye had come this way?

Jonah took a deep breath. He knew that the longer he wandered the tunnels, the more likely it was he would be caught. And the fear he felt suggested to him quietly on some level that perhaps he wasn't as ready to chuck his life away on some mad, final gesture after all.

'What else can I do?' he muttered, not wanting to be seduced by reason.

What the hell use is reason in a life like mine, he thought, sitting down on a box. It sagged under his weight – not as sturdy as he'd imagined. He peered inside – and found a crimson robe, like the one he'd seen the Scribe wear in Chamonix. If he wandered the corridors dressed in this, he might still get nowhere – but at least he wouldn't stand out so much . . .

Jonah sighed as he struggled into the vestment. 'That's one up to reason,' he supposed.

But as he rose, ready to resume the search, he heard movement in the passage outside – measured, confident footsteps clopping on the rock. He stole quietly over to the door and peered out through the grille.

A jolt went through Jonah as he saw Coldhardt

coming. The old man looked suave and assured in a sharp black suit and a pale blue shirt, open at the neck. He was carrying a stunning bouquet of exotic white orchids in his arms, the beautiful flowers strung on long slender stalks, like ice to the fire of the crimson-robed guards escorting him.

I could kill him, thought Jonah suddenly. *Cheat Saitou and Street of their moment of glory. Break his neck for what he's done to us.*

He remembered Sadie bursting in to kill Budd and Clyde without hesitation, right in front of him. The memory led to one of him seeing Tye in Geneva after the killings in LA. '*I'm never gonna be cut out for this life*,' he'd reflected back then, '*am I?*' All that was half a world away . . . and what felt like half a lifetime ago.

No one ever knew what was round the next corner. You just had to keep going and find out.

Letting himself back out of the cell, Jonah trailed after his former boss with his heart well into his mouth. Whatever lay ahead, he felt a reckoning for them both was soon on the cards – either in this world, or the next.

Tye stood on the balcony in her disguising crimson cowl, her hands cuffed behind her back, the hood hanging down over her features. She was grateful for it – it was like wrapping herself up in a cocoon, a place where she could hide away from reality. But the cold prod of Sadie's crossbow pistol in her back kept finding her.

The low drone of chatter whispered around the

arena like flies. Tye thought she recognised some of the faces here today, gathered in the sunshine spilling down from the window of blue sky above. It seemed such an unassuming day; Tye had been expecting the sky to fall in around them at any moment, or jagged bolts of lightning to strike them all down. Instead there was the salt-fresh tang of the sea in the air, the sun warming her robes, and the cold scent of lilies in their strewn piles of purple and gold. They might be tied in the shape of the Knot of Isis, but Tye knew the old significance of the shades from her upbringing. They were funeral flowers.

Coldhardt will never admit he's sorry, Tye thought nervously. *He'll never give them the satisfaction.* So what would Saitou do to him? How swiftly would the beautiful arena become a coliseum, the crowd baying for blood, the big emperor turning down his thumb as they threw Coldhardt to the lions . . . ?

Then suddenly Bree ran out into the middle of the circle, standing beside the sinkhole of water in magnificent crimson robes of her own. She held up her hands and the chatter in the gallery died down, the features of the onlookers fell away into folds of fabric as cowls were adjusted.

Bree quickly disappeared again into the mouth of one of the tunnels. Tye felt her stomach lurch as the Scribe rose from his chair, as Saitou donned his bronze face mask, as Heidel wrapped himself in dark blue and black silks and took his place in the Mage's throne, ready to make his shock guest appearance when cued.

This was it.

Coldhardt was about to arrive at his own funeral.

Jonah had lost track of Coldhardt and his escort in the labyrinth of tunnels, together with all sense of which paths he had already taken. His leg was so painful he could barely stay standing. His fear of discovery was growing more pronounced with every painful step.

Suddenly Jonah jumped at the sound of strange music starting up, an atonal blast of pipes. He realised it was coming from a room further along the passage. The temple chic was made a little homelier here – a rich red carpet had been put down, and the tunnel walls were plastered white in thick, artisan sweeps.

Disguising his limp, trying to act as if he had every right to be here, Jonah ventured inside the room. It was like entering the back of a small, dimly lit cinema. Rows of plush seats, most of them occupied by maybe fifteen suited and booted guests, faced a huge high-definition TV screen that was even bigger than the one back home (he caught himself with a grimace – *the one back at Coldhardt's base, you mean*). The screen showed a front-on view of a rocky amphitheatre. A miniature pool sat in its centre, and three thrones stood towards the rear. Jonah didn't know who the figure was in blues and blacks sitting on the biggest chair, but he felt a shiver as he saw the Scribe sitting to its left and Saitou, in his dark robes and bronze mask, on the right. Acolytes were looking down on the flower-strewn scene from a balcony stretching almost clear around the arena. The music was coming through the TV's speakers, lifelike in its fidelity.

A guard in red robes like Jonah's stood near the

front of the room beside a buffet table loaded with drinks and food, but his attention was fixed on the screen in rapt silence, as was everyone else's – no one turned as Jonah stepped cautiously closer and leaned against one of the high-backed chairs for support. These people must be guests of Saitou's, he realised. They could make good hostages, bargaining pieces to get back his friends . . .

But before he could even begin to work out a plan he saw Coldhardt appear on-screen with his guards and flowers, striding into view from beneath the camera – it must be fixed above a main doorway. Jonah seemed alone in his startled reaction – his fellow audience members didn't move or whisper, they just sat grimly in their chairs as if poised for some catastrophe.

The music stopped. Jonah could only see the back of Coldhardt's head and wondered what expression sat now on the craggy face. A look of triumph, of goals accomplished? Would there be even the faintest trace of remorse?

Jonah watched, his nerves tightening, as the robed figure sat to the left of the big throne shucked off his hood. It was the Scribe, and now he rose slowly to greet Coldhardt. 'You stand in the temple of Isis, the light of the goddesses,' he began, the rocky arena sweeping his deep, halting tones up to the sky. 'At her will, the planets of the air, the wholesome winds of the seas and the silences of hell are disposed. Do you praise Isis?'

'I praise her,' Coldhardt responded, still clutching his flowers.

'Do you embrace the wisdom and purity of the

goddess Guan Yin,' boomed the Scribe, 'do you feel her thousand arms around you?'

'I feel them,' Coldhardt returned, stooping to place the flowers at his feet. 'And I offer her orchids, "the plant of the king's fragrance".'

The Scribe nodded as if satisfied. 'And do you welcome the healing touch of Hiiaka, kind friend and fierce warrior . . .'

They're winding him up, ready to blow him out the water, Jonah realised. He felt conflicted – a part of him couldn't shake the old thinking that he should race to help Coldhardt and stand by him in there, the other part was saying '*Watch him suffer. Watch him fall.*' Jonah thought of Patch's body lying sprawled on the charred deck, thought of how it had felt to imagine he finally belonged somewhere, how all that had been changed and taken. He felt his nose start to run and tears scalding the backs of his eyes. *Can't do this,* he thought dismally, *can't do any of this*.

Too late he realised the guard at the table had turned to regard him. Before Jonah could react, the robed figure burst into life and charged towards him, arms outstretched, fingers clawing for his face.

CHAPTER TWENTY-TWO

The hands yanked at Jonah's cowl, pulling away his disguise. Jonah grabbed hold of the bony wrists, twisted them aside.

'Jonah, it's me!' protested a voice beneath the cowl.

He stared, let go of her wrists. '*Maya?*'

She pulled off her own hood and beamed, her fine red hair in disarray. 'Nice disguise,' she said, embracing him tightly. 'We really do think alike, don't we?'

Jonah broke free of her grip, turning to the people in their seats and backing off, expecting a real fight on their hands. But still no one moved, just slumped there staring at the screen.

'They'll sleep for some time,' said Maya briskly. 'I'd just taken care of them when you showed up. I thought you were a real guard till I saw your trainers.'

'What did you use?' asked Jonah.

'A kind of knock-out gas – odourless, invisible – a cocktail of halothane and fentanyl, most likely. Motti had a small canister with him.'

'He must have taken it from that booby-trap on board the *Aswang*,' Jonah muttered. 'So he escaped? Is Con with him?'

'I set them both free,' Maya assured him. 'Now

they're looking out for Coldhardt.'

Jonah stared at her, suddenly suspicious. 'How the hell did you get in here, anyway?'

Maya gestured to the big screen – Saitou and the Scribe were skirting the circular pool in different directions to converge on Coldhardt. 'That sinkhole is connected to a nearby cave. A tough swim, but an excellent means of access when you're not expected.' She shrugged. 'I found Motti and Con quite quickly, but I didn't see you and Tye.'

'Tye was taken away, and Patch has – well, Patch is . . .' He glowered. 'Hang on, when you say Motti and Con are looking out for Coldhardt, d'you mean they're trying to find him or trying to protect the old bastard?' The words fell out of Jonah's mouth in a gabble. 'After what he did to –'

Maya put a hand over his mouth. 'Just two things you need to know, Jonah,' she said, quietly and urgently. 'First of all, Patch is in a bad way but he's *not* dead. Not yet, anyway.'

Jonah stared. Time seemed to stand still in the air about him. 'Not dead?'

'You saved him. You and Con.'

'We *what* –?'

As his mouth started to flap open she closed it with her palm. 'And the second thing you need to know?' She looked at him, something hard and glinting in her eyes. 'This is such a long way from being over. Now, *move*.'

Tye stared down at Coldhardt as the litany of goddesses and demi-goddesses to whom he had to swear service finally ended. She wanted to look away; it was like waiting for a car crash you knew was going to happen. But whenever she looked down, the jab of Sadie's bolt in her back forced her eyes back to the drama unfolding in the arena.

'Now, Coldhardt,' the Scribe announced, 'in the presence of our brethren, in the gaze of scholar and novice alike, let it be known you have made a great gift to our Mage.'

'I have fulfilled that which was asked of me,' said Coldhardt simply. Tye searched his face for any flicker of emotion. Nothing.

'Your gift has been well received.' The Scribe paused impressively and smiled. 'And now the Mage shall receive you . . .'

An absolute hush seemed to descend on the arena; the audience holding their breaths, the birds wheeling away into the deep sky, even the sea seeming to calm in anticipation.

What was that the Scribe had just said, she thought dumbly, her own heart thumping in her throat? *The silences of hell are disposed.*

Saitou, still safely disguised in mask and costume, remained seated in his chair as Heidel rose from the throne and stepped slowly forward, walking round the periphery of the sinkhole towards Coldhardt, head bowed beneath the blue hood to conceal his face, his dark silks brushing the floor.

'Kneel,' the Scribe commanded. 'Avert your eyes.'

Coldhardt did as he was bid, sinking to his knees slowly and carefully.

Heidel let the silks hiding him fall away. Then he cleared his throat.

As Coldhardt looked up, Heidel kicked him in the jaw and knocked him sprawling on to his back. There was a breathless pause as the sight sank in, then someone started drily to applaud. Tye stared around, disgusted, as the lone clap was taken up and suddenly everyone in the gallery was joining in, clapping, jeering, laughing. Coldhardt stared round in confusion, a trickle of blood leaking from the side of his mouth. His two guard escorts pulled automatic weapons from beneath their robes and trained them at his head.

Saitou held up his arm for silence, and reluctantly the crowd piped down. Tye watched Coldhardt down there, looking suddenly pathetic, and wanted so much not to care. She'd always believed the whole world lied to you, and yet she'd been so desperate to be proved wrong. Coldhardt had become her world, but he'd turned his back on her and the others. So screw him. He'd made this bed of nails for himself, now he could just lie on it, get what was coming. And yet despite it all, still she wanted to run to him, to fend off the jackals and vultures, to help him escape.

The only thing that stays the same is that everything must change, she'd thought, that perfect picnic day. But some things didn't change easily.

'Heidel?' she heard Coldhardt whisper, the arena amplifying the slightest breath. 'How did you . . . what does this . . . ?'

Saitou crossed to join the Scribe and Heidel, facing Coldhardt as he knelt among his scattered orchids. 'I'm glad you're on your knees,' he announced. 'My friends and I have waited a very long time for this moment.'

'Karl?' As the mask came off, for a few moments Coldhardt stared up in naked astonishment at his former associate. Then he seemed to recover himself, forcing a small, resigned smile to his face. 'The man-at-arms in Chamonix. It was you . . . *You* killed the boy, Sorin.'

'That's right.' Saitou let the mask slip to the floor with a clatter, and smiled like the cat who'd got the cream. 'You are on my island. It belongs to me – not to some shadowy, crackpot cult.'

'And so this is an impostor . . .' Coldhardt stared at Heidel. 'And yet I tested your belongings, your fingerprints . . .'

'Genetic detritus from thirty years ago.' Saitou could barely contain himself. 'Your doctor was Heidel's doctor too, remember? And such an old hoarder, kept a souvenir of all his patients . . . He was very cooperative in helping us create the illusion.' He stabbed a finger up at someone on the balcony opposite Tye. 'Weren't you, Draith?'

Tye saw Draith reluctantly pull back the folds of his gown to reveal his drawn, bony face, like a tortoise poking its head from its shell.

'*Et tu*, doctor?' Coldhardt stared up and around at his surroundings as if seeing them for the first time. Then he smiled – but it seemed to Tye the smile of a little man trying to be bigger, of a fool trying to save face. 'So. All a trick. I really must hand it to you, Karl – it's a brilliant, meticulously planned set-up.'

'I'm glad you appreciate it,' said Saitou. He gestured again to the balcony. 'It's taken a lot of people a good deal of time and investment to make it work.'

'And how delightfully barbaric of you to invite them to join you for the kill.' Some of the people on the balconies had removed their disguises, clearly revelling in seeing Coldhardt so cut down to size, and wanting him to see who had helped make it possible. 'Well, well . . . All the old faces.' Coldhardt held up a hand to his enemies in salutation, and this time his smile was wider, stronger. 'I detect Bree Matthews' organisational flair in this, do I not?'

'Mine too.' David Street swaggered out from the tunnel to Coldhardt's right, Bree following on a couple of steps behind. 'Payback's been a long time coming, Coldhardt. You cheated us.'

Coldhardt tried to rise. 'I never cheated either of –'

'Shut up.' Saitou kicked him this time, the point of his boot cracking against Coldhardt's ribs. '*We're* speaking.' Tye winced as Coldhardt fell hard again on to the rocky ground. She looked away but Sadie hissed warningly in her ear, pressed the point of her bolt hard up against Tye's spine.

Bree held back, observing as Street took his place between Saitou and Heidel. He looked sweaty and edgy, not quite all there. 'You cheated us, Coldhardt. I'm not talking about Heidel's money or contacts, none of that crap. You cheated us of *family*.'

Coldhardt shook his head feebly. 'No.'

'Yes.'

Without warning, Street pulled a handgun from his pocket, jammed it to the side of Heidel's head and jerked on the trigger. Tye gasped as the bang thundered round the arena, as blood spattered into the sinkhole and Heidel's body collapsed to the ground.

She shut her eyes, willed herself not to be sick. The crowd wasn't laughing now. A heavy silence had fallen over the amphitheatre.

Street hadn't even bothered to watch what he'd done, too busy glaring at Coldhardt. Tye focused on Coldhardt too. He was still kneeling on the floor, his face bloody but his eyes bright.

'Was that how easy it was for you, thirty-two years ago?' Street shouted, spraying spit in Coldhardt's face. 'Bang, bang, you're dead, move along? The man who pulled us out of the gutter, who had faith in us . . . A bloody genius who made us better than we ever could have been . . .'

He ranted on, and whispers started up again around the gallery. Tye saw Bree swap looks with Saitou and the Scribe, caught the unease in her face. She got the impression that killing Heidel hadn't been part of the plan. Street had gone off-script, he was ranting like a maniac.

'. . . so you tell me, Coldhardt,' Street raged on, 'you ever learn to live with yourself? You ever look back and feel good for what you did?'

Coldhardt stared back at him, his voice measured, eyes placid. 'To be honest, Street, I'm wishing I'd killed you when I had the chance instead of giving you a flesh wound.'

Street swung the gun round and aimed at Coldhardt's head. 'Don't give me that. You *meant* to kill me.'

'You fired the first shot,' said Coldhardt, frighteningly calm. 'And Saitou fired the second. I shot back to save my own life but I had no desire then to take yours.'

'Lies!' Street screamed.

The whispers and gasps in the gallery grew louder; someone called out in protest. Saitou quickly hit Street on a pressure point in the small of his back, striking a nerve so that the gun clattered from his fingers. Street cried out, then rounded on his partner. 'What the hell was that?'

'You need to step back,' said Saitou tersely. 'We didn't spend all this time planning for you to ruin everything with your goddamn temper.'

'Have you forgotten how it *felt*?' Street turned from him and addressed the gallery now as if trying to win the audience over to his side. 'Thirty-two years ago Coldhardt shoots the *real* Heidel, not some shite imitation . . . then he helps himself to the boss man's money and screws us out of every penny. Blows up the systems, wipes out every last file, every last trace of him . . .'

'And that's precisely what we're going to do to you, Coldhardt,' Saitou interjected. Tye sensed how anxious he was to regain control of both Street and his big event. 'Computers have come a fair way since the 1970s, but we're inside your networks right now. We'll be helping ourselves to all those little offshore bank accounts of yours, and splitting the proceeds between the members of the consortium . . .'

'And I suppose you'll be getting that information from the microprocessor you concealed in that rather splendid gold ring of mine,' Coldhardt surmised. 'Is that so?'

Tye felt her insides twitch as Coldhardt climbed determinedly to his feet. Nervous mutterings started to build around the arena, and judging by Bree's frown and the look Saitou and Street shared, things were once again going not-as-rehearsed.

'Don't make out you knew about it,' Street began savagely. 'It was hidden –'

'– beneath the enamel, yes,' said Coldhardt, wiping the blood from his mouth on the back of his hand. 'Naturally, I've moved any sensitive files to a non-networked computer. My experiences with you both taught me never to take anything at face value.' He straightened to his full height, nodded to Heidel's gory corpse. 'Take him, for instance. I've known for certain he was a fake ever since you and your "Scribe" visited my safe house at Chamonix.'

'Sure you did.' Saitou sneered, but Tye saw him glance nervously up at the displeased crowds above.

'The footage my Talent took of your impostor in action only made me more certain,' Coldhardt went on. 'But I couldn't tell *them* that because I knew that Jonah Wish and Maya Marisova had been bugged – despite dear Dr Draith assuring me of their rude health.'

'Sure, you knew all that,' said Street, 'and still you came blundering in here.'

'Once I saw you in the surveillance footage outside the auction house, of course I realised you were involved. But, like Saitou, you lack the imagination to contrive such a splendidly sordid affair on your own. You would have needed help and funding.' Coldhardt straightened his collar and glanced round at the onlookers. 'I was intrigued to know who my greatest enemies were. Though I must admit I didn't expect to find quite so many of you in attendance . . .'

'That's enough,' snapped Saitou. He gestured to Bree, who spoke into a tiny radio, and a few moments later Tye saw two robed guards enter the arena from two different tunnels. Each was armed with electric shock prods. 'Whatever you claim you knew,' Saitou went on, 'you were still a fool to come here alone.'

'But I'm not alone, am I?'

Tye was still concealed beneath her robes but Coldhardt looked straight at her and smiled.

'I sent my Talent here ahead of me.'

'You betrayed them!' Bree objected.

No, thought Tye, the hairs on her neck rising, *that's what you* said *he did*. She wondered for a moment if she were dreaming, if should pinch herself at this point; but the arrow point in her back was pinch enough, and already Tye's every muscle was tensing for action. She shrugged off her hood and he nodded to her – a nod she took to mean *Be ready*.

Coldhardt seemed to have taken control of this little gathering – and the onlookers weren't liking it. The guards with the prods stepped closer to him uncertainly.

'Kill him now,' someone shouted.

'Gloating's getting us nowhere,' a woman added.

'She has a point,' said Coldhardt drily. 'And I'm a busy man, so –'

'Just shut it, Coldhardt.' Saitou flexed his fingers as if getting ready to put them to use. 'You're mine now.'

'*Ours*,' said Street thickly, picking up his gun. 'You know what, Coldhardt? You're going to apologise to us for all you've done.'

Saitou looked up at Tye. 'And you'd better mean it.'

Coldhardt looked down at the crushed orchids at his feet, stooped to pick up one that was intact. 'I'll always be sorry for what I did that day,' he said quietly, and Tye could see at once he *did* mean it. 'More sorry than you could know.'

'Oh, we can know a *lot* of sorry,' Saitou's smile was chilling as his fingers curled to dangerous points.

Coldhardt nodded. 'But if I hadn't killed Heidel, he would have killed me.'

'Oh yeah?' Street sneered.

Facing up to the gun, still gripping the orchid, Coldhardt stepped towards them. 'How'd you think I knew for certain your Heidel replacement wasn't for real? If Nomen Oblitum had him in their care for thirty years, if he'd talked about me every day, if his thirst for revenge was so very unquenchable . . . don't you think he'd have told them what he never told you? The same thing I tried to tell you that day it all fell apart . . . only you were too busy trying to kill me for all that you *believed* I'd done.'

'He's tapped!' jeered Street, but Tye could tell he was speaking angrily to mask his nerves. 'Trying to talk his way out of –'

'Heidel wasn't just my boss,' Coldhardt snapped, his words ringing out around the ancient rock. 'He was my father.'

CHAPTER TWENTY-THREE

For a second, no one spoke in the arena, as Coldhardt's words bounced around the bare rock. *His father?* Street and Saitou were staring, disbelief written all over their faces.

But even from this distance, Tye had seen the flash of pain in Coldhardt's eye and knew he was straight on the level.

Then she noticed that the guard with the prod who'd been standing nearest Coldhardt was moving slowly, purposefully towards Bree and the Scribe. The other guard was edging closer to Saitou and Street. With a jolt Tye saw that these guards were wearing Converses. She bit her sore lip, not daring to hope. *It couldn't be . . .*

But Sadie must have seen them too. She couldn't shout a warning but her bolt would scream for her. The girl's face pressed up to hers for a moment, dark eyes burning, mouth twisted in a savage grin. Then Tye gasped as she was shoved to the ground, as Sadie leaned forward with the crossbow.

Desperately, Tye scissored her legs tight around Sadie's ankles and lifted them with all her strength. Sadie fell forward and toppled right over the balcony rail. She plummeted to the ground ten metres below, hit heavily. The impact must have triggered the bolt. Tye heard the murderous whoop of its flight through the air . . .

And a thunk as it embedded itself between Saitou's ribs. Saitou gave a hoarse cry and staggered sideways under the weight of impact.

'As good a cue as any,' Coldhardt shouted, and thrust his orchid into Street's face. It was clearly no ordinary flower – Tye saw a cloud of white mist spray out from inside the petals. Choking, clawing at his eyes, Street sank to his knees.

At the same moment, as the gallery filled with noise and scuffling feet, the guard behind Bree zapped her with the electric prod, stunning her. Then he quickly grabbed her in an arm lock with one arm and pulled off his restricting hood with the other – it was Motti. The Scribe started forward but Motti jammed the tip of the prod into Bree's ear.

'Back off,' he spat, glaring round at anyone else who might try to rush him. 'Or it won't be pretty.'

'Let go of me,' Bree hissed, as Saitou groaned, clutching his side. 'He needs medical help.'

'Aw, I think I just cried the world's smallest tear,' said Motti. 'Now tell these assholes to drop their guns!'

The guards hesitated, looked to Bree for guidance. She nodded curtly, and the guns were duly thrown to the ground.

Con had already shrugged off her own heavy crimson robe and dropped her own prod to grab one of the fallen weapons. Tye watched her friend fire awkwardly into the air to bring those in the gallery to order.

'Everyone be still,' Con yelled, 'yes?'

Tye wanted to call out to her and Motti but suddenly realised how vulnerable she was. Many people up here – Draith for a start – must know she was part of Coldhardt's team and so prime hostage material herself. She held still for now, not wanting to draw attention.

'I'm blind! Damn it, Coldhardt, what did you do?' Street shouted, rubbing furiously at his eyes. 'I can't see!'

'Just a little pepper spray variant,' said Coldhardt briskly, looking down at Saitou's prone body. 'I knew I couldn't smuggle a conventional weapon in here, but with an atomiser hidden in the bloom and a nylon wire threaded through the stem . . .'

'Show's over now, folks,' Motti shouted up at the winding gallery. 'We're getting out of here so everyone stay nice and –'

'No!' Street bellowed. 'Nobody's leaving till we finish this.'

'It *is* finished,' said Coldhardt, and did Tye imagine the note of regret in his voice? 'And so are you.'

'Guards,' snapped Bree suddenly. 'Change of orders. Pick up your guns and shoot Coldhardt.'

Motti scowled and tightened his grip on the prod. 'You crazy?'

'They're thieves, not killers,' Bree ground out, 'they don't have the guts. *Do it!*'

'No!' Con fired at the discarded guns on the ground, sent rock and shrapnel flying. But the Scribe had circled round Motti and Bree and now grabbed

Con from behind, wrestled her over backwards. Con's finger was still on the trigger and the gunfire raked upwards, bullets slamming into the rock walls and the balcony.

At once, total, bloody pandemonium broke out.

The gallery erupted as the onlookers upped and ran – *Every evil bastard for himself* seemingly the order of the day. For a few seconds the noise of the gunfire drowned out everything. Stone chips peppered Tye's back, and her wrists burned as she strained against her cuffs. Someone stepped on her ankle, and she rolled desperately to the edge of the balcony for cover to avoid being trampled.

Then the firing stopped. What the hell was happening down there now? Staring out through the stone balusters at the war zone below, Tye found her eyes flicking between different scenes of chaos, as if channel-hopping on Mayhem TV.

Lithe and catlike, Con was fighting the Scribe and another guard both at once, trying to keep them from the weapons on the ground, but –

flick

– out of her reach, another guard had scooped up his rifle. He aimed it at Coldhardt, but Motti shoved Bree savagely into the line of fire –

flick

– which left Motti with no shield and another two guards coming for him. Motti managed to zap one with the prod, sent him staggering back into his mate, then ran for the thrones at the back of the arena, diving for cover as a hail of gunfire exploded all around him and –

flick

– Coldhardt was hugging the ground behind Saitou's body as Street went on bellowing with helpless anger, as –

'We can take the old man ourselves!' one man shouted as he started down the staircase to the arena. 'You with me?'

And at his words Tye jumped out of her terror trance, felt a rush tear through her, as if her body was suddenly nine parts adrenaline. If these onlookers joined in, some of Coldhardt's biggest enemies . . . She was up on her feet and running for the staircase before she even consciously realised it. Even with her hands behind her back, she had to do something. Bree would have the keys to the cuffs, so if Tye could get to her . . .

She forced her way down the steps through the scrum of bodies, saw Draith was just ahead of her, trampling a woman who'd stumbled in his haste to get down. 'You're a doctor!' she shouted in outrage, as if this might shame him into helping anyone.

'He'll kill me,' Draith gasped hoarsely, hobbling out into the arena. 'If we don't kill him first.'

She charged after him, had almost caught him up. And then his gaunt frame danced suddenly in a storm of bullets. He pitched forward, and Tye hurled herself to the ground beside his body. Peeping over Draith's bony shoulder, she saw with horror that Street had got hold of an M16 and was firing wildly and sporadically in a sweeping semicircle, still blinded by the pepper spray. All around, consortium members danced and jerked in a gruesome, bloody ballet as bullets tore into their bodies. Behind her Sadie's limbs twitched with stray impacts, each movement rippling the black-red moat widening around her broken skull.

'You're not beating me again, Coldhardt!' Street shrieked, his eyes streaming.

'Stop it!' Bree yelled behind him, now struggling with Con. 'You idiot, Street, you'll kill us all!'

Feeling sick and frozen inside, Tye shut her eyes and curled up tight as a child, trying to make herself as small a target as possible as the ground was shot up in shards all around her, as the madness went on.

Jonah felt a sense of rising elation as he ran towards the arena with Maya. They'd just taken control of Saitou's computer systems. This whole island would be going offline soon, no communications, no lights, no security – nothing. He couldn't believe they'd got away with it – but if Patch truly was still alive, then that was the real miracle. This was just luck.

Luck that could run out at any time.

Jonah skidded to a halt at the sound of running footsteps ahead, coming their way. He motioned to Maya to hide in an alcove in the wall, while he did the same on the opposite side.

They needn't have worried. The Scribe ran straight past them, his robes soiled and bloody, a dark-haired woman trailing behind him. 'Saitou's got guards on the perimeter,' the Scribe was saying. 'We'll get back-up . . .'

'Looks like things have kicked off in there,' said Jonah.

'Come on,' said Maya simply.

They hurried along the tunnel, the rattle of gunfire echoing weirdly as they grew closer. Jonah swore under his breath. He knew Coldhardt's plan now, and flying bullets weren't a part of it.

More people fled past them. Jonah followed Maya to the tunnel's end, looked out into the arena – and almost hurled his guts. It was a massacre. Dead ahead, facing away from them, Street was firing an M16 in deranged, screaming sweeps. Corpses lay scattered like the blood-spattered flowers, and Jonah was afraid to study them too closely for fear of recognising someone he cared for. Bree was yelling something, sat astride Con, who struggled beneath her. And close to Jonah's right, about the only guard left standing was firing at the thrones. He saw someone hiding out down there.

'Motti,' he breathed, a sense of helpless panic rising. 'What can we do?'

'Want to know a secret?' Maya looked at Jonah, her eyes dust-grey. 'Follow me quickly, while Bree and Street are distracted . . .'

I'm going to die, I'm going to die, Jonah thought, tearing after Maya, terrified that any moment Street would turn and the bullets would tear into them too. He watched as Maya ran up behind the guard and jabbed her fingertip against his neck, while striking him around his kidney with the flat of her other hand.

She can do it too. Jonah just stared. *Saitou's trick.*

The guard froze, still clutching the gun but apparently unable to fire it. Then Maya raced on towards the thrones, and Jonah hared after her. They reached Motti, chucking themselves behind the thrones.

Jonah stared at her, shaken up. 'Just who the hell *are* you, Maya?'

'Skip it,' said Motti, sparing Jonah the tiniest nod in greeting. 'Right now, how the hell are we gonna save our family?'

Body tensed, still hugging the ground and straining against the cuffs, Tye couldn't help but wonder if she was already dead and this was her hell – the gunfire going on for ever. *He's got to run out of ammo soon*, she told herself. *He's* got *to*.

Then the firing broke off. Bree's bellow filled the ringing silence that followed. 'Street, for the last time – put down the gun!'

Street lowered the rifle. He looked exhausted, his breath coming in ragged gasps. 'Can't . . . bloody see . . .'

'Give me the gun and *I'll* kill Coldhardt!'

'No!' That was Con. Tye raised her head cautiously and saw her friend flat on her back, writhing underneath Bree, trying to stop the girl from reaching for Street's rifle. 'Coldhardt, run!'

Tye scrambled up from behind Draith's body and sprinted over to help. At the same time, her heart leapt to see Jonah, Motti and Maya racing towards Con and Bree too, from the opposite direction.

Closer than either group, Coldhardt got up from behind Saitou's body; for a few supercharged seconds it seemed they would all converge on Street and Bree, save Con and kick some collective ass.

But a sudden flash of movement showed Tye that Saitou wasn't out for the count after all. He propped himself up on one elbow and reached out, grabbing Coldhardt's ankle with gory fingers. With a cry of pain, Coldhardt fell down.

Tye pushed herself faster, harder.

But she couldn't outrun Street's fingers as he swung round blindly at the sound of Coldhardt's voice, aimed low and opened fire. And he couldn't see that his old-time partner was between him and his target.

'Saitou!' Bree screamed, hair askew, bleeding from a gash in her cheek, all composure lost.

The bullets meant for Coldhardt struck Saitou point blank in the neck. Thick spurts of blood slapped against the ground and a few seconds later he followed them, quite dead, dark eyes staring from his face.

Jonah quickened his step as Saitou took the bullets – Street still had the gun, and surely couldn't miss again? But just then Bree broke free of Con's struggling grip and hurled herself at Street, began wrestling the gun from him.

'You killed Saitou!' she hollered. 'You stupid, *stupid* –'

Tye reached Street first. Her wrists were cuffed behind her back but it didn't slow her down. Lightning fast she kicked the gun away with one foot, and planted the sole of the other in his jaw. He fell backwards and lay still. A moment later Jonah caught up to Bree and hurled himself on to her back, pinning her to the ground. She bucked wildly beneath him, but Tye joined the fight. She brought her knee down hard on the back of Bree's skull, knocking the girl's forehead into the rock floor. The struggles abruptly halted.

Jonah looked deep into Tye's eyes. *Who cares who's watching*, he thought, as he grabbed her tight as hell and they just kissed. He wondered if he tasted as rough as she did. *Probably*, he decided. But still it was the sweetest kiss of his life.

'Gee, guys, that's a big surprise to no one at all,' drawled Motti, checking the fallen bodies around him. 'But if you guys are planning on going further, I'd wait till Patch is around. You can sell him tickets.'

Tye broke off as if stung and glared at him. 'Patch is –'

'Alive, we are told,' Con told her happily, helping Coldhardt pull clear of Saitou's lifeless fingers.

'It's true,' Jonah whispered, smiling and nodding his head, searching out Tye's gorgeous brown eyes as they filled with tears. 'Maya says Patch is OK!'

'He was when we left him,' said Maya briskly. 'But we must return, and quickly.'

'But how *can* he be OK?' Tye demanded. 'Jonah, you said –'

'Maya is an uncommonly skilled student of the Order,' Coldhardt announced.

Jonah looked at her sharply. 'Order?'

Maya shrugged off the crimson robe she wore to reveal a plain black swimsuit beneath, still wet from her swim through the sinkhole. Then she pulled down the top a little way to expose the tattoo that sat over her heart, the same tattoo Jonah had glimpsed before when he shouldn't have been looking. But now he was staring, like everyone else, at a familiar symbol.

'The Knot of Isis?' Tye breathed.

Maya nodded. 'I am a scholar-priest of Nomen Oblitum.'

Jonah stared at her, a chill prickling down the length of his back. He wanted to phrase a hundred questions in his mind but got nowhere with any of them.

Tye shook her head dumbly. 'First we find out Heidel is Coldhardt's father, then we –'

Jonah stared at her. '*What?*'

'I'm sure we all have questions,' Coldhardt said heavily. 'But there is no time.'

Suddenly, it was as if something in the air changed, as if a noise in the background that Jonah hadn't even registered had cut off. 'Maya and I shut down the island's power systems,' he said. 'Death of an island.'

'The timing is apt,' said Coldhardt. 'Our business seems to be concluded here.'

'Once we get these cuffs off me,' said Tye, pointing to a key on Bree's silver charm bracelet. Jonah snapped the thin silver chain and soon had the cuffs unlocked.

'The Scribe went to fetch the perimeter guards,' said Maya, restlessly. 'They could be on their way now.'

Tye looked round sadly at the devastation in the arena, rubbing her wrists. 'Maybe they can organise some first aid for the survivors.'

Con didn't seem so impressed with that idea. 'Come. It is time to go.'

'What about Street?' Motti nudged the man's shoulder with his foot. 'You just gonna leave him here?'

'Why not,' said Coldhardt. 'Let *him* meditate on

what it is to kill one you care for.'

'But he could come after you in the future,' Con argued. 'Any of these bastards could. Given the chance, they'd kill you.'

Coldhardt glanced at Maya, as gulls high above shouted their shrill complaints at the strengthening blue sky, and gave a heartfelt smile. 'Where I'm going . . . no one will ever find me.'

CHAPTER TWENTY-FOUR

Jonah followed Coldhardt, Tye, Motti and Con, walking quickly through the dark and twisting tunnels out of Saitou's labyrinth, trying to stave off his thoughts and questions and stay alert.

He was armed with a pepper-spray orchid in case of trouble. Jonah supposed it was a measure of what he'd lived through that to be holding such a bizarre weapon now seemed perfectly reasonable.

Maya lagged behind him, hanging back from the others. Jonah put that down to her secret being out now. Maybe she felt awkward for not telling them sooner, or maybe she had simply stopped pretending to be normal. He had felt quite close to her when they'd been just a couple of hackers working an overclocked computer. Now so much made sense suddenly – no wonder she'd known so much about Nomen Oblitum, no wonder the Scribe's oh-so-knowledgeable pronouncements in Chamonix had left her less than impressed . . .

Jonah felt stupid and small-minded. He wasn't used to that, and he didn't like it. Maya had come through for them, but with what agenda Jonah wasn't sure. Could they trust her?

With Patch's life in the balance, he reflected, *can we afford not to?*

The atmosphere was muted as they emerged into daylight. They had won, but more through chance than skill. And the fact remained: Coldhardt might not have sold them out as such but he'd still let them run into the dragon's den without warning them of the situation, purely to suit his own agenda.

Where do we go from here? Jonah wondered.

The answer, of course, was to get help to Patch as fast as possible.

They met no one on the way out to the harbour.

Coldhardt had apparently made the last leg of his journey here in a small speedboat, from which Maya had jumped ship and swum for shore. But that couldn't accommodate them all. Tye started searching for an alternative among the many luxurious boats, and Jonah wondered how many of the owners had survived.

'How did you find Patch?' Motti asked Coldhardt.

'I was monitoring your progress on Jonah's transmitter, just as Saitou was.' Coldhardt stared out over the calm and glittering sea, sounding matter of fact as ever. 'Maya's skills and upbringing have left her well-attuned to her own body. She was aware of the transmitter placed beneath her skin, and was able to remove it. Once she accepted my need to talk candidly, she left it carefully out of hearing range while we discussed the situation – and what to do about it.'

'While the rest of us stayed in the dark,' Jonah muttered, itching the lump on his neck.

'My own aims and Coldhardt's coincided.' Maya

hovered at the periphery of the group. 'We were already on our way out here when the explosion went off on board the *Aswang*.'

'And you stopped off to collect Patch?' Jonah challenged. 'Even though you thought he was dead?'

Coldhardt met his gaze. 'You think I would leave his body to rot on that ship?' he asked quietly.

Maya stepped in. 'Con's instruction to the *Aswang*'s captain as she mesmerised him – that he should do all in his power to aid and protect anyone not a part of his crew – saved Patch's life. That and the titanium blanket he was *still* wearing around his midriff.'

'That one-eyed pussy,' said Motti, half smiling.

'The captain administered first aid and kept him alive, until I arrived.'

Tye had re-emerged from the cabin of an especially sleek boat and now started untying the mooring rope. 'I heard Street say the *Aswang*'s cameras had picked up a masked "man" on board,' she said. 'You know, Bree had you down for a pirate, looting the bodies.'

'I had to take the chance I would be spotted. Your friend Patch was in a critical condition. His body was shutting down and only drastic action could help him.' Maya looked at Tye. 'Now, if you are ready, we should go. Quickly.'

'This is a Skater 46 Supreme,' Tye told her stiffly, crossing to the captain's seat. 'It does one-fifty miles an hour on twin thirteen-hundred hp engines. We'll be quick.'

Con got in the seat beside her, while the others piled in the back. Jonah felt slightly uncomfortable, sat between Maya and Coldhardt. They were the ones with all the answers, but how far could he trust either? He felt a groaning wave of tiredness overwhelm him, and his burns stung in the sunlight.

Coldhardt discussed directions with Tye. Then she gunned the powerful engines, and the speedboat soared away over the calm ocean.

Jonah turned to Maya. 'I'm still waiting to hear how I helped save Patch.'

Maya's grey eyes fixed on him. 'Your breakthrough with the circles in the manuscript was timely.'

'You mean the way they relate to the dark ink strokes beside them?'

She nodded. 'When you pointed out that not every redrawn circle was perfectly drawn, that some had very particular start points, I studied them closely.' She started drawing in the air. 'If you bisect the circle horizontally, then that's your nought-degree line. And if you draw a line from the start point through to the centre of the circle, then you get an angle. It's that easy. When two or more circles follow on you simply add the angles together. Then you take the first darker ink stroke that follows and rotate it by the same value.'

'And what does it get you?' Jonah demanded. 'What do all those different line-strokes make when you put them together – new pictograms? A key to understanding the manuscript?'

'They make sense of the appendix,' Maya told him. 'Only it's not really the appendix – it's more like the *heart* . . . the heart of the Bloodline Cipher.'

Jonah wanted to shake her for the answers. 'Well?'

She closed her eyes and shook her head. 'It's more

easily demonstrated than explained. And I'm going to need my energy for what's ahead.'

Motti looked at Coldhardt. 'Then I guess it's your turn. Care to share about you and Daddy?'

Jonah didn't for one moment believe that Coldhardt would answer. He seemed to have fallen asleep, his head angled back so his pale face caught the sun.

Con turned round in her seat to look at him. 'Did Street and Saitou really not know that you and Heidel were . . . you know . . .'

'Heidel was no more his name than Coldhardt is mine,' the old man said with unexpected candour, loud enough for them all to hear over the engines' diesel symphony. 'His own father invented an identity for him from an early age . . . a tradition he continued. He considered our relationship a weakness, didn't want anyone thinking they could get to the father through his son. And so I became Nathaniel Coldhardt. Just another member of the team.'

'Until you popped Poppa,' said Motti bluntly. 'Was it like Street said?'

Coldhardt said nothing.

Maya opened her eyes for a moment. 'Tell them,' she said, and it sounded to Jonah more an order than a suggestion.

'Heidel told us he needed to go away on business,' Coldhardt began reluctantly. 'To lie low for a while, he didn't know for how long. He told us we would be needed to run things in his absence. I went to see him, to say goodbye to my father one last time . . .' He paused. 'And I learned – against his wishes – that he was very sick. That he was leaving to join a secret society named Nomen Oblitum, that the entrance fee was three-fifths of his total wealth, and that in fact he might never return.'

Con had turned round in her seat, her eyes wide. 'He hadn't told you?'

'Perhaps it slipped his mind – along with the fact that he was selling off his team.'

Jonah stared. 'He what?'

'As soon as he was safely out of the way, he planned to send the signal to our purchasers to come and collect,' said Coldhardt. 'He'd set data bombs inside the computer systems to erase all records of the business, his contacts, our bank accounts . . . He was planning to take everything away from us. Our freedom . . . my birthright . . .'

'God,' Jonah muttered.

Coldhardt half smiled. 'Oh, he'd taken God away from me many years before that.'

'He could sell his own son?' Con shook her head. 'You were right to shoot him.'

'He shot me first,' said Coldhardt matter-of-factly. 'I returned fire, caught him in the chest. Then I crawled away and passed out. When I woke again, he'd gone. But the amount of blood, the scream he'd given . . . I knew he had to be close to death.' Coldhardt looked at Jonah, eyes piercing, who felt a chill despite the baking sunshine. 'Street and Saitou found me in the hub. The computers had blown. Everything was lost. I must have convinced them about Heidel's death, but before I could say much more, Street started shooting.'

'I'm seeing a pattern here,' said Motti drily.

Coldhardt didn't react, seemingly miles away. 'Street and Saitou thought I'd killed him simply to take everything for myself . . .'

'So there was a gun fight,' said Con. 'And you won.'

'No one won,' said Coldhardt heavily. 'Each of us went to ground to recover. Indeed, that was the only thing that saved us from being "collected" by those who had purchased us.'

'Looks like Street and Saitou didn't exactly find it easy to move on,' Tye called back over her shoulder.

Coldhardt said nothing, but he glanced at Maya, an impatient look that seemed to say, *Satisfied?*

'Those who do not remember the past are condemned to repeat it,' Maya muttered, just loud enough for Jonah to hear.

But even if you knew the truth all along, can moving on ever be easy? Jonah reflected. *When you've tasted a life so vivid and real . . . when you've run so deep into the darkness but raced back with glittering treasure time and again . . . Whether it's taken from you or you choose to walk away – how can you ever adjust to a different life?*

He thought of Patch with a note of anxiety. *It's harder still to move on when you're in a coffin.*

'How long till we reach this island?' Jonah asked. There was an empty feeling inside him now, despite the weight of Coldhardt's secret history. As a story it had filled only a few minutes of their journey, and yet its repercussions ran on. Dozens of lives had been lost in the long aftermath of those events. And if Patch died because Coldhardt had let them blunder into a trap instead of telling them the truth sooner . . .

Jonah looked down at his white orchid, at the sinister mechanism peeping out from the beautiful façade. He reached past Maya and threw it overboard to be chewed up in their wake, the white scratch they were leaving in the veneer of perfect blue.

Tye took them into a white sandy bay on some insignificant speck of land; there was no jetty, but a protruding spire of rock in the shallows allowed them to moor the boat and wade ashore. All except Coldhardt, who elected to remain on board, alone with his thoughts.

A stiff breeze was blowing up, and the waves broke noisily on the shore. Jonah's insides felt like a mosh pit and his bad leg stung evilly through his wet clothes, as Maya led them to a small cave in the cliff face on the shore. 'Not exactly BUPA, is it?'

'The cave is cool, there is no unpleasant animal life –'

'You dumped a dying boy in a cave.' Tye glared at Maya accusingly. 'Why not divert to a conventional hospital?'

'They would have undone my work,' said Maya stiffly. 'Conventional treatments can do nothing for your friend right now.'

'We've only got your word for that.' Motti lowered his head to speak in her ear. 'If anything happens to Patch . . .'

The threat went unspoken as they entered the cool, wet half-light of the cave. A small figure lay on a stretcher, only his bloody, blackened face protruding from beneath a blanket.

'Oh God,' Tye whispered.

Jonah clutched her hand tightly as she started to cry. He noticed that Motti had taken Con's hand too.

Within moments, Jonah caught the familiar taste of tears at the back of his throat. When Maya had told him Patch was alive, he'd allowed himself to believe things would be OK. But to see him like this – that cheery, lively, horny little bugger he'd come to know as a friend this last year, as *family* . . .

'Patch?' Tye approached the body on the stretcher warily, letting go of Jonah's hand.

'He actually looks better than he did,' Jonah murmured, his voice cracking on the last words and so fooling no one, least of all himself.

'Of all of us . . . Patch is the one who deserved this least,' said Con softly.

'Wait.' Tye turned to Maya, suddenly frantic. 'He's not breathing.'

Maya knelt beside Patch. 'He *is* breathing. I have put him into a deep trance, slowed down his autonomic reflexes, to divert all his energies into coping with his injuries.'

Motti wiped his running nose crossly. 'You did all that by tapping him with your fingers?'

'Just as Guan Yin gave her eyes to blind and wicked men to redeem them in the old stories, so the teachings of "her" manuscript open *our* eyes to our true potential. They explain how the meridians and pressure points of the body may be manipulated.' Maya smiled serenely as she pricked at Patch's ruined flesh with her fingertips. 'But I was wrong before, Jonah – it's *not* the ultimate medical handbook. Not until you factor in the appendix, anyway.' Her eyes were aglow. 'That spiel about junk DNA the Scribe came out with in Chamonix, that was sheer invention . . . Our cells are full of chemical magic, sure, conjuring life, creating energy. And what the mages of Guan Yin's devotional cult *really* discovered was a means to master that energy within our bodies more fully than any doctor or shaman had before or since. Knowledge so powerful, so dangerous, it had to be kept the most strictly guarded secret.'

'So they came up with the Bloodline Cipher,' said Jonah.

'And at last, it is secret no longer.' Maya looked over at Jonah. 'A bloodline means a group of related individuals with shared characteristics. And what's the largest group of all?' She smiled. 'The human race. In the old stories, Guan Yin reached out to them all in their misery, ignorance and sickness in the hope she could make them whole.'

'And the shared human characteristics are blood and veins, bones and breath and sinew,' Jonah realised suddenly, 'just as the pictograms said.'

'But the bloodline also refers to something far simpler in a way. Remember, this is being translated from old, old language . . .' Maya's grey eyes were agleam with excitement as she went on prodding and poking at Patch's skin. '"*The life of a creature is in the blood*," – that's what the title page said, remember? "*Thy flesh be stitched with threads immortal.*" ' She looked at Jonah. 'The flesh is threaded with veins. Veins like lines. Lines of blood, or . . .'

Jonah stared back at her. 'Blood lines?'

'And the blood carries energy, powers the body. The angled pen-strokes you discovered, Jonah. When arranged in the intended design they don't form a pictogram – they form a *diagram* of those lines of blood . . . A visual guide to manipulating key pressure points around the body in ways unheard of, in order to achieve . . .'

'What?' Jonah urged her.

'I'm trying to put it in terms you would appreciate.' Maya looked at him. 'Just as you and I overclock our computers . . . so the Bloodline Cipher allows us to push human potential to the next level.'

Jonah felt the others' eyes on him, as if awaiting his reaction before deciding what they felt themselves. But he felt frozen, as if the dark chill of the cave had somehow stolen inside him. The sound of the sea outside, the warmth of the sunlight, they seemed suddenly miles away.

'If we could increase the speed and performance of the mind and body, we could achieve higher states of understanding and physical ability, right? It's obvious.' Maya looked to be growing impatient. 'But without a cooling mechanism, mind and body would burn out – just as an overclocked computer will burn out if its processors are not cooled.' Her eyes were shining. 'Now, with the cracking of the cipher, we have the breakthrough.'

'The information tells you how to "overclock" the human body to run its programmes faster?' Jonah swallowed hard. 'So instead of ordinary, natural healing you get Healing version 2.0?'

'If you like.'

Jonah's mind was swimming. 'That's the maddest thing I ever heard.'

But it was followed by the sweetest, as Patch opened his cracked lips and whispered weakly: 'While you're down there, babe, I've got a wicked itch in me balls . . .'

'Patch!' Tye cried, falling to her knees beside him, reaching for his hand.

'No,' Maya commanded. 'You must not touch him, not yet. Balance is all. The procedure has left his energies in a fragile state.'

Jonah, Motti and Con crowded in to see Patch, to speak to him. But already his eye had closed again and he was asleep. But this time his chest was rising and falling more normally.

Con looked at Maya. 'He will pull through, yes?'

'His condition should stabilise shortly,' Maya agreed. 'Then you can take him to one of *your* hospitals.' She got up abruptly. 'There are other matters I must attend to.'

'Why did you help us?' Con demanded.

Maya shrugged. 'Patch was an ideal subject upon which to test a little of this newly acquired knowledge.'

'You used him as a guinea-pig to check you'd cracked the cipher correctly?' Motti glared at her. 'Is that it?'

'Would you rather I had let him die?' Maya turned back to Jonah and inclined her head a little. 'Besides, without Jonah I might not have cracked the cipher. This is his reward.'

'Don't mention it,' Jonah murmured, watching the

steady rise and fall of Patch's chest. 'Anyway, what d'you mean, other matters you must attend –?'

He broke off suddenly as a heavy shadow fell over the entrance to the cave. Jonah spun about, heart suddenly knocking at his throat.

Two men stood in the cave mouth, watching them. In their linen suits they looked like ordinary middle-aged businessmen – save for the large, spreading birthmarks over their chins and necks.

Maya went to stand with them. 'Coldhardt,' she said. 'We must attend to Coldhardt now.'

CHAPTER TWENTY-FIVE

'Wait,' said Tye, pushing her way past Jonah and Motti to challenge the strangers. 'Where did you spring from?'

'Our helicopter touched down nearby,' said the man to Maya's right in the same accentless English.

Tye realised now that she could hear the whirr of the rotors stealing in over the hissing rush of the waves on the sand. 'And what do you mean, "attend" to Coldhardt?'

'He has bought our services,' said the man simply. 'Like his father before him.'

'Heidel did reach us, but badly wounded,' said the other man, to Maya's left. 'He could not be saved. And yet, now it seems we may yet save his son.'

'Save him from what?' Con demanded.

'From the fate that awaits him,' said Maya. 'Heidel passed to him a genetic disorder. As he grows older, so it grows stronger . . . a condition that conventional medicine cannot cure.'

'And so he turned to . . . *un*conventional medicine.' Jonah glanced at Tye. 'The occult kind?'

'And made deals.' Tye shuddered. 'Sold his soul . . .'

'Or *believes* he did,' Jonah said firmly.

The first man smiled. 'Now the Bloodline Cipher has been decrypted, many new approaches will become possible. A solution to Coldhardt's predicament may yet be found.'

'He never told us . . .' Con swallowed. 'He never said that he was so ill.'

'That is why I decided to come with you after you broke into Blackland's place in search of the manuscript,' Maya explained. 'When I learned Coldhardt was involved . . . It was a chance to study him up close – the son of the father we could not get through to.'

Jonah looked at her. 'A different kind of bloodline cipher.'

'If you like,' said Maya. She put her hand to the tattoo on her chest ruefully. 'Coldhardt's cameras at the safe house allowed him to glimpse this, our symbol. He suspected then I was no ordinary university student, I think. That, together with my knowledge of Nomen Oblitum . . . Well. He soon grasped the possibilities I represented. Once you had left for Zamboanga, he approached me.'

'And now it is time to begin his treatment,' said the man on the left. 'Payment has been agreed and made – three-fifths of his total wealth and assets, so that we may further fund our exploration into the ancient sciences.'

'With discoveries such as this still waiting to be unearthed, the work may never cease. Coldhardt's wealth will enable us to achieve much . . .' The first man inclined his head, and his birthmark fell further into shadow. 'Of course, as business assets, the five of *you* count as a part of that wealth . . .'

Tye swapped an uneasy look with Jonah, tensed herself for trouble. 'Meaning?'

'Meaning Coldhardt would not strike the deal until you'd been captured by Saitou and his associates.' Maya smiled wanly. 'Technically you were no longer his assets and exempt from inclusion in the deal.'

Con's eyes held the kind of brightness she usually reserved for piles of cash. 'Then *that's* why he sent us out there?'

'Son of a bitch,' said Motti quietly. 'The old man wouldn't sell us after all.'

'He gives you this.' The first man handed Tye some sheets of folded paper.

'Why?' she said, taking it. 'Why not give it to us himself?'

'Because it is time to part now,' said Maya softly, turning and leading the way from the cave.

'Now hang on a sec,' said Jonah angrily, 'you can't just turn your back on us!'

'We can waste no more time,' said the first man.

'You have the boat. Take Patch to heal in Zamboanga.' Maya paused. 'When the time comes for you to renew your acquaintance with Coldhardt, rest assured you will be found.'

'But – at least – I mean . . .' Con was staring round in confusion. 'Why can't we see him now?'

'Because he has already left,' said Maya, leaving the cave. 'And now we must follow.'

Tye ran out after them with Jonah, Con and Motti just behind. She saw the speedboat was now empty. A helicopter was disappearing into the distance, while another had landed further along the tiny strip of beach.

'Wait!' Con yelled as Maya and her companions crossed quickly to the copter, braving the rotor wash and climbing on board. 'You can't just . . .'

'Go,' whispered Jonah, as the copter took off into the faultless blue sky. The wind had dropped, and all was calm again.

'Coldhardt split,' said Motti, incredulous. 'Just like that.'

Tears were rolling down Con's cheeks as she stared after the copters. 'Never even said goodbye.'

Tye took her hand. 'That's because he's coming back.'

Con tried to nod bravely but the sobs were already coming. Tye gave her a hug, and Motti came over, clumsily grabbing them both. Jonah piled in to the sweaty, snot-stained embrace, and for a long while they just clung together on the empty beach, until the tears stopped coming and their shaky breaths evened out, like the slow wash of the sea on the shore beside them.

And then Patch's voice floated out from inside the cave. 'You sods gonna leave me in here all day or what?'

EPILOGUE

In the Geneva hub, Tye stared at Coldhardt's parting note for the hundredth time. A hastily scrawled list of names, addresses and instructions. No words of kindness or farewell. No thanks. Just a plan of action from boss to employees.

Jonah sat beside her at Coldhardt's computer, his fingers tapping away over the keyboard. For now, it was just the two of them. Motti and Con were keeping Patch company in a Filipino private hospital while he slowly recovered.

It had been four days now, and it seemed that poor Patch's hands had been the worst damaged by the explosion – Motti found it doubtful he would ever pick locks again. Then again, Tye reflected, miracles had been known to happen. Although Con had rejected all calls to wear a PVC nurse's outfit, she *was* letting him fumble with the zips and fasteners on her clothes three times a day – the more he managed to undo, the more he could goggle at. Tye suspected that an incentive like that might see Patch making a full recovery yet.

'How're you getting on?' Tye asked Jonah.

'Getting there,' he said distantly, itching the scar on his neck where an astounded Filipino surgeon had removed the transmitter. 'I just can't help thinking . . . All that stuff we learned about Coldhardt and I feel I know less about him now than ever.' He sighed, his fingers tapping over the keys. 'We don't even know his real name.'

'Or what's wrong with him,' Tye agreed moodily. 'I just hope he's being well looked after.'

'He will be.' Jonah's reassuring smile shifted into something a little more pointed. 'Who'd risk messing with such a perfect example of a devious mind? The man's a genius!'

The chip in the gold ring that had allowed Saitou to hack into Coldhardt's computer system was, it turned out, a double-edged sword. It was now allowing Jonah a back door into Saitou's own server. And since all the onlookers in the temple had contributed funds to the enterprise and were expecting to receive a percentage of Coldhardt's cash assets, Saitou had their financial records on file as well as his own – allowing Jonah to clean out every last member of the consortium and divert the funds into the Talent's personal bank accounts.

Coldhardt's orders.

A farewell gift to the 'children' who had given him so much? Or simply not wishing Nomen Oblitum to lay claim to three-fifths of his cut and planning to reclaim the funds at a later date?

In a way, she hoped it was both those things.

Thinking of the NO men, she decided to ask Jonah the question on her mind. 'Do you miss Maya at all?' she asked falteringly. 'The Maya you thought you knew, I mean?'

'Hmm,' said Jonah, smiling. 'Wonder what the correct answer here would be.'

'Seriously though. I mean, you could talk to her about all kinds of techy stuff.'

'I can talk to *you* about all kinds of anything.' He smiled. 'And besides, I know she was our age, but . . . she seemed way older. And she had a go at me once for not believing you could hold back aging.'

Tye frowned. 'Coldhardt sourced a picture of her for her college pass, and she was dressed in 1960s stuff with make-up to match. I'd put it down to her trying out the retro look. Now I'm wondering . . . what if that picture was actually *taken* in the 1960s?'

Jonah raised his eyebrows. 'You mean that birthmark of hers might be a *rebirth*mark? Weird how her NO mates had them too, maybe –'

'Maybe she was just trying out the retro look,' said Tye firmly. Then she half smiled. 'Speaking of retro, what about Coldhardt in that old picture!'

'You can knock his fashion sense, but not his business sense – as this little project just proved.' Jonah shut down the computer with a flourish. 'All done. My last act of thieving.'

'Oh?' She shot him a look. 'Going to become a saint on me now, are you?'

'Nope,' he retorted, smiling into her eyes. 'But when this little diversion of funds is noticed, there'll be an awful lot of angry people after us.'

'I get you.' Tye nodded. 'Best keep a low profile for a bit.'

'Uh-huh.' Jonah's smile became a grin. 'Besides, we've just become so mega-stonkingly rich we won't need to steal, beg or borrow anything again . . . or not for a long while, anyway.'

Tye tutted and shook her head. 'Clearly you don't know how quickly I can get through money.'

'I *want* to know, though. I mean, I want to find out . . .' Jonah blushed slightly, looked away. 'Now we're free agents – you and me, Motti, Con, Patch . . . well. I suppose there's nothing official to keep us all together, but I thought, you and me . . . If you wanted to, we could maybe get more official. Hang with the others still, but . . . be *more* together.'

'Huh?' She frowned. 'Are you talking in code?'

'I'm nervous as all hell, throw me a bone here!' He looked at her hopefully. 'You know what I mean. So is it cool?'

She tutted and shook her head again. 'Clearly you also don't know just when to shut up and kiss me.'

'I *want* to know,' he said again, smiling the crooked smile she knew so well and wanted to see always. She leaned in and they kissed, getting into it.

'Snogging in the boss's chair,' Jonah murmured. 'What would he say?'

'Well, *I'm* the boss now, and you'd better not forget.' Tye pulled gently away, eyeing the chair and feeling a little funny. 'I don't want us to stay here, Jonah . . . It's Coldhardt's place. And now he's not around.'

Jonah nodded thoughtfully. 'Then . . . I suppose we'll have to find our own place.'

She raised her eyebrows. 'Just like that?'

'Life's still short, whatever people like Maya may say.' Jonah jumped up from the chair and ran to the lift. 'What are we waiting for?'

Tye lingered for a few moments, looking around the hub. The cluster of blank TV screens was like a dark eye watching her. The rush of the air con was like a long, unending breath. This place would live on without them. Waiting.

She turned out the lights, and the lift sighed as it bore them upwards.

A few minutes later Jonah led the way across the grounds to where Tye's BMW was parked outside the stables. The car aside, they were leaving all their old belongings and starting again. Only their smokestones were coming with them. Theirs, and Motti's, Con's and Patch's.

Their world may have cracked apart, but family didn't break so easily.

Jonah felt a buzz in his back pocket. 'Hang on,' he told Tye, and pulled out his mobile. A text had just arrived from the other side of the world. 'It's Con.'

The message was typically succinct: *You have all the money, yes?*

He smiled and texted her back: *We won*

As he hit the send key, Tye took his hand, ready to set off again. But Jonah lingered for a moment, taking in the shadowy grounds of the place he'd called home, filing it all to memory: the sheen of the moonlight on wet slates, the outbuildings like neat stone packages tied up with ivy, the dark, silent pattern of the paths and hedgerows. In the distance, the uncertain boundaries of fields and hillsides, fixed beneath the stars in the wide-open night.

Then Jonah felt his phone buzz again. This time it

was a picture message – Motti and Con sitting either side of Patch's hospital bed with goofy smiles and two huge bottles of champagne, while Patch himself was giving a bandaged thumbs-up.

We'll keep some on ice for you, read the accompanying message. *Come on home.*

'Home,' Tye murmured, as they walked over to the BMW. 'Wherever that is.'

'Finding out could be fun,' said Jonah. 'Don't you think?'

Tye squeezed Jonah's hand. The two of them kissed, got into the car and drove away into a new morning.

ACKNOWLEDGEMENTS

Gratitude is due – to Jill Cole, for patiently enduring the endless late nights and early mornings of the writing process, and for appreciating the twists. To Ele Fountain, Ian Lamb, Suna Cristall, Susannah Nuckey, Georgia Murray, Isabel Ford and Diana Hickman, for all their hard work and support. To Philippa Milnes-Smith, without whom . . . To Captain Denis Dallaire, copter adviser (and Sand Dalek sculptor). To my dad, Tony Cole, for wanting to read what I've done, and to Mum, Nat, Cassie and Nathan as ever. To Justin Richards, Paul Magrs, Mike Tucker and Jason Loborik for being there. To Linda Chapman for so much help and reassurance. To Dominic Barker for laughs and no mirrors. To Paul Grice and Tony Fleetwood for such a rewarding way to get tinnitus. To Editors, Acid House Kings, Mobius Band, The Postal Service, Snow Patrol, Feist, A Certain Ratio, Feeder, Faces Fall and so many others for informing the mood. To Tobey, for always. And to those who have read the books, and those who have written.

Thanks for coming with me, all of you.